Janet cupped the ball in both hands and peered into it. Gradually a scene began to take shape. Mark Jamison was seated at his desk, reading a tattered, yellowed manuscript and taking notes.

"What are you searching for, Mark Jamison?" Janet whispered.

She was shocked when the figure in the ball turned abruptly and looked over his shoulder. He got up and went to the door and looked out. He returned to his desk, shaking his head in puzzlement.

Janet couldn't believe what she had seen. Mark had reacted as if he had heard her whisper! "Mark … Mark Jamison," she thought urgently.

"Damn it! What's going on? Who's calling my name?" the man said.

Janet almost dropped the crystal ball as the sound of his voice came clearly into her mind. The image faded and she shakily replaced the crystal ball on the table.

She said to the empty room, "Okay, David. You told me to use the crystal ball and not to be afraid. Why, David? Does this man have the key to something I want or need?"

Janet mentally listed the things she needed and wanted: the answer to why David had been killed and who had done it; to stop whoever was stealing and selling artifacts; and to pursue rumors of an ancient Roman settlement in the Southwest.

Did Mark Jamison hold the key to these questions?

Other Books by the Author

A Practical Guide to Past Life Regression

Visions of
MURDER

A Novel by
Florence Wagner McClain

1996
Llewellyn Publications
St. Paul, Minnesota, 55164-0383 U.S.A.

FIRST EDITION
First Printing, 1996

Cover painting: Beth Fortune
Cover design: Anne Marie Garrison
Book design, layout, and editing: Connie Hill

Library of Congress Cataloging-in-Publication Data
McClain, Florence Wagner, 1938
     Visions of murder : a novel / by Florence Wagner McClain
     p.   cm.
     ISBN 1-56718-452-9
     1. Indians of North America—Antiquities—Collectors and collecting—Fiction. 2. Women archaeologists—Oregon—Fiction. 3. Black market—Antiquities—Fiction. 4. Occultism—Fiction. I. Title.
PS3563.C3392V57   1995
813'.54—dc20   95-45090
                                                      CIP

Printed in the United States of America

Llewellyn Publications
A Division of Llewellyn Worldwide, Ltd.
P.O. Box 64383, St. Paul, MN 55164-0383

For Terry —
Friend, lover, and husband.

Prologue

"Those clever bastards." The data on the CRT in front of David Manning left no doubt that millions of dollars from the sale of stolen antiquities had been laundered in a brilliantly simple manner.

David logged off and broke the phone link. He was relieved that his search was finished. His repeated excursions into the Houston firm's data banks couldn't have gone unnoticed and he would be one of the first to come under suspicion.

David wrote one cryptic sentence on the last page in a small leather notebook and slipped it into his coat pocket. If anything happened to him before he had an opportunity to tell Janet about his discoveries, she would understand where to find his personal records. He'd almost told her during breakfast that morning, then decided to verify this last bit of data first.

The security guard at the elevator checked his badge. David glanced at the time. He was well ahead of the crowd. Plenty of time for a leisurely dinner at home with Janet before their kendo class. He grinned at the familiar thrill of anticipation. Ten years of marriage had only made their time together more precious and exciting.

One more badge check let him out of the building. He broke into a run as he crossed the parking lot toward his car, anxious to put the thirty miles between him and Janet behind him.

Shot to Death

Dallas — A 33-year-old Denton County man was shot to death in an execution-style slaying Tuesday afternoon in the parking lot at Southwest Data-Comm Corp. where he was employed. Chief Systems Analyst, David Lee Manning, was pronounced dead at 5:30 p.m. at Parkland Memorial Hospital of gunshot wounds to the head and chest. SDC security guards told police that Manning was checked out of the building at 4:07 p.m. His body was discovered at 4:25 p.m. by an unidentified SDC employee.

The dead man's wife, Janet Manning, has been taken into custody for questioning.

J anet sat under an oak tree in her back yard, staring at the great blue heron wading in the shallows of Lake Lewisville. Stress and grief made her appear older than her thirty-two years. Dark shadows detracted from her unusually beautiful dark eyes. Her shoulder-length dark hair had lost its natural luster and curl. The months since David's murder were written in the lines of her face.

The heron took flight suddenly, startling Janet from her mental stupor. The sound of its wings beating the air brought a fleeing smile to her lips. She rose to her feet and shook herself. *Sitting and staring won't find David's killer*, she mentally chided herself. *But where do I look next?*

The police detectives had grudgingly cleared Janet of the murder. Since then, their line of investigation had been a brutal joke. David involved in organized crime? David executed for double-crossing his accomplices?

Rage at such slander had spurred Janet to do her own investigation. Fury had gradually turned to sadness and frustration, as friends and colleagues made it plain to Janet that they wanted nothing to do with anything which might touch their lives with scandal. Janet's faith in David remained unshakable.

Now Janet had reached a point where there were no more leads to follow, no new questions to ask. But she still had a promise to keep.

"I promise I will find your killer, David," she said aloud as she entered the back door of her house. "I will! But where do I look now?"

Janet wandered through the house, asking herself again a question no one had been able to answer. What was David working on just before his death? His little leather notebook should provide the answer. It was missing.

As she entered their bedroom, Janet realized she hadn't searched David's bedside stand. Even the book he had been reading the night before his death lay undisturbed under a thick coat of dust.

A quick glance into the drawer of the stand revealed nothing but an untidy jumble of what David had called his "good junk." Fighting tears, Janet closed the drawer and picked up David's book. She hugged it to her chest, smearing dust on her blouse.

A small pad of paper and a ballpoint pen marked David's place in the book. With trembling fingers, Janet opened the book to see what David had written.

It took a full minute for her mind to process what her eyes were seeing. That name. Agness. Not a person. A place. A place from her past. Agness, Oregon.

Now she knew where to look for David's killer.

Chapter 1

Janet reached the outskirts of Mountainair just at
sunset. She turned her Toyota 4x4 pickup into the
parking lot of the first motel and sat with the engine
running, hands gripping the wheel. The big black Lincoln sped past.

"You really did a number on yourself, Janet. You
ought to hang a sign around your neck: Warning —
Rampant Imagination."

She had to admit that the damned car had given
her reason to be edgy. First it had appeared behind her
about two miles out of Denton, well before dawn, blinding her with bright headlights in her rearview mirror.
Then it stayed behind her all day across West Texas. By
the time she crossed the state line into New Mexico,
she had a full-blown case of the jitters. She had
detoured on the truck route through Clovis. The Lincoln had been a block behind her.

On the long, sparsely traveled highway between
Clovis and Mountainair, she had become increasingly
uneasy and just a little angry. Between Clovis and Fort
Sumner she had driven 80 mph. Her shadow had
stayed a steady quarter of a mile behind her. From Ft.
Sumner to Vaughn she had slowed to 40 mph. The

black Lincoln had maintained the quarter-mile interval. A dozen possible scenarios raced through her mind, each more bizarre than the last, as she drove the lonely road between Vaughn and Mountainair. Now she felt foolish.

"If I could see who was in the car," she said aloud, "it would be different. Those damned tinted windows."

Well, it was over with now. Janet pulled into a parking place and killed the engine. She rented a room at the motel/RV park and then drove on into the small downtown district in search of a hot meal. She scanned the few cars parked along the street. Somehow she wasn't quite ready to write off the whole frightening day as coincidence. There was no sign of the Lincoln.

During a mediocre meal of overdone steak and underdone baked potato, Janet carried on a mental debate with herself. Part of her wanted to drive through town and check out the other motel parking lots for the black car. Another part of her just wanted a hot shower and eight hours of sleep. She compromised by driving and looking until she found an open gas station where she had her pickup serviced before returning to the motel.

Janet awakened abruptly several times during the night. Twice she automatically reached out for David. The empty space beside her was a momentary shock. Her sense of David's presence had been so strong that for a split-second she was convinced she was awakening from a six-month nightmare. In the grey hour before dawn, Janet sat on the edge of the bed and smoked one cigarette after another — a habit she had resumed the week after David's murder, after a five-year abstinence. Apprehension battered the carefully constructed defenses in her mind.

I won't give in to fear, Janet thought. *Why should I be afraid? I'm not exactly defenseless and the worst thing which could possibly happen to me happened when David died. No damned black car or anything else is going to keep me from the truth about that.*

Twenty minutes later Janet was headed west on U.S. 60, canceling her plans to spend a couple of days at Mountainair exploring the nearby Saline Missions of Abo', Quarai, and Gran Quivira, ruins of seventeenth-century Spanish missions and older pueblos. She refused to acknowledge it, but she was running. Tiny tendrils of fear had crept through her defenses. She was afraid of whoever or whatever was in that black Lincoln.

Thirty miles west of Mountainair, Janet glanced in her side mirror. Her hands tightened on the steering wheel as adrenalin hit her bloodstream. That blasted car!

The black Lincoln settled in behind her at a steady hundred yards.

"Damn you!" Janet hit the steering wheel with her fist as she shouted aloud. "Who the hell are you and what do you want?" If only she could see through those tinted windows and put a face to her pursuer.

Janet's mind raced. Within a few miles she had to make a choice. Interstate 25 was just ahead. Should she turn south to Socorro and pick up U.S. 60 west again, or should she turn north to Albuquerque and try to lose the Lincoln in the city traffic? There was always the chance she could find a highway patrol car on the Interstate.

A lot of good that would do me, she thought. *What could I tell them? "Say officer, that black Lincoln is following me. No, no one has made any threats." That would be just terrific*, Janet continued her mental monologue. *I'd have to explain about David if I wanted them to take me seriously and even that wouldn't be any guarantee. Face it, Janet, whatever happens, you are on your own.*

She made a sudden decision to turn south when she sighted the Interstate. The highway west from Socorro was more familiar to her than the road from Albuquerque to Gallup. If the need arose, there were several narrow dirt roads running south into the Gila Wilderness which she and David had explored — roads not intended for big black Lincolns.

"I have my guns. I could trap the bastards and kill them." Janet was startled by the harsh sound of her voice and shocked by the momentary hatred which engulfed her.

"Oh, my god. What am I thinking of?" she continued in a whisper. "Could I really kill another human being?"

Janet was afraid to answer her own question, even in the privacy of her thoughts. Fear and anger were stripping away another layer between the self she knew and a self which had begun to surface during the months of grief, frustration, and vicious accusations following David's murder. Prior to that time she would never have considered the possibility of taking a human life, even though she and David had always carried guns on their backpacking trips, more for defense against a possible human predator than a wild animal.

Troubled thoughts occupied Janet's mind throughout the twenty-eight miles to Socorro. She was through Socorro and almost to Magdalena before she realized that she had turned west again onto U.S. 60. She didn't bother to look back. She knew the car was behind her like some scavenger trailing a wounded animal. She raced through Magdalena and on across the Plains of San Agustin, only glancing at the vast array of mobile radio telescopes looking like a field of moonflowers turned toward the sky. The questions in her mind were eclipsed by the sharp and painful memories which the familiar terrain invoked, memories of a dozen wonderful adventures with David, and the dream of a ranch on the fringes of the Wilderness so nearly realized.

She drove unseeing through Datil and Pie Town. Janet was exhausted from the emotional barrage by the time she pulled into a service station in Quemado. Her legs trembled and barely held her weight when she slid out of the pickup. She told the attendant to fill it up and headed for the restroom. A splash of cold water on her face helped, but her whole body was shaking.

She stared at herself in the mirror. "Are you really that afraid?" she whispered. "No, no I'm not," she answered after an inventory of her emotions. "I'm a little afraid, a little angry, more than a little sad, and very hungry," she ended with a nervous laugh. Dinner had been her only meal the previous day and she hadn't eaten since.

Inside the station Janet bought a bag of chips and a candy bar, paid for the gas, and got change for the drink machine. While she traded quarters for two cans of Pepsi from the machine outside, she casually glanced at the black car parked on the shoulder a short distance down the road, hoping to see the occupants. Sunlight glared on the windshield. Under the guise of examining a Christmas tree-shaped structure constructed of deer antlers in the yard next to the station, Janet tried for a clearer view.

The service station attendant stepped outside and watched Janet with an expression somewhere between curiosity and suspicion. She noticed his scrutiny.

"Hunting must be good around here," she said, pointing toward the deer antler tree.

He silently stared at her. Janet shrugged and climbed into the pickup.

The cat and mouse game continued through the remainder of the day, with Janet alternately immersed in her troubled thoughts or involved in trying to make life miserable for her shadow by taking detours over rugged side roads. After the second detour, the driver of the Lincoln simply waited near Janet's point of reentry onto the highway.

In Kingman, Arizona, Janet called a halt to the game when she stopped at a motel for the night. She was too tired to eat. She showered and fell into bed.

A noise awakened her a few hours later. Janet abruptly opened the motel room door and saw a shadowy figure run from the back of her pickup. Scratches on the tailgate made it obvious that someone had tried to force the lock on the camper top.

Janet threw on her clothes and tossed her things in the pickup. "Bastards, bastards! What do you want?" she mumbled angrily as she cruised the streets of Kingman looking for the black Lincoln. Daylight came without a sighting of the car.

Janet headed out of Kingman toward Needles. The Lincoln appeared behind her as she crossed the state line into California.

Fatigue and lack of food dulled her senses. She knew it wasn't rational behavior when she allowed her instinct to run to overrule her reason. But Janet felt as if she and the faceless occupants of the black car had entered a dimension separate from the rest of the world. She allowed herself to become the relentlessly pursued quarry. Fear and dread of a confrontation spurred her on — both fear of the pursuers and fear of herself. She was afraid that a confrontation might bring the answer to her question, "Could I kill?"

Janet didn't stop until almost empty gas tanks forced it on her. She paused only long enough to have them filled.

Late that evening, approaching San Jose, the unexpected happened. Janet glanced in her rearview mirror just as the Lincoln turned onto Interstate 880 toward Oakland. She continued toward San Francisco with a strange feeling of emptiness, a feeling that she had been deprived of a climactic resolution, an explanation which was her due. Three days of fear and anger, and now nothing.

Janet drove the streets of San Francisco for an hour, expecting, almost hoping, that the black Lincoln would appear behind her. Then, when she was finally convinced that her adversary was gone, a wave of relief swept over her. She laughed through her tears. The mood left as suddenly as it had come, replaced by the sober realization that she had ventured far too close to the outer limits of her sanity. Her mind and body were leaden with fatigue.

Janet stopped at the next hotel she saw. Oblivious to the desk clerk's disapproval of her disheveled appearance and distracted manner, she barely remembered to tip the bellhop when he dumped her suitcase just inside the door. As soon as he was gone, she sprawled across the bed without undressing and slept for twelve hours.

Janet awakened rested and ravenous, feeling completely sane and rational for the first time since leaving home. After a hot shower and a huge room-service breakfast, she lingered over her third cup of coffee and a cigarette.

She thought back over her reactions and the emotional atmosphere which had permeated the experiences of the past few days. The past six months had left her vulnerable. One by one the people she had trusted had proved false. She wasn't entirely certain that she was following a valid clue to David's killer. Perhaps she was simply using the doodles on the slip of paper left in the book David had been reading the night before he was killed as an excuse to run away. Maybe her mind had latched onto the idea of a pursuing car as a justification for running

"No. That's a bunch of bunk," she said aloud. *I had the bad fortune to cross paths with some sicko jerk who gets his kicks from playing games with women traveling alone*, she continued mentally. *He must have really gotten his jollies from the stupid way I reacted. If I'm serious about tracking down David's killer, I can't ever allow myself to fall apart like that again.*

I'm smarter than that. I won't make the same mistakes again. I can't allow myself to be vulnerable to anything.

Sometime, somewhere, Janet knew that she would pay a price for all the emotions she had bottled up inside her, but not now. When David's killer was dead would be time enough. Now was the time to allow that other self — the hard and ruthless Janet who could consider killing — to take control.

Janet repacked her bag and checked the room. The telephone reminded her of the McVeys. She placed a credit card call through the hotel switchboard to Agness, Oregon.

"Hank, this is Janet Manning. I thought I'd better let you and Maggie know that I'm running ahead of schedule. I'll be there late this evening. I hope that isn't a problem."

"Not at all, Janet. Maggie has had everything ready for a week. We're looking forward to seeing you. Drive carefully."

"Thanks, I will. See you this evening."

The early morning drive north toward Eureka was pleasant, even though the sky was masked by a thick layer of clouds. The threatening rain deepened Janet's dread of the long miles of dirt road which would be the grand finale of her trip to Agness. A slow, steady drizzle marked her entry into the redwoods in northern California. It only increased Janet's determination to have a closer view. All her plans to visit favorite places along the way had been abandoned with the appearance of the black Lincoln, but she wasn't going to let a little dampness deprive her of the redwoods. She glanced in the side mirror as she prepared to stop.

"You S.O.B.! Where did you come from?"

The drizzle turned to rain as the Lincoln settled in behind her. They were close enough that, in the absence of reflected light, Janet could see through the windshield well enough to determine that two people, probably men, occupied the front seat. She smiled.

"I don't know how you found me, fellows, but the rules of the game have changed. Now we play it my way, at my pace."

The seed of a plan began germinating in her mind. For now she would ignore them. Let them chew on that for awhile. She intended to play them like a fisherman working one of those big salmon in the Rogue River. When the time was right, she would reel them in.

"David always said that I was a mixture of Machiavelli, Nancy Drew, and MacGyver. We'll see!"

Janet stopped in Crescent City, just a few miles south of the Oregon state line, and topped off her gas tanks. Then she pulled through the drive-in lane of a fast food place for a burger and fries and had her Thermos filled with iced tea.

She drove at a leisurely pace, dividing her attention between the highway and her food. Mentally she was examining her plan from every angle. It stood up under scrutiny and would exact a satisfactory revenge. Fifteen years ago a logger had used the same trick on the sawmill hand who was romancing his wife on the sly. Janet grinned and poured some tea into her spill-proof cup.

Janet left the main highway at Bandon and cut southeast to Coquille, then south through Broadbent, Gaylord, and Powers. In Powers she stopped just long enough to lock her wheel hubs for four-wheel drive and slip her revolver from its hiding place before she turned into the water-filled ruts and potholes of the old logging road to Agness. She watched the Lincoln turn onto the narrow road behind her.

"The advantage is mine now, guys. You may know where I'm going, but I don't think you know this road. We're about to find out if your fancy black Lincoln has four-wheel drive."

The first few miles were easy curves into a gentle climb, but she shifted the pickup into four-wheel drive. She increased her speed to the maximum for the road, hoping the other driver would do the same. He followed her lead and kept close behind. She was going to gamble everything on a fifteen-year-old memory, her driving skills, and just a bit of luck. There wouldn't be a second chance. Her plan would either succeed or precipitate a confrontation. She unconsciously touched the gun beside her.

It was farther than she remembered. Her reactions were instantaneous when she saw it between swipes of the windshield wipers — a nasty little piece of road, subtly banked the wrong way just before a sharp curve into a switchback.

Janet stomped her brakes, then accelerated as she skidded into the curve. The driver behind instinctively slammed on his brakes. Janet laughed through clenched teeth, then held her breath as the Toyota fought for traction on the first switch-back. She felt a fiendish sense of satisfaction as in her mirror she saw the Lincoln sideslip off the road into the fender-deep rush of mud and water of the South Fork of the Coquille River.

There wasn't time to gloat. The switchbacks came hard upon each other — steep, sharp, made almost impassable by the deep mud. Janet skillfully drove the fine line between too fast and too slow. Each turn brought her sliding within inches of the steep dropoff.

The flash of a much-weathered board nailed to the trunk of a Douglas fir sent a shudder through her. She hadn't seen the name, but the years hadn't made the crudely lettered signs any less eerie. Other names began a litany in her mind: "Neilson was here," "Willis was here," "McCaudle was here." Memorials to logging truck drivers who had lost their lives on this road. Janet had seen it happen once. Tons of logs suddenly gone berserk. A truck and driver pushed over the edge and crushed.

The tall pine and fir trees flanking the narrow road made the rainy evening even gloomier. Memories crowded in and Janet lost awareness of time and distance. There was little to distinguish one difficult mile from another. What Janet did know was that each mile brought her closer to the one piece of road she dreaded above all others.

The stretch of level road through the high meadow took her by surprise. She stopped the Toyota and leaned over the steering wheel. She was trembling. Her neck and back were aching knots of muscles. After a few minutes she stretched, poured a cup of tea, and lit a cigarette.

Janet smiled at the memory of the swift, muddy water swirling around the Lincoln. "I won't see them in my rearview mirror anytime soon," she said aloud. "If they survive, they won't have any doubts about where to find me, though. There's only one place at the end of this hellish little road. They must have some idea where I'm headed, though, or they couldn't have picked me up outside San Francisco. Who in thunder are they and what do they want?"

There was no reason for the Dallas police to follow her. She had finally convinced them that she had nothing to do with David's murder. And she had told them where she was going. The hotshot reporters had lost interest. They had exhausted all their venom and innuendo during the first few weeks. One of them, she supposed, could still be convinced that she and David had organized crime connections, but this hardly seemed the style of an investigative reporter.

Janet checked off the possibilities and could only come to one conclusion. The actions of the occupants of the Lincoln were an addition to a long list of things which didn't make sense. She had to believe that they had something to do with David's murder. She must finally be on the right track. No one had shown any overt interest in her detective work until now. This trip to Oregon was a longshot, her last resort in an effort to track down David's killer and find out why he had died.

A sudden bleak loneliness caught Janet off guard and triggered painful scenes which played through her mind like a video tape on fast-forward: David's sheet-wrapped body in the medical examiner's office at Parkland Memorial Hospital, the unexpected hostility from David's parents at the funeral. weeks of questions and accusations from police and press, the sinister little man who claimed to be from Southwest Data-Comm making demands for David's personal papers, fair weather friends, and a dozen leads which had been dead ends.

"Oh, damn it, David. Why?" Janet caught her breath in a half sob. "No! Stop it!" She hit the steering wheel with her fist, then shoved the pickup door open and jumped out. "Damn all of you," she screamed at the rain-filled sky.

Janet was engulfed by an explosion of anger and pain. Her wordless, feral howls might have come from a rabid wolf or some Neanderthal woman hurling her agony toward the heavens.

The outburst frightened Janet to the depths of her being. She looked around her, trying to identify her surroundings, refusing to acknowledge the emotional eruption, striving to bury it in memories of other times.

There, at the edge of the meadow. That vague shape among the trees. Wasn't that the little one-room red schoolhouse which had always stirred her imagination? She walked along the edge of the meadow. Hadn't there been a marker in the meadow? Wasn't this the site of a battle between the U.S. Army and the local Indians — another Custer's last stand for a troop come to remove the natives, who chose not to go and whose descendants were still here?

The cold rain finally penetrated into Janet's awareness. She felt empty, wet, and very cold. She climbed back into the pickup, used half a roll of paper towels to dry herself, and changed into dry jeans and sweater. Then she sat behind the wheel and smoked one last cigarette, reluctant to start the engine, wondering if she had the courage to go on.

You certainly can't go back, old girl. The longer you wait, the worse it will be. The road can't really be as bad as you remember it. Come on, Janet. It's Agness or bust.

Chapter 2

The road rapidly deteriorated into a ribbon of mud clinging to the canyon wall. It was every bit as bad as Janet had remembered it, and worse.

All of the anxious emotions of her first trip over these last few miles were there with sudden clarity in Janet's mind. It had been the summer before her senior year in high school. It had been raining then, also. The headlights of her father's car had spotlighted a seemingly endless trail of mud which appeared too narrow for his big old Buick. She had been plunged into an emotional nightmare of terror of the road and anger at her parents for dragging her to this remote corner of the world.

The road had been well-maintained then by the logging company which had headquartered at Agness during the summers. At its best, it had been awful. The logging company had long since moved on, leaving, as the center of activity, the two lodges which catered to summer fishermen, a few hunters in the fall, and occasional tourists who came up from Gold Beach on the mailboat for the day. Even during the logging boom there hadn't been much in Agness. A few people, mostly Native Americans, lived scattered through the mountains surrounding the confluence of the Rogue and Illinois rivers. There had been a tiny post office and a shabby frame building, grandly called the City Hall, which had been used for everything from community picnics to funerals. Agness, Oregon. Population 13.

Hank McVey had told Janet that nothing much had changed in fifteen years. He was wrong. Now, somehow, Agness held the key to David's murder.

Janet closed a mental door on her memories. The road demanded her total concentration. Almost every curve revealed mud slides, some minor, some almost obliterating the track. Twice Janet thought she was trapped. In two different places, culverts crossing under the road had caved off into the river a hundred feet below, taking much of the roadbed with them. As she maneuvered around these areas, Janet was convinced that only sheer will and perhaps a hint of levitation kept her and the pickup from disappearing forever into the bottom of the river. The 4 x 4 slipped and slid from one near disaster to another. Janet felt her reserves of energy dwindling from the demands of each new challenge.

She almost missed the turn for the narrow track which led through the center of Agness. There were only weeds and a foundation on the corner where she had expected Cougar Lane Store. With a great sigh of relief, Janet stopped the pickup and gave herself a few minutes of rest while she mentally recreated the small log building with cougar skins nailed to the wall, fifty-pound wheels of cheese, old prospectors trading aspirin bottles filled with gold dust and tiny nuggets for sacks of flour and beans. It had been another world.

Janet brushed her hair and put on a touch of lipstick while she was reminiscing. No point in appearing at the McVeys looking like a half-drowned waif.

The main street, the only street, was a series of muddy ruts and rock ledges designed to give nightmares to the manufacturers of lifetime-guaranteed shock absorbers. To Janet, it was heavenly. There was flat, solid ground on both sides.

A short distance down the track, Janet saw the gates facing each other on either side of the street and laughed aloud. Agness Municipal Airport — a grass strip which started on the slope of a mountain and continued through a horse pasture, crossed the road through the gates, ran between two rows of trees in an orchard, and ended abruptly on a bluff above the Rogue River, just across from another mountain. Not a place for fainthearted pilots.

Janet felt a strong sense of coming home when she saw the rambling log house with its wide verandas lined with rocking chairs. She turned in at the narrow gate next to a sign proclaiming "McVey Hunting and Fishing Lodge." The porch lights were on. Hank McVey, lean, weatherworn, dressed in a plaid flannel shirt and overalls, rose from the porch swing just as a plump little woman, encased in a snowy white apron over jeans and a red flannel shirt, burst through the kitchen door.

"Oh, Janet, you're finally here. I can't tell you how glad we are to see you. Gracious, you're all grownup and ladified. And you used to be such a tomboy." Maggie enveloped Janet in a hug perfumed by the smell of freshly baked bread. "It's so good to see you after all these years."

"Woman, for goodness sakes, stop talking and let her in the house. She's gonna drown out here if we both don't starve to death first," Hank growled, and then winked as he shook Janet's hand.

"You don't know how good it is to be here and see both of you. I hope you didn't wait supper for me."

"Oh, you know Hank. He has to eat six meals a day with snacks in between or he thinks he's starving. Dadgum six-foot hollow beanpole," Maggie said affectionately.

The beautiful old lodge seemed to wrap Janet in a warm aura of peace. She felt safe and secure and truly welcome somewhere for the first time since that horror-filled March night. Janet's tension began to slip away as Maggie fluttered and fussed over her.

Maggie found it difficult to hide her dismay over the strain and fatigue mirrored on Janet's face and the haunted look in her eyes. Maggie knew that Janet's husband had died suddenly, but neither Janet nor her mother had said anything beyond that in recent phone calls. From the shape Janet was in after six months, Maggie suspected that there was a great deal which hadn't been told.

"Put your things there on the chair, dear. You know where to freshen up. Then come on into the kitchen. We mustn't let Hank waste away."

Janet joined Maggie and Hank in the lovely, old-fashioned kitchen a few minutes later.

"Goodness, is this feast just for the three of us? I haven't seen a meal like this since I left here. I could gain five pounds and plug up my arteries just from the smells."

"Won't hurt you any," Maggie replied as she loaded Janet's plate with venison steak, hot biscuits oozing with homemade butter, mashed potatoes with cream gravy, and a huge baked apple stuffed with brown sugar, cinnamon, and walnuts. "From the looks of things, you could stand some coddling."

"Coddling maybe, but this is more like fattening a pig for the slaughter."

The conversation lagged as the three of them gave the meal the attention it deserved. Maggie nodded her approval as Janet ate everything on her plate.

"Now, dear, there is pie and coffee."

"I couldn't eat another bite, Maggie. It was wonderful."

"Never seen the time you would turn down my huckleberry pie," Maggie said as she placed a large wedge topped with thick fresh cream in front of Janet.

Janet groaned. "Maggie, how can you do this to me? I haven't seen fresh cream from a real cow in years, much less huckleberry pie. "

"Healthy food never hurt anyone. You'll need plenty of energy for running up and down the mountains."

"Shame on you, Maggie. It'll be your fault if I grow out of all my clothes. "

"Never did care for skinny women," Hank said. "They don't warm your bed worth a durn on a cold winter night."

"And what would you know about skinny women in bed, Mr. McVey?" Maggie snapped with a twinkle in her eyes. "Now, dear," she turned to Janet, "I know what you told us on the phone about why you want to lease the old log house, and we've prepared it just as you requested, but why are you really hiding yourself away up here in the wilderness so far from your family and friends?"

"Maggie, for goodness sakes, let the gal finish her pie and tend to your own business."

"It's all right, Hank. Maggie has a right to ask." The question, though, had snapped Janet back into the reality of why she was in Agness. She wanted to tell Hank and Maggie the whole truth, but the past six months had made her wary of even those she believed to be the best of friends.

"I've had a difficult time since David's death but I'm not running away from life. You know how well-intentioned Mom is, but she has always thought of me as her baby girl and now it's even worse. I had to have some time away from everything and everybody to do some serious thinking about what I want to do with my life now. All of my goals for the future involved things that David and I wanted to accomplish together. I could have gone to our favorite place in New Mexico, but I'm not quite ready to deal with all the memories yet. Agness seemed to be a good choice. It's familiar, neutral territory, and nicely out of Mom's reach."

Hank and Maggie nodded their understanding.

"You mentioned to Hank that you plan to do some writing while you're here."

"Yes," Janet continued her carefully rehearsed cover story. "I have been working as a special research assistant at a university in Denton. They had quite an involved Texas history project under way. I exchanged research for office space and full access to their research facilities for a personal project."

"Are you going to write about Texas history?" Maggie asked.

"Partly. While digging into old documents and records, I found a great deal of interesting information about some of the lesser-known early explorers of the Southwest. I want to try my hand at a couple of historical novels, and this seemed like the ideal time and place to make a start in that direction."

"Seems I remember your mother writing us that you had sold some stories or something."

"Well, not exactly, Hank. I have had several articles published in some of the historical and archeological journals, but that's a whole different world from writing novels."

Janet was ashamed of the half-truths she had told the McVeys. She had taken some notes and made some outlines before David's death, but she had no intention of writing now, except for a few pages as a cover for her investigations.

"That's enough about me. Tell me about Agness. Are there many new faces around here?"

"No," Maggie answered. "Most of the folks you and your parents knew are still here. Some of the kids moved away after they grew up. Of course there have been a few deaths. Old man McHenry died last year at ninety-six. Jane Willis and Joseph Riegel both died several years ago. Other than that, Agness is pretty much the same. The mail boat is still our main excitement."

Maggie refused Janet's help with the supper dishes, but extended an invitation for her to spend the night at the Lodge.

"Thanks so much for supper and the invitation, Maggie, but I'm eager to see the log house again and get settled in. The rain seems to have let up for the moment, so I think I'll say goodnight and go now."

Hank insisted on leading the way in his battered pickup. Janet was surprised to see that the road to the house on the bluff overlooking the river appeared to be little used. Now that she thought about it, she was also surprised that there were no guests at the Lodge. September had always brought a crowd of fishermen to Agness.

Hank helped Janet unload the Toyota. He had built a fire in the living room stove earlier so the house was warm. He added a couple of small logs and laid a fire in the cookstove for morning.

"If you need anything, be sure to let us know. It's been raining pretty hard up in the mountains so your water line may be washed out in the morning. If it is, let me know and I'll go up and fix it, unless you want to try your hand at it."

Janet laughed. "I haven't forgotten how. I certainly had plenty of experience when we lived here and I won't mind having an excuse to go roaming tomorrow. Is it still the first creek to the west and up about a mile?"

"Yep, exactly the same place."

Hank started for the door, then stopped and looked at Janet. A faint red flush crept over his face as he groped for words to express his thoughts.

"I'm real sorry about your mister, Janet. I know you're hurting something fierce. These mountains can be a mighty healing place and Maggie and me are glad you came to us. We'll do our best to see that no one bothers you."

"Thank you, Hank."

Hank nodded and mumbled a goodnight. As Janet heard his truck rattling off up the track, she wanted to call him back and tell him the truth about why she was here. She hated lies. Maybe tomorrow.

Janet opened her billfold and looked at the slip of paper which had brought her here. Somehow the words didn't carry the impact they had before her arrival.

"How could this peaceful, remote place and these good people have any connection with David's murder?" she said aloud. "Did I make a mistake? Did David mean something else?"

Janet was tired but still somewhat keyed up from the day. She wandered through the house in an effort to unwind.

It was like stepping back into yesterday. She couldn't believe how little had changed in fifteen years. The same pot-bellied stove heated the living room. The same old scruffy desk sat in the corner. Only the couch with its faded flower pattern was different, but it looked just as lumpy and uncomfortable as its predecessor. Best of all, the Jolly Brown Giant still occupied its place of prominence in front of the stove.

Some pioneer craftsman had fashioned a beautiful myrtlewood rocking chair with a seat so deep and broad that no ordinary person's feet could touch the floor. Janet remembered the many rainy afternoons she had spent curled up in old JBG with a pillow and a good book.

Janet had only pleasant memories as she inspected the house. The two downstairs bedrooms, separated by a bathroom, were simply furnished with antique iron beds and handmade chests. Maggie had brightened them with two of her lovely quilts.

In the kitchen, the Atlantic Queen cookstove, freshly blacked and polished, dominated the room. Beside it a woodbox decorated with faded Pennsylvania Dutch designs was filled with kindling. The cupboards were filled with a winter's supply of groceries. On a top shelf, Janet spied several jars of Maggie's home-canned huckleberries and smoked salmon from Hank's smokehouse.

Janet grinned. As a teenager she had earned quite a reputation for her capacity for huckleberry pie and smoked salmon. Hank had once jokingly threatened to put a padlock on his smokehouse door.

Janet filled a couple of gallon jars with water in case Hank's warning about the water line proved true. Then she remembered the reservoir on the stove and filled it with water which would heat the next morning while she cooked breakfast. She could at least have a hot sponge bath in the morning. As an afterthought, she put a full kettle to heat on the living room stove while she continued her tour.

She marveled, as she had in years past, at the loving care which had gone into the building of this house. It was constructed of hand-hewn logs, and the ground floor was paneled and floored with polished redwood.

Janet saved the best until last. She was almost afraid to climb the narrow stairway from the kitchen to the second floor, which had been her domain. At the top of the stairs on the left there was a small, dark room where her mother had stored apples during the winter. To the right was a bathroom containing a huge enameled tub with claw feet.

What a pain it had been, toiling up the stairs with buckets of hot water when she wanted a leisurely bath instead of a quick shower in the downstairs bathroom.

Janet flipped the light switch for the large room which occupied the remainder of the second floor. Thank god, nothing had changed. The gorgeous antique brass bed stood between the two front windows on the same enormous braided rug. What fantasies she'd had after hearing that Clark Gable had spent two weeks here in the summer of 1954 and had slept in that bed.

The warm sheen of the myrtlewood paneling and floor gave the room a special glow, even without Gable. The slope of the roof had been walled off for storage down both sides of the room except for an alcove under a dormer window, which had a cushioned bench on three sides and a small myrtlewood table. The rainy darkness obscured the lovely view of the mountains on the far side of the river.

Janet lingered for a few minutes, thinking of happier times, then went downstairs, made a cup of hot tea, and settled into the Jolly Brown Giant. The black Lincoln and the treacherous road from Powers seemed part of another lifetime. She knew the decision to come here had been a wise one, even if it didn't lead to the answers she was seeking. She could already feel the healing effects.

Chapter 3

It was a beautiful autumn day, but, true to Hank's warning, there was no water. Janet had a breakfast of ham and biscuits with wild blackberry jam. She ruefully pinched a couple of excess inches at her waistline. No matter what she did there always seemed to be an extra ten pounds, but the lure of huckleberry pie was too much to resist. She made a pie with a jar of Maggie's home-canned berries and put it in the oven to bake while she took a sponge bath.

Janet vacillated between immediately heading for the mountains to repair the water line and doing part of her unpacking first. She finally decided to unpack so that she could feel free to spend the rest of the day exploring.

For the present, she decided to use the downstairs bedroom where she had slept the night before. She put her clothes in the closet and chest and added a few personal touches to the room. She arranged her favorite books, tapes, and tape-player on the desk in the living room, and rather enjoyed the whimsical touch of her sterling silver candelabra in the center of the oilcloth-covered kitchen table.

Janet took her typewriter and writing and research materials upstairs and arranged them on the myrtle-wood table in the alcove. As a finishing touch, she placed a little pot of ivy she had brought from home on the ledge above the window seat and put David's favorite glass paperweight on a stack of blank paper.

It was mid-morning when she wrapped the left-over biscuits and ham in foil and tucked them in one pocket of her jacket. First, she had to drop by the Lodge and telephone her parents to let them know she had arrived safely.

Janet dreaded the conversation. Her father had understood and respected her need for independence since early childhood. Her mother had always been annoyingly over-protective. It was a strange situation which Janet had never understood, since her mother was a very independent and adventurous woman who admired those traits in others. Somehow, when it came to Janet, she had never given up the hope that Janet would be Betty Crocker, living in *House Beautiful*, clad in frilly aprons, with at least four bouncing babies. That just wasn't Janet's nature.

Janet detoured by the old apple orchard on her way to the lodge and found a tree still heavy with fruit. She stashed a couple of apples in a pocket and headed up the track while munching a third.

David would have loved this, Janet thought. He would have particularly appreciated the ingenuity which brought running water to the log house. A hose was buried underground for several miles cross-country to emerge in a fast-flowing creek far up on the side of a mountain. The last few feet of hose were anchored in the stream bed with large rocks. A piece of fine-meshed wire was tied over the end to filter out debris;

ingenious, but somewhat subject to the whims of Mother Nature. Janet laughed. David would have found a solution to that right away.

As Janet paused on the steps of the rear veranda of the Lodge, she heard loud and angry voices.

"Damn it, Hank, how could you let her come here? I told you to call her back and tell her not to come. She can't stay. I won't allow it."

"The Warners are our friends, Jim. We've gone along with you so far. The Lodge is empty. We've turned people away who have been coming here for twenty years, but there comes a time when a person has to draw the line."

"Well, it shouldn't have been with her, of all people. If you won't tell her to leave, I will."

"No, Jim. I forbid it. She stays. You only have to look at her to know how much she needs to be here and how much she needs some friends. You just keep this damned mess that you're involved in away from her."

Janet's heart pounded as she backed away and ducked behind the nearby trees to work her way deep into the forest. Jim and Hank were fighting about her. The Warners were her parents. And Jim — she had recognized Jim's voice after all these years. James Scott had been her best friend and first love when she was seventeen.

Janet's head was whirling with questions. Why was Jim so angry about her presence in Agness? Why had he said, "her, of all people?" What terrible thing was he involved in that would make the McVeys willing to turn guests away from the Lodge?

A possible answer still eluded her an hour later when she found the end of her water line. The heavy run-off from the rain had dislodged the anchor rocks and the filter was clogged with bits of leaves and pine needles. She restored everything to proper working order within a few minutes.

Janet replayed the conversation she had overheard once more in her mind. She simply could not believe that whatever Jim was doing had anything to do with her. David had never been to Agness. David and Jim had never met. It had been fifteen years since she had seen Jim, and almost fourteen years since they had corresponded.

Whatever was involved, Janet felt certain that a confrontation with Jim was imminent. She didn't have any idea how to handle the situation. She finally decided that she would just allow events to unfold as they would. In the meantime, she intended to carry on with her plans for the day.

The ruins of an old water-powered sawmill were a short walk farther up the mountain. Twenty minutes later Janet was perched on a huge stump, daydreaming. *The ruins surely dated back to the earliest settlers*, Janet thought. In her mind's eye she could see the mill as it had once been — a busy place with people scurrying about sawing logs for houses and furniture, perhaps even for her log house and the Jolly Brown Giant.

"Janet! Janet!"

The voice shattered her reverie. She turned toward the sound and caught her breath. She hadn't expected the confrontation with Jim to happen quite this soon.

"Over here, Jim," she called.

I'll just have to play it by ear, she thought. *For now I'll just act like anyone seeing an old friend after many years*. Jim strode toward her. She shook her head as she watched him. He was almost a Hollywood stereotype of a lumberjack: tall, broad-shouldered, narrow-hipped, curly black hair, brilliant blue eyes framed by handsome, deeply-tanned features.

"My, my, you've grown into a big one," Janet said, grinning up at him.

"Well, ma'am, you know how it is here among the tall pines. We keep trying to stretch up to see the sun. You haven't done so shabbily yourself. Scrawny little tomboy grown up into a beautiful woman."

"Appearances are deceiving, Jim. The tomboy still lives. What on earth are you doing in Agness? I thought you would be in some glamorous part of the world digging up ancient bones."

"I was for a while. You see before you Dr. James Scott, archeologist, anthropologist, and world traveler, for what it's worth," Jim said caustically.

Janet was startled by Jim's harsh manner. She had evidently hit a sore spot. A change of subject seemed in order.

"Jim, I've thought so often of those two summers. No two kids ever had as much fun as we did. What a rare experience those magic days exploring the mountains with old Sam and his dog. And that last summer, remember the little girl who tagged around after you like a lovesick puppy? What was her name?"

"Ginny Carmichael. Ginny Carmichael Scott. She's dead."

"Good lord, what happened?"

Jim turned his back on Janet as he answered. "I married her at the end of my junior year in college. A couple of years ago I took over a dig in Arizona for a colleague who got sick.

"Eighteen months ago Ginny and two of the students were killed in a rock slide. She's buried on the bluff between the rivers."

"I'm so sorry, Jim. I had no idea. I do understand how you feel."

Jim turned to look at Janet. She was frightened by the expression on his face.

"Yes, I know. I heard about your husband." His voice was harsh and angry. "Why in hell did you come here, Janet? Why did you have to come *here?*"

Janet was shaken. She wondered if Jim had heard about David from the McVeys or if he had gotten his information elsewhere. Did he know all of the vicious accusations that had been made against her and David? Did that account for his anger? She didn't know how to answer Jim, so she countered with a question.

"Why are you here, Jim?"

"It's my home. What's your excuse?" he snapped.

"Home." Janet repeated the word. She felt deep sadness and a stirring of resentment as she considered the word.

"Home. Nice word. I don't have one right now. No husband, no home. Friends who turned out not to be friends when I needed them. Everywhere I could think of to go were places which had been special to David and me. The memories hurt too much. Agness seemed to offer peace and solitude and a chance to put my life together again. I even thought I might still have a friend or two here. Was I wrong?"

Jim didn't answer. The ravages of grief on Janet's face and the quiet agony of her words touched Jim, reminding him that Janet was not his adversary.

The contrast between the young tomboy he had known and the woman who faced him was like the difference between a proud, high-soaring eagle and a robin with a broken wing, hurt and vulnerable. Jim was angry with himself for hurting her more, for being so centered on the problems her presence might cause that he had ignored her pain. He searched for the right words, kind words, but they eluded him.

Janet was moved to compassion by Jim's obvious distress. She reached out to him and took his hand.

"Jim, I know the awful anger one feels at pointless death. I know how it feels to want to lash out and hurt others to make up for losing someone you love. It doesn't help. Sometimes it is a damned rotten world. Since we're in the same situation, can't we be friends instead of hurting each other?"

Jim put his arms around Janet and held her. "You're right, Jan. I've become a real bastard and it's a hard habit to break. I've forgotten how to let anyone get close. Friends?"

"Friends."

Janet and Jim strolled through the woods and quickly slipped back into the easy camaraderie they had enjoyed as teenagers. Both made an effort to keep their conversation on safe ground. "Are you living with your parents, Jim?"

"No, they sold out and moved to Grants Pass a few years ago. I bought the old Joseph Riegel place from his widow."

"Riegel? Was he the one called 'German Joe', the one who packed the washing machine and refrigerator up that awful trail to his cabin?"

"Yeah, that's the one. And it was a refrigerator, washer, and dryer. No one ever figured out how he did it."

"I guess you've put in a road by now."

"No. I had a temporary road put in while I was fixing the place up and putting in new appliances and a new generator. When I got it all done, I had the road bulldozed and trees planted. I park my Jeep at the old logging camp and walk from there. I don't get a lot of uninvited guests that way."

"I can understand why," Janet laughed. "I remember that trail. Built for and by mountain goats."

They walked and talked for an hour and then sat on the trunk of a fallen tree to enjoy the forest sounds. After a few minutes Jim sniffed the air.

"Ham. That's what it is. I smell ham."

"Nonsense. You're having delusions. Where would you find ham in the woods?"

"Perhaps hunger has made me delirious," Jim teased.

Janet casually pulled a clean bandanna from her jeans and spread it on the log between them. Jim grinned in anticipation. Janet slowly removed her Swiss Army knife from the chain around her neck and placed it carefully on the bandanna. Then she took two apples from her jacket pocket and put one in front of Jim and bit into the other.

"Lunch is served."

"Damn! I could have sworn I smelled ham."

Janet shrugged and continued devouring her apple. Jim looked at his apple and sighed.

"Drat! When a fellow's mouth is all set for ham, an apple just doesn't do it."

"I really shouldn't share this with you," Janet said as she pulled the foil packet from another pocket. "And I won't until you tell me how you knew. You couldn't possibly have smelled it."

"Guess I'll have to confess. I saw Hank this morning and he told me you had driven in last night. He said you would probably have to fix the water line this morning. Just thought I'd be neighborly and dropped by to offer to do it for you."

I'll just bet, Janet thought as he continued.

"When I stuck my head in the kitchen door, I smelled ham and saw the biscuit pan. You never used to venture out without a snack stashed somewhere on you. No reason to think you had changed. That was a great looking pie on the table."

"I spend fifteen years trying to become a woman of mystery and in five minutes you know all my secrets."

"I doubt that. That I know all your secrets, I mean."

"There was a time, Jim, when we didn't keep secrets from each other. Times change, people change." Janet took a deep breath and continued. "You evidently have, Jim. I overheard part of your conversation with Hank this morning. Why don't you want me here? Why have you forced Hank and Maggie to close the Lodge?"

"Damn you, Janet," Jim exploded. "Just stay out of it. Mind your own business. It has nothing to do with you personally. We just don't need any outsiders here right now. We'd all be a lot happier if you would just pack your bags and leave."

Janet grabbed her knife and bandanna and faced Jim defiantly. "I don't know what your problem is about my presence here, but I am here to stay whether you like it or not. Don't worry, I know how to mind my own business."

She walked away at a fast pace, her mind a jumble of thoughts. She was furious with Jim, but she was also afraid that he was in serious trouble. She slowed her steps when she heard Jim following her. *Was it possible*, she wondered, *that he might unknowingly have some answers about David's death?*

"Jan, wait. I'm sorry. I shouldn't have exploded like that. I have a lot on my mind that I'm not free to talk about. Can we just put some subjects out of bounds for now and still be friends?"

"I think so, Jim. I've told you my reasons for being here and there really isn't anything else to say on the subject. I won't pry into your affairs."

Not much, I won't, Janet added to herself.

They continued their walk in silence, both gradually caught up in the beauty of their surroundings. Each had an eye for tiny details missed by most, and read the story of the forest inhabitants like most people read a book.

"Cougar," Jim challenged, nodding toward a series of tracks.

"Stalking a rabbit," Janet answered, pointing to a few hairs caught in the huckleberry brush. "Rabbit got away."

"You haven't lost it."

"Nope. Once a woodsman, always a woodsman. Or should I say woodsperson?"

Jim groaned. "Don't tell me you're one of those liberated women."

"As far as I know, I was never unliberated. Think we can find enough safe subjects to talk about through dinner?"

"We can try."

"Good. I'll cook. You do the dishes."

When they arrived at Janet's back door, Jim volunteered to bring in some firewood from the shed. Janet went inside and took a quick look around. She chuckled at the sight of the pie, then bit her lip as she stopped in the living room doorway. Her billfold was on the desk where she had left it, but it had been moved slightly and a tiny corner of yellow paper was visible. Jim must have seen the slip of paper which had brought her to Agness. Had the words meant anything to him?

"Oh, Jim," she whispered, "what have you gotten yourself into?"

Janet took a deep breath and breezed across the kitchen just as Jim struggled to open the screen door.

"James Scott, you're a thief as well as a snoop!"

Jim's face flushed a deep red as he dumped the logs into the woodbox. "Aw, Jan, you're convicting me on circumstantial evidence. How do you know I took that piece of pie? It could have been a passing fisherman."

"How do you know I'm referring to the pie?"

Janet noted his furtive glance toward the desk, visible through the doorway.

"Well, I guess you caught me. But I did leave a fair exchange." He pointed toward the screened-in box attached to the outside of the kitchen window which served as a refrigerator. There was a basket filled with huge blue-black prune plums. "I'll never forget how funny you and your mother looked years ago, sitting under that tree eating plums until you both got sick."

"That's a horrible thing to remember. It makes us sound like pigs. We were having a serious mother-daughter talk about you, if you must know, and didn't realize we'd eaten so many."

Damn, Janet, Jim thought, *why are you here? You can't be involved in this mess. But that damned note in your billfold ...*

Gave you a good scare, didn't I Sonny-boy?, Janet was thinking. *You can't expect me to stay out of your business if you won't stay out of mine.*

After dinner, Janet made coffee while Jim rummaged through her tape collection and chose a Chopin tape. She wondered if he realized that she was the pianist.

Jim picked up a book — a rare work on early archeology — just as Janet told him that his coffee was ready. She curled up in JBG while he occupied the other rocking chair. They drank coffee, smoked, and listened to the music in companionable silence. Jim stubbed his cigarette in the ashtray and opened the book and noted the nameplate.

"Hm ... Are you friends with this J. W. Manning? I noticed his name on the tape and now on this book."

"Yes, I know J. W. fairly well."

"What do you think of his theories?"

"Well, unless something terribly strange has happened since the last time I looked in the mirror, he is a she. And I like my theories just fine, thank you."

"*You* are J. W. Manning?"

"Janet Warner Manning at your service."

"You're J. W. Manning! I never heard your married name ... but the music ... I should have known. I just read that article you wrote about the eleventh-century traveling bird salesman peddling parrots and macaws to the Indians across North America. That was the funniest piece I have ever read in one of those stuffy journals. I don't know how you ever got them to print it, but you almost made a believer out of me by the time I finished the article."

"Only almost?"

"Well, okay, I couldn't find any fault with your research. I must say that some of your other theories are still open to question. I can't believe that you're involved in this field. I thought you'd do something with your music."

"You shouldn't be so surprised. It's all your fault."

"How can it be my fault?"

"Besides having repeatedly told me that with my imagination I should be a writer, you infected me with two incurable diseases during my two summers here — a love of tobacco and a fascination with history and archeology. I can forgive you for the history and archeology, but for the tobacco — never."

The hours slipped away as Jim excitedly questioned Janet about some of the articles she had written and her future plans for writing. They had a slight disagreement over the date of an obscure historical event and Janet took him upstairs to search through some of her research material for verification of her statement. She found the material and handed it to Jim. While he was reading, she unconsciously picked up David's paperweight.

Jim looked up at her curiously. "Janet, you don't believe in that occult stuff, do you?"

"Me? No. Why do you ask?"

"That crystal ball."

"This isn't a crystal ball. It's just an old glass paperweight that my husband kept on his desk."

Jim took it from her and examined it closely. "This isn't glass. It's a crystal ball made from a very fine piece of quartz. I'll bet it's quite old and probably worth a tidy little sum. A piece of quartz that clear and flawless is rare. Probably belonged to some old gypsy who was the seventh daughter of a seventh daughter and born with a caul over her face," Jim said laughingly.

"Well, as far as I'm concerned, it's a paperweight."

Jim placed it carefully on the table and returned to his reading. He became immersed in one of Janet's outlines. For an hour the only words she could elicit from him were "um" and "uh huh." He finally closed the notebook, stood up, and stretched.

"What do you think? Is there material for a historical novel there?"

"Can't tell you right now. I'm having withdrawal symptoms. Forgot to tell you that I'm an addict," he answered shakily.

"Drugs? Jim, I don't believe it!"

"Nope, not drugs. Huckleberry pie."

"James Scott, I could shake you. Huckleberry pie! You had two pieces at supper, plus the one you swiped this morning."

"One more piece will probably pull me through."

Jim told one uproariously funny story after another while they finished the last of the pie. Janet started to offer him another cup of coffee when she noticed that it was midnight and a spate of raindrops hit the kitchen windows.

"It's going to be a dark, wet walk home for you," Janet said pointedly, "but you have your pie to keep you warm. Can I loan you a poncho and flashlight?"

"No, thanks. My Jeep is parked out by the trash pit. I'll just spend the night at the Lodge." He leaned over and kissed Janet on the cheek. "Jan, thank you for the first happy day I've had in a long time."

"It was fun. I enjoyed it, too. Goodnight, Jim."

Janet sat at the kitchen table a long while after Jim left, wondering how much of the boy was still in the man. The teenaged boy she had known and loved had valued truth and honesty above all else. People changed in fifteen years, but did their basic values change? Janet was still asking herself that question when she went to bed.

Jim was asking questions, also. Just how had David Manning died, and was there some connection to the despicable people with whom he was involved? Did the note in Janet's billfold mean that David had drawn her into this nasty business? Jim determined to start getting some answers to his questions the first thing in the morning. It was just possible that his life and Janet's might depend on it.

Chapter 4

Janet's mood, when she awakened, didn't match the beautiful, sunny day. Breakfast was a pot of tea and half a pack of cigarettes. She paced the floor and wondered what her next move should be. She kept coming back to the same answer: Maggie. If she couldn't trust Maggie McVey, then there was no one in the world she could trust. She could talk to Maggie about David in the way she had needed to talk about him since his death.

Twenty minutes later, Janet stuck her head in the door of the Lodge kitchen. "Hey, Maggie. Is Thursday still your baking day?"

"Come in, dear. Yes, I'm a creature of habit. Pour yourself some coffee. Let me set these loaves to rise and I'll join you."

Janet sipped her coffee and watched Maggie shape the dough into loaves. Maggie was the epitome of the true pioneer woman, as far as Janet was concerned. She was about five-foot-two, with a plump little figure encased in a pretty print dress and a big white apron. She had golden-red hair curling out of a bun on her neck and every visible inch of skin was sprinkled with golden freckles. She ruled the sometimes rowdy fishermen who came to the Lodge with an iron hand. They minded their manners and their language around Maggie and loved every minute of it.

Janet knew Maggie as a lady of many dimensions. Besides being wise and kind and having a sixth sense for anyone with a problem, she was well-educated. Maggie had a master's degree in music, was well-read, and could intelligently discuss any subject from nuclear energy to Zen. She could deliver a baby or a calf, splint a broken bone, and shoot a bear, butcher and cook it. There really wasn't much that Maggie couldn't do and still maintain her facade as a sweet, rather naive, little mountain granny.

Maggie set a plate of hot cinnamon rolls in front of Janet as she joined her at the table.

"I don't know what you did to Jim yesterday, but he came in here last night whistling so loud he woke us. He was so distracted this morning at breakfast that I had to ask him three times if he wanted a piece of huckleberry pie to finish up on."

"Jim is part of the reason I'm here, Maggie. You're the one person I feel free to talk to who may have some of the answers I need.

"To begin with, I accidentally overheard part of the argument that Hank and Jim had yesterday morning. I know that Jim wants me to leave because of something that's going on in Agness. I also know that you and Hank went against his wishes by letting me come.

"I have a great deal to tell you and you may want me to leave when you know the truth. If you ask me to leave, I will, but I hope you will allow me to stay."

"Janet, dear, I can't think of anything you could say which would make us ask you to leave. Jim doesn't run our lives. Tell me whatever you want to, but don't feel that you have to tell me anything. As to what questions you may have about Jim and his situation, I can't promise to answer them."

"Thank you, Maggie. First about Jim and yesterday. We had a little battle of our own out in the woods, but we called a truce and found some common ground in our losses. We ended up having dinner together and sharing a very pleasant evening discussing our mutual interests in history and archaeology. If my reasons for being here were only those that I told you, then there wouldn't be any problem. I could mind my own business and stay out of Jim's way and probably manage a pleasant relationship with him. Unfortunately, that's not the case."

Janet stopped to catch her breath.

"Take your time dear. Jim left early this morning and I don't expect him back for a couple of days. Hank went up the Illinois to fish and I packed him a huge lunch, so we have several hours to ourselves. Just relax. Why don't you begin by telling me about your David. That's what this is all about, isn't it?"

"Oh, Maggie, I miss him so. He was my best friend as well as my husband. No marriage is perfect, but I think ours came very close. It seemed like no matter how much time we had together, it was never enough. Even after ten years we rushed home to each other every evening like newlyweds."

"I understand, dear. Even after forty years Hank and I never seem to have enough time together. That's how love is."

"Then I think you'll understand when I say that David and I not only shared a deep love and respect, but we were catalysts for each other's minds. It was so exciting to discuss our ideas with each other. Somehow we broadened each other's capacity for insight and creative thinking. I don't quite know how to put it into words. David somehow caused me to reach into facets of my mind that I didn't know were there, and he said I did the same for him. I had a capacity for reasoning and thinking when he and I were discussing a subject that I don't have on my own."

"I think you said it very well. Now, tell me about David the man."

"I don't think I have idealized him. He wasn't perfect, but he never betrayed a trust, and he was honest and good. In all the years I knew him, I never knew him to tell a lie. He was creative and inventive and kind. But he wasn't a prig, a goody-goody. He was a man who never felt that he had to prove that he was a man. He was never interested in a night out with the boys. What we did, we enjoyed doing together. We had so many grand adventures.

"You can't have the kind of relationship I had with David and not really know a person. That damned police detective told me that no wife ever thinks her husband could be mixed up in criminal things. But, damn it, Maggie, I knew David. Not just on the surface. I knew the whole fabric of his being. I ..." Janet choked on her tears. "Oh, Maggie, someone murdered my David."

"Oh, Janet, my dear. My poor dear. I'm so sorry. I had no idea."

Janet brushed her tears away and took a deep breath. "I'm just so angry, Maggie. I've been so angry ever since it happened, not just because David was killed, but because of what the police have tried to do to both of us since then. They say that David was killed by a professional hit man.

"At first they accused me of having killed David, but after they questioned the people at the university and found out that I had been there all afternoon, they decided that I had hired a killer. When they couldn't find any reason or proof, they decided that David, or David and I, had been involved in some type of criminal activity. They even tried to tie us into organized crime. They haven't really tried to find out who killed David or why. They have spent all their time trying to prove that we were criminals."

"Do you have any idea why David was killed?"

"None. I thought I had some leads, but they didn't take me anywhere, and no one has really been willing to help. Our so-called friends hold the attitude that 'where there's smoke, there's fire' and don't want to get involved."

"What about family?" Maggie asked.

"David's parents have shown nothing but hostility toward me. I can't understand their lack of faith in their own son. They believe that I'm responsible for his death — that he wouldn't have gotten involved in whatever led to his death if I hadn't somehow influenced him."

"What about your parents, Janet?"

"My parents? Well, their belief in both of us is unshakable, but you know Mother. She wants me to move in with them where she can wrap me in cotton-wool and protect me. She just wants me to forget it all and be her baby girl. Dad understands that I can't leave it alone, that I have to find out why David was murdered and who did it.

"That, Maggie, brings me to why I am here. You are free to tell what I have told you so far, as you feel necessary. The remainder of what I have to say, I will ask you not to tell anyone, with the exception of Hank."

"You have my word, Janet. I don't give it lightly. I also want you to know that I believe in you and your David. I think you knew your husband very well, and if you believe he was incapable of criminal activities, then I have to believe it also. "

"Thank you, Maggie. You don't know what a relief it is to talk to you. I think you understand that I can't just walk away and let David's killer go free."

"Yes, Janet, I do."

"That is why I am here, Maggie. The very last clue I have brought me here."

"To Agness?"

"Yes, as strange as that might seem. David doodled and wrote notes to himself, the way I talk to myself, when he had a problem he was trying to resolve. For several days before he was killed, David was excited and preoccupied with something. I knew he would tell me about it when he had it all put together.

"The night before David was killed, he was reading in bed while I was translating some old documents which seemed to shed some light on a theory I have been trying to prove. I noticed that he was taking notes as he read.

"By the time I finished and went to bed, David was asleep. It wasn't until a few days before I called you that I found the paper David had been writing on in the book he had been reading. There were some doodles and the word 'Agness' several times. Then he had written, 'The key to the whole thing has to be Agness. It's somebody in Agness. Talk to Janet about Agness.' So you see, I had to come."

"Yes, I can see why you came. And now, since, you overheard the conversation between Hank and Jim, and since Jim has made it plain that he doesn't want you here, you wonder if there is any connection between Jim and the note."

"How could I help but wonder under the circumstances?"

"I don't know if there is any connection, Janet. I can't discuss what Jim is involved in with you. I gave my word. But, if you will answer some questions for me, I think I can tell you if there isn't a connection."

"That's as much as I could ask. What do you want to know?"

"Who did David work for and what did he do?"

"David worked for Southwest Data-Comm in Dallas. I'm sure you've heard of them even way up here."

Maggie nodded.

"He was the chief systems analyst, but that doesn't really describe his job. He had a great talent for devising tamper-proof computer systems for companies and for being able to track down computer frauds. He had a very quiet fame in his field. He was often called in by large companies, and even a couple of times by the government, to track down people who had breached computer security. He seemed to have a sixth sense for such things."

"Tell me about his hobbies."

"We essentially had the same hobbies. We took classes in various martial arts including judo, karate, and kendo. We loved backpacking and rock climbing —

anything to do with the wilderness. We both loved flying, history, geology, photography, exploring ghost towns, old Spanish missions, and Indian ruins. For years we dreamed of owning a ranch at the edge of the Gila Wilderness in New Mexico. We were just about to buy it when David was killed. Does that tell you what you need to know?"

"Yes, I think it does. I don't see any connection between David's work and hobbies and Jim's situation."

"Maggie, are you sure?"

"I just don't see how there could be, dear. If David's note means what you think it does, then there has to be something else going on in or around Agness that we don't know about. And Janet, don't judge Jim too harshly. Things are not always what they appear to be."

"If you say so. I'm relieved that Jim isn't involved. I won't say that I'm not curious about what is going on, but I'll leave it alone if it doesn't concern David. Can you think of anyone around Agness, perhaps someone who hasn't been here long, who might be worth investigating?"

"I need some time to think about that, Janet. The problem is that there really aren't any new faces around here except the forest ranger and his wife and three little boys. They have been here about a year. Unless my judgement of human nature has completely deserted me, I can't think of a less likely couple to be involved in anything underhanded."

Maggie got up to check on the loaves in the oven. It was evident that she was doing some heavy thinking, so Janet remained silent, wondering if her trip to Agness was another dead end.

"Janet, dear, why don't you go into the parlor and play the piano for me? I want to do some thinking and the music will help."

Janet nodded her assent. She went into the parlor and seated herself at the old upright piano and ran her fingers over the keys. To her surprise, it was in perfect tune.

"Had it tuned when you decided to come," Maggie called from the kitchen. "I don't play much anymore, but Hank and I thought we might have some music while you are here."

Janet played a Chopin nocturne, then a waltz. By then she had forgotten where she was and was totally immersed in the music. Janet hadn't played since David's death and now she vented her emotions through the music. She played for more than two hours before a muscle cramp in one hand ended a Chopin prelude. She could see Maggie and Hank sitting on the front porch. Maggie was peeling apples for a pie and Hank was rocking and smoking his pipe. Janet joined them.

"That was mighty nice, Janet," Hank said.

"It certainly was a treat, dear. I'm beginning to get a touch of arthritis in these old hands and they don't always do what I want them to on the piano these days." Maggie set the pan of apples aside. "Janet, I took you at your word about telling Hank what you told me. I thought we needed his ideas about this."

"That's fine, Maggie. I just want to apologize to both of you for not telling you the truth in the beginning. I've gotten out of the habit of trusting anyone the past six months. I hope you can understand and forgive me."

"You had good reason for what you did," Hank said. "Maggie and I certainly understand, and it's forgotten. I think I may have a little different viewpoint to offer on the note your husband wrote. It's possible that he had uncovered some type of computer fraud but didn't have the complete picture. He may have had reason to believe that someone living around Agness or connected to Agness in some way had the additional information he needed. The thing is, that person may not know that he or she has the information. Does that sound reasonable?"

"Yes, it does, but does it bring us any closer to knowing who?"

"Not at the moment. Neither Maggie nor I can think of anyone who might have connections to anything in Texas. The only possibility we can think of is that it could be some of the people who have summer cabins around here. Most of them have been coming here for years, but we really don't know them all that well. On the surface they all seem like good folks.

"Let me see what I can find out, without attracting too much attention. It may take a while."

"Thank you, Hank. You don't know what it means to me to finally have someone to talk to whom I can trust."

"Dear," Maggie said, "have you explored the thought that David might have been killed for revenge by someone whose criminal activities he had uncovered in the past?"

"Yes. That was one of my first thoughts. I investigated the possibility the best I could. David always confided in me about his work, so I knew of several people who might have a motive. None of those leads proved out.

"David's immediate superior believed in David, to a degree. He gave me as much help as he could. He also checked out David's most current project. It seemed to be a straight-forward job of designing a security set-up for the computer system of a reputable company in Houston. I know David was working on something else, but no one seems to know what it was."

"I'm sure you checked David's things for any other notes he may have written," Maggie said.

"Yes. There wasn't anything. The small leather notebook David used for notes about current projects and access codes and related information has never been found. He always carried it on him. The note about Agness is the only clue I have."

"Hank and I will help you every way we can. Now, dear, you are worn out and Hank tells me that he ran into Jim down the road and invited him to drop by later for supper. You are welcome to stay, but I suspect you'd rather not."

"You're right, Maggie. I am tired and I think I'd rather spend the evening alone. I may even write a little just for the heck of it."

"You just sit here with Hank for a minute and let me get some things I want to send home with you."

Maggie disappeared into the kitchen, only to reappear almost immediately with a heavily-laden basket. "Here's your supper and something I think you can use."

"You didn't need to do that, but thank you. Thank you both for everything."

"Now, honey, you know you're welcome. Hank and I will do everything we can to help you. You feel free to come up here any time to talk or play the piano or whatever."

Janet gave, Maggie a peck on the cheek. "The pair of you are a real treasure."

"Go on and get out of here. Put all of this out of your mind for now. It would probably be good for you to do some of that writing you were talking about."

"I think I will."

Janet was halfway down the trail before she realized that she hadn't mentioned the black Lincoln that had followed her from Texas. She decided that it wasn't worth going back to the Lodge. She could tell Maggie and Hank later.

She was ravenous by the time she walked into her kitchen and took the cloth off of Maggie's basket. There was enough food for several meals: a loaf of freshly baked bread, several cinnamon rolls, chicken-fried venison steak, deviled eggs, potato salad, and half a huckleberry pie. In the bottom of the basket was a small electric hot pot. There was a note tucked inside: "Thought this might make life easier for a city girl. Love, Maggie."

Janet loaded a tray with food, the hot pot, and instant coffee and carried it upstairs to the bay window. She sat with her feet on the window seat, the plate balanced on her knees, devouring the view and the food. A great burden had lifted from her. The talk with Maggie and Hank had been the best medicine she could have for her heartache. Now she didn't feel quite so alone.

After coffee and a cigarette, Janet leaned back in drowsy contentment. David's paperweight caught her eye. It was a pretty thing. She wondered where David had gotten it. She wondered, also, if Jim knew what he was talking about when he identified it as a crystal ball.

She held it up to the window, catching reflections of the river, mountain, and sky, intrigued by the upside-down images. She was almost hypnotized by the effect when the sharp images became blurred and were replaced by the face of a young man — a handsome, deeply-tanned face framed with sunstreaked hair. She stared in fascination at his beautiful dark blue eyes.

"Oh, my god. What's happening?" Janet dropped the ball on the window seat and ran down the stairs. She paced the living room, almost afraid to think. She stuck a tape in the player and turned the volume up all the way, but she couldn't tolerate the noise and turned it off.

"Enough, Janet. You promised yourself you wouldn't fall apart at the least thing. Now get a grip on yourself. There has to be a very simple, logical explanation for what you think you saw."

She sat down at the kitchen table and took several deep breaths. "You are a sane, reasonable, rational human being, Janet. Remember that. Sane, reasonable, and …" An involuntary yawn interrupted her monologue. "Tired," she continued, "but sane, reasonable, and …" In the middle of a second yawn, a rational explanation did occur to her.

"Of course, you ninny. You were drowsy. You dozed off and dreamed it all. It was the power of suggestion from Jim's talk of crystal balls and gypsies."

Janet climbed the stairs to retrieve her supper tray. She tried to ignore the faint uneasiness tugging at her mind. She resolutely picked up the paperweight and replaced it on the table, not quite daring to look at it.

Downstairs she rinsed her plate and mug and put them in the drainer. It was too early to go to bed. She got a pillow, chose a favorite book, and settled into the Jolly Brown Giant in front of the stove. She was determined to read, but she found it difficult to concentrate on the book. Gradually she drifted off to sleep.

David was standing beside her chair with the crystal ball in his hands. He spoke to her.

"Take it, Janet. Don't be afraid, darling. It's my legacy to you. Use it." He held the crystal ball toward her.

Janet took the crystal ball from David's hands. It felt wonderfully warm and comforting. David turned and walked away. Janet forgot the crystal ball and called after him.

"Don't go. Please don't go."

Janet awakened, calling David's name aloud. Her cheeks were wet with tears and the room was dark and cold.

The dream was as real as anything which had ever happened to her. She turned the lights on and saw that she had slept for several hours. She was shaking with a heavy chill. The dream had taken away all her fears of the crystal ball, but she was too cold to think about anything but getting warm.

Janet stirred the coals in the pot-bellied stove and added several sticks of wood. Her chill was bone deep. She wrapped herself in a blanket and curled up in JBG until the blazing fire warmed the room.

As she sat there, Janet had the feeling that David was in the room, that if she turned her head quickly enough she could see him. It was a strange feeling. Not bad, just strange. It was a feeling she had never experienced before, that she didn't know how to react to or explain.

Janet began to explore her memory for information about such things. She believed that the mind had wondrous potentials which lay dormant in most people. She believed, also, that some intangible part of a person lived on after death. She had read a few popular books on ESP and related subjects and knew that some reportedly reputable people had claimed to have had some rather bizarre experiences. Most of what she had read hadn't impressed her, particularly the idea of communicating with the dead. Now, however, the part of her which was normally questioning and skeptical was thoroughly convinced that David had somehow reached across whatever barrier separated the living from the dead and presented her with a strange legacy.

"Now the question is," Janet said aloud, "what will I do with it? What can I do with it?"

Janet brewed herself a cup of tea and returned to her warm nest in JBG to think. She wasn't really aware of the thought process she went through, but her conclusion was that she would accept David's legacy and not be afraid. She was a rational adult with free will. She could choose the extent to which she would explore the phenomenon of the crystal ball and whether or not she would allow herself to be affected by it. David wouldn't urge her to do something that would be harmful to her, but the choice was still hers.

Chapter 5

Friday. What the thunder was significant about Friday? Through breakfast and a second cup of tea, Janet tried to remember. It was midmorning when the sound of a outboard motor struggling against the river current answered Janet's question. The mail boat.

Twice a week during fall and winter the mailboat made the trip up the Rogue River from Gold Beach. Mail day was always something of a social occasion, bringing the scattered inhabitants of the area by boat, horseback, and foot to the tiny log cabin which served as a post office. Janet wasn't interested in the social aspect, but she did need to mail a letter.

Janet hadn't telephoned her parents. They didn't expect her to be in Agness for a few more days, so she decided to avoid an emotional conversation with her mother by writing. She also wrote a note to Madge Yanek, the neighbor who was taking care of her house.

After a quick swipe with her hairbrush and a dab of lipstick, Janet headed the Toyota toward the post office. She arrived just in time to have her letters included in the outgoing mail and to say hello to several people she vaguely remembered from years past.

There were two couples who had been special friends of her parents. When they showed an inclination for a lengthy conversation, Janet murmured that she had a great deal to do to get settled in and would visit with them later. She headed for her pickup, but getting away wasn't going to be that easy.

"Janet. Janet, dear."

Janet turned to see Sarah Peale, the diminutive postmistress, waving several envelopes in her direction.

"Your mail, dear. You mustn't forget your mail. Quite a lot for your first mail day here. Some of it very official looking," she chirped.

Janet thanked Sarah and reached for the letters, trying to ignore the blatant curiosity of the bystanders. Sarah Peale was not about to relinquish the right she claimed as distributor of the U.S. Mail. Janet gritted her teeth and steeled herself for the well-remembered ritual.

"Here you are, dear. Here's one from Mr. and Mrs. Warner, your parents."

As if I don't know who they are, Janet thought.

"And how are they these days?"

"Very well, thank you."

"Here's another. Hm ... Madge Yanek. One of your friends?"

"My next-door neighbor back in Texas."

"How nice of her to write. Oh, dear. I hope there isn't a problem. There are two official letters here. One is from the Denton County Sheriff's office and the other is from the Dallas Police Department." She was almost twittering with excited anticipation of what she might learn. Everyone else was straining to hear.

Janet couldn't take any more. She snatched the remaining letters from Sarah's hand.

"You're all so damned curious. You just can't keep your noses out of other people's business. Well I'll tell you about those letters. My husband was brutally murdered six months ago and the police are still looking for his killer. Are you satisfied now?"

Janet was immediately ashamed of her outburst when she saw the expressions of embarrassment and sympathy on the faces of the bystanders. Old Sarah looked as if she was about to cry. Janet patted her on the shoulder.

"I'm sorry. I'm really sorry, everyone. I know you didn't mean any harm. Please forgive me. I'm not fit company for anyone right now."

Janet ran to her pickup before anyone could react. She was almost to the Lodge when she met Jim in his Jeep. She waved but ignored his gestured invitation to stop and talk. Maggie was on the back veranda as she drove by the Lodge. She waved, but Janet was too embarrassed to stop and tell Maggie what she had done. Maggie would understand her rudeness this once. Janet determined that she would stop and think before she opened her mouth from now on. She had to realize that these people were not like the ones she had left behind.

Her hands were shaking as she curled up in JBG and perused the envelopes. In addition to the letters Sarah had commented on, there was one from Eric Baren, the professor she had worked for at the University of North Texas in Denton.

As she read one letter after another, her emotions ranged from bewilderment through indignation to anger. Her house had been broken into and ransacked the day she left. Even the wood paneling in the den had been ripped from the walls. As far as Madge and the Denton County sheriff could determine, nothing had been taken. Her office at the university had been treated in the same manner. Several file folders of research material on rare Indian artifacts had been taken from the office.

The two fingerprints found in her house were identified as belonging to a Roscoe Carrac, a man with organized crime connections who was wanted for questioning as an accessory to several murders. Again, questions were raised about the possibility of David's involvement in criminal activity.

All the old anger and frustration came welling up in Janet, but the thing which shook her to the core was the enclosed mug shot of Roscoe Carrac. He had introduced himself to Janet with a different name, and had pretended to be a junior executive at Southwest Data-Comm. He had demanded the right to search David's personal papers in case they contained confidential information about his work. Janet had angrily assured him that David never brought confidential documents home and had slammed the door in his face. Janet's faith in David was unshaken. Everyone else seemed to have already tried and convicted him. He had only Janet to defend him and find the truth, but she didn't know where to start.

All at once the house seemed dark and stifling. She grabbed her windbreaker and ran out the front door toward the river. *There had to be some answers somewhere*, she thought. *But, damn it! Where?*

She paced the river bank with mounting anger and frustration, which finally gave way to feelings of desolation and helplessness at the thought of her violated home. She was so achingly alone.

She dropped to her knees and beat her fists against the rocks, crying out her pain and giving vent to all the dammed-up emotions she'd held in check for weeks.

Janet was unaware of Jim's presence until his strong arms suddenly encircled her from behind and her battered, bloody hands were imprisoned in his firm grip.

"No, Janet. No. Scream and rage and throw things, but don't harm yourself."

"Oh, Jim . . . "

"I know, dear. I know."

He held her for a long time while she cried. When she was empty of tears, she moved self-consciously away from him. He lit a cigarette and handed it to her. She noticed that his cheeks were wet.

"Don't be embarrassed, Janet. I understand much more than you might suppose."

Janet nodded and concentrated on the cigarette in an attempt to regain her composure.

"How did you find me?"

"Hank explained to me about David after Sarah Peale told me what happened at the post office. I had the feeling you might need someone. If you want to talk, I'll listen. If you want me to leave, I will."

"Thank you. I ... I don't know what I want. I don't want to be alone right now, but I'm not sure I want to talk. I ..."

"That's okay. What you do need is a cup of coffee and some attention to those hands."

Janet's hands were oozing blood in several places and beginning to throb. Her eyes were swollen and her face was streaked with dirt. Outwardly she was a mess.

Inwardly she felt better than she had in months. She allowed Jim to pull her to her feet and followed him as he walked toward the log house.

Jim was silent until they reached the front door. As they entered, he put his hands on Janet's shoulders and propelled her toward the bathroom.

"Wash your face and hands. I'll make some coffee."

When Janet reentered the living room a few minutes later, Jim had placed a tray with coffee and cinnamon rolls on the footstool between the rocking chairs. The letters which Janet had scattered across the floor were neatly stacked on the desk. "Let me see your hands. Did you put something on them?"

"Yes. They aren't as bad as they looked. They will probably be stiff and sore tomorrow, though."

"The next time you feel like hitting something, beat the hell out of your pillow. Okay?"

Janet nodded.

Jim wisely didn't question Janet and appeared to be content to sit in companionable silence. It wasn't long before Janet began to tell him about the vandalism of her home and office and the accusations against David.

"I'm really sorry you've been through such hell, Jan. Please don't misunderstand my question, but I have to ask. Are you absolutely certain within yourself that your husband couldn't have gotten mixed up in something without your knowledge?"

Janet stifled the resentment which was her automatic response to Jim's question. Intellectually she knew that he didn't mean it as an accusation. She looked Jim directly in the eye.

"I'm absolutely certain. David and I were extraordinarily close. He wasn't involved in anything which didn't include me."

Jim frowned, obviously disturbed by her answer.

"See you later," he said, and abruptly left.

Janet was baffled by Jim's behavior. She thought about it for a few minutes, then put it from her mind. She was restless, but not in the mood to leave the house or talk to anyone. She didn't even want to think about any of it at the moment. As a last resort, she retreated upstairs.

Janet spent the afternoon sorting through notebooks of plot outlines and stacks of research material. Perhaps she would try her hand at writing a novel, she thought. At least it would give her something to do, something to think about when she couldn't spend anymore time thinking in circles about David.

David. The crystal ball was on the table. Had it been only yesterday that she had seen the face in the crystal ball and dreamed of David? His legacy to her. What did that mean?

She cupped the ball in her hands and looked into it. For a long time there was only the reflection of her own face and the room around her. She was surprised at how relaxed she felt when the image of the young man began to take shape. He was laughing. She examined his face thoroughly and experienced only pleasant, happy feelings. In a few minutes, the scene changed. The young man was seated at a desk. Janet felt a thrill of excitement as she recognized familiar objects on the desk: pottery sherds, magnifying glasses, reference books she recognized, maps, and an odd assortment of hand tools and brushes. He was an archeologist, or worked in a related field.

Janet watched him examine a large rectangular slab of fine-grained, gray volcanic rock with a magnifying glass. There appeared to be marks etched deeply into the surface of the stone. He stopped, picked up a book which Janet recognized as a reference work on ancient languages, and search for something. The search was successful. He compared an entry in the book with the marks on the stone and gave an excited shout.

Janet could make out only "O V I" just before the young man turned the stone over. She recognized it then as a finely shaped metate. The ancient grinding stone was worn thin from generations of use.

The scene shifted. The young man was standing behind his desk, making notations on a map tacked to the wall. There were already numerous arrows, x's, and undecipherable words written on the map. Something about the map and the marks Janet had seen on the bottom of the metate tugged at her mind. The overall appearance of the map was familiar, but she just couldn't see it well enough to identify its location. And those marks — she had seen those same marks before as a part of something else.

Slowly the scene faded. Janet thoughtfully placed the crystal ball on the table and went downstairs. *Well, David,* she thought, *I followed your instructions and used the crystal ball. Now if I could only understand what I saw and the purpose for it. If I could only be certain that I'm not having mental aberrations.*

Janet wandered aimlessly around the kitchen. She was hungry but she couldn't decide what to cook. She found that the water in the reservoir of the cookstove was still warm, so she opened the valve which allowed it to drain into the insulated tank connected to the shower. She refilled the reservoir and promised herself a nice hot shower as a reward for building up the fire to cook a meal. A second reservoir of hot water would insure that her shower wouldn't end with an icy blast from the mountain stream.

Her hands were stiff and sore as she prepared her meal. When all other ideas for a meal failed, there was always what she and David had called "camp breakfast." She peeled a potato to dice with bacon and onion. When the potato and bacon were done, she drained the grease and stirred an egg into the mixture. She brewed a cup of tea and sat at the kitchen table to eat. By this time, her hands were aching.

That was really a stupid thing to do to myself, but maybe it was worth it, she thought. *I've been an emotional time bomb poised to go off. Now I'm exhausted and my hands hurt, but the sense of emotional relief makes me feel as if I've cleared the decks for battle and am ready to accomplish something.*

After a hot shower, Janet went to bed and slept until almost daybreak. She lay in bed for a while after waking and tried to formulate a plan of action. Hank and Maggie would do their best to get information for her, but she couldn't sit around waiting for something which might not exist. No plan came to mind, so she decided a leisurely walk might help her think.

Within half an hour, Janet had dressed and breakfasted on a cinnamon roll and glass of orange juice. As she stepped out the kitchen door, she noticed the tips of clouds edging over the mountains to the northwest, promising rain later in the day.

She decided to explore upriver toward the confluence of the Illinois and Rogue rivers. If rain came sooner than she expected, she would be only a few minutes walk from the house.

The quiet stillness of the forest at early morning was pure delight to Janet. The lofty pine and fir trees perfumed the cool air. This time, when the daylight denizens of the forest were still in their dens, holes, and nests, had always evoked an almost mystical feeling in Janet, a feeling of excited anticipation, as if the coming day promised grand adventure. That feeling was always the same, whether the forest was in Texas, New Mexico, or Oregon.

Janet couldn't pass up a fallen tree with a moss-covered trunk. She sat down and leaned back on a convenient limb, lazily watching the forest come to life.

The momentary serenity connected her present self with the person she had been before David's death. She was not pleased with the comparison. Emotions were controlling too much of her behavior. She was reacting to events, rather than using mental and emotional discipline to generate a suitable response.

Janet left her mossy seat and continued upriver. "There is nothing wrong with grieving for David," she told herself. "What *is* wrong is using grief as an excuse to be mentally lazy, as an excuse for allowing myself to be emotionally manipulated by the actions of others — especially the S.O.B. who trashed my house!"

"No more," Janet promised herself, as she stood watching the clear blue waters of the Illinois join the swift red waters of the Rogue. "No more!"

She looked across to the craggy bluff which reared from the juncture of the rivers. She felt a momentary sadness at the sight of the small mound which was Ginny's grave, suddenly wondering if Jim had told her the whole truth about Ginny's death.

Janet turned away and climbed out of the river bottom. *Even if he hasn't*, she decided, *Ginny's death has nothing to do with me.*

She headed in the general direction of an old vineyard she remembered. A good book and a bunch of grapes, and she'd be set for a pleasant rainy afternoon.

The vineyard was still there, hidden among the trees and brush. Someone, probably Hank McVey, had tended the vines at the proper times to insure continued production. The vines looked incredibly old. The trunks were the size of large trees, knarled and weathered grey. Janet had no idea how long a grapevine could live, but she wanted to believe that some pioneer family in a covered wagon had cherished delicate cuttings over hundreds of terrible miles and had planted them here in this bountiful land, where they still flourished.

Two of the ten rows of vines were laden with bunches of grapes so huge that each cluster must have weighed close to twenty pounds. The individual grapes were the size of plums.

Janet used her Swiss Army knife to cut one bunch. It was immediately apparent that there was no easy or neat way to carry the grapes, but she was determined to get them back to the house.

By the time Janet was in sight of the log house, she had grape juice all over her windbreaker and dripping down the neck of her shirt. She kept trying to think of the word which described the way she felt — something associated with Roman feasts and orgies — but the word eluded her. The moment she saw Hank and Jim sitting on her back porch, her thoughts turned to embarrassed amusement at the ridiculous picture she must present.

Both men were wiping away tears of laughter by the time she stepped onto the porch.

"Gentlemen do not laugh at ladies. A gentleman would open the door for a lady before said lady deposited her grapes in his lap."

Jim leaped to his feet and opened the back door. "Captured them all by yourself, did you? Looks like they put up a vicious battle."

Janet turned and shoved him out of the door with one foot. "You sit on the porch while I clean up. I'll deal with the two of you later."

She dumped the grapes in the sink and retreated to the bathroom. When she was somewhat cleaner and wearing a fresh shirt, she joined them on the porch.

"Durn," said Hank. "I never have a camera at the right moment."

"I might have known that there would be someone around to see me, even in a remote place like this," Janet laughed. "I feel like a little kid caught with jam on my face. Now, what brings you down this way? It must have been something besides a chance to see the sideshow."

"Jim and I wanted to warn you that the electricity will be off most of the day and maybe part of the evening. We need to overhaul the generator and replace the bearings before winter sets in. Maggie sent a couple of kerosene lamps."

"Give her my thanks. I brought one kerosene lamp and a big box of candles from Texas. I didn't think to bring kerosene, though."

"No problem," Jim said. "There's a five-gallon can in the woodshed. I've already filled the lamps and that should see you through the day. Just in case, though, maybe I'd better set the kerosene can on the porch. It looks like rain."

"Thank you. It does look as if it might get drippy."

Hank stood up. "Well, Jim, I guess the entertainment is over for the day. We might as well get at that generator."

"Yep, only one show a day. Next time there will be an admission charge," Janet quipped.

Jim grinned. "I'll pay my admission ahead of time. I'd really enjoy having you come up to my place for lunch tomorrow if the weather clears."

"That sounds like fun, Jim."

"Great. If something happens to change your mind, there's a buzzer system between my place and the Lodge. We use a simple code. Hank or Maggie can let me know if you can't make it."

"When you say, 'give me a buzz,' you're really serious."

"It beats smoke signals."

J anet hurried to carry in a supply of firewood before the rain started. She set out candles and kerosene lamps in strategic places. A heavy rain started just as the electricity went off. Janet changed into her velvet robe and wool-lined squaw boots and curled up in JBG to bask in the coziness of her domain while she enjoyed some giant grapes.

The patter of the rain, the warmth of the fire, the soft light of the lamps, and the hominess of polished wood and braided rugs all gave her a feeling of peace and contentment. She had more than her share of problems, but most of them were things she could do little about at the moment, so she intended to enjoy the good things as the opportunity arose.

When Janet went to the desk to get a book, she noticed that none of the books were in the order she had placed them. Her tape collection had been left in disarray.

With growing anger and apprehension, Janet took a lamp and examined the log house, room by room. In the spare bedroom, the stack of empty boxes she had stored there after unpacking had been tossed around the room. She skipped the bathroom. She would have noticed anything out of place when she changed into her robe and boots.

The clothes in her bedroom closet appeared undisturbed, but she was filled with fury when she opened the drawers of her chest and saw the tangled mess of lingerie.

Her hands were shaking when she placed the lamp on the kitchen table. The thought that the intruder had handled her intimate apparel was disgusting. She calmed down a little as she opened the kitchen cabinets. Everything there appeared to be in order.

She picked up the lamp and turned toward the stairway. The door was closed. She always left it open. "Oh, my god!" she whispered, "whoever did this may still be here."

She set the lamp back on the table and dropped into one of the chairs. She should have thought of that first. What if she had blundered up the stairs and been attacked? It was time to control her anger and use her head.

She sat at the table a few minutes longer. *Well, she thought, either you learned something during ten years of martial arts training or you didn't.* There was a flashlight in the kitchen drawer. She put it in the pocket of her robe and picked up the cast-iron handle used to lift the pot hole lids in the wood cookstove. *Too bad it wasn't a poker, but it should be lethal enough.*

Janet quickly opened the door to the stairs, poised for attack. There was no one there. The lamp in one hand, her makeshift weapon in the other, she slowly climbed the steps. It was an effort to keep her breathing slow and steady, as adrenalin raced through her body. She was afraid and angry, but she was in control.

At the head of the stairs, the light from the lamp was enough to confirm that neither the small storage room nor the bathroom harbored an intruder. She held the lamp up at arm's length as she entered the main room. A quick survey assured her that no one else was there. She placed the lamp on the myrtlewood table. With her flashlight, she swiftly checked the latches on the doors to the storage areas on both sides of the room. The latches could only be fastened from the outside. Every latch was securely in place. Just to be certain, Janet opened each door and flashed her light inside. Each cubbyhole was empty, except for the one where she had stored her camping gear and rifles. They appeared undisturbed.

She collapsed on the cushioned bench in the alcove and heaved a major sigh of relief. "Damn, that was scary," she said aloud. "But someone has been up here." She grimaced at the sight of the once-carefully organized research material now scattered across the floor. "You bastard! Who the hell are you and what are you looking for?"

Janet immediately dismissed the possibility that Jim and Hank had searched her house. They had no motive and they would have made a neater job of it. Whoever had searched her house was either too dumb or in too much of a hurry to put things back the way he had found them. Or, maybe he didn't care if she knew he had been here.

She wondered if the occupants of the black Lincoln had finally caught up with her, or if that slimey Roscoe Carrac, who had left his fingerprints in her ransacked home, had also followed her from Texas.

She was angry that her privacy had been invaded, but she didn't feel that she was in any personal danger — for now. She was also excited by the knowledge that someone had made a move. *As Sherlock Holmes would say*, she told herself, *"the game's afoot."*

Janet locked the front and back doors and wedged a kitchen chair under each doorknob. There was nothing wrong with a few precautions. She wondered if she should confide in the McVeys and Jim about the search. She thought about the situation from every angle as she prepared lunch and finally decided to keep the information to herself for now. There was always the slight possibility that some child with nothing better to do had wandered by and decided to satisfy his or her curiosity about the newcomer.

Janet didn't believe that, but she decided to wait and see if anything else happened during the next few days. She didn't see any point in getting everyone excited about something that might not be important. Besides, if any strangers were wandering around

Agness, Maggie and Hank would be quick to notice and tell her.

After lunch, Janet went upstairs, found an empty spiral notebook and began a journal of the odd happenings since David's death, in the hope that some significant pattern would emerge.

A.   Roscoe Carrac had pretended to be from Southwest Data-Comm — demanded access to David's personal papers.

B.   Someone had followed her from Texas to Oregon.

C.   Roscoe Carrac had ransacked her home and office — info on rare Indian artifacts taken.

D.   Someone had searched the log house, apparently interested in her books, tapes, chest of drawers, and research material.

As she read and re-read the list, Janet thought she did see a common thread between the events. Someone seemed to be searching for written or taped information which David might have passed along to her. She hadn't the slightest clue what it was, or even if it existed. But that had to be the reason for the search of her home and office in Texas and the search here.

Why had Roscoe Carrac stolen her research material on rare Indian artifacts? The information was available to anyone who wanted it. That didn't fit the pattern.

Why had she been followed? Perhaps the men in the Lincoln had been afraid she would pass on whatever information they thought she had, or hide it. Maybe they had intended to frighten her into giving whatever it was to them.

Janet thought about the situation from every angle. The only thing David might have had was information, and that should have been in his little leather notebook. The police hadn't found it on him. It hadn't been found at his office or at home. Someone had the notebook and either couldn't decipher the information or didn't know it was there. Or, maybe David hadn't written it down. In that case, there wasn't anything to find.

I seem to find more questions than answers, Janet thought. *David was so excited that last week. If only I knew what he was working overtime on. If only I had asked him what was going on, instead of being so wrapped up in my own research.*

That import-export company in Houston — the job he did there sounded routine, but that's when his overtime and excitement started. Maybe I missed something when I investigated them.

If only — no! This won't get me anywhere. I've been through the "if only" bit a hundred times. It only makes me feel guilty for being human. I'll let this all kick around in my head awhile and maybe I'll see something I overlooked.

Janet had a long evening to get through. She decided to put the time to some constructive use and restore order to her research material. As she sorted the papers, she found the first chapter of a novel she had started before David's murder. It was about Marcus de Niza, a Franciscan priest who was called one of the twelve apostles of the New World, and his adventures in Peru and what was to become New Mexico. As she read the material, she became excited about the idea all over again. The electricity was still off, so she substituted a pencil for her typewriter, and began the second chapter.

Janet wrote until late in the evening. She was pleased with her work when she read over it. It felt good to be doing something creative again. She was beginning to come alive again as more than just a human being bent on revenge. Revenge she would have when she found David's killer, but she was beginning to see a faint glimmering of the possibility of a productive life on the far side of that revenge.

The electricity came on and Janet's high spirits stayed with her as she put out the lamps and made herself a sandwich and a cup of tea. A short while later she checked the doors and windows, then went to bed with the satisfaction of a day well spent.

Chapter 6

The rain stopped early Sunday morning and the sky cleared rapidly. The sunlight was captured in millions of tiny raindrops clinging to the needles of the pine and fir trees around the log house. There was an almost melodic sound from the dripping vegetation.

Janet felt poetic about the morning, right up until the moment she turned on the bathroom tap to rinse the toothpaste from her mouth and got only a tiny trickle of water. When the water continued to trickle but didn't in fact stop, she realized that the hose was probably still anchored but the screen must be clogged with debris. This was no good; she was determined to find some way to fix the problem. Rain was a way of life in Oregon, especially during the winter, and she had no desire to take a daily walk up the mountain in order to have running water.

The problem of what to do about the water line occupied her mind while she dressed and prepared breakfast. She tried to think what David would do. He had always had an answer. She finally decided on what seemed to be a workable plan. It was going to be wet and muddy work, and it wasn't the way she had intended to spend her morning, but she might as well deal with it now.

Janet knew that she couldn't finish her construction work and come back to the log house in time to change clothes and keep her lunch date with Jim. She went upstairs and got her day pack and walking stick from the closet where she had stored her camping gear. She packed it with a change of clothes and shoes, a poncho, flashlight, and a miscellaneous assortment of items. She and David had learned to expect the unexpected when dealing with Mother Nature. She intended to cross the mountain to Jim's cabin rather than backtracking to the trail. She was unfamiliar with that area, so it was only reasonable to carry some basic survival items and dress so that she could adapt to changing weather conditions and her level of activity.

On impulse Janet wrapped the two chapters of her novel in plastic and managed to fit them into her pack. She put her pack and walking stick in the Toyota and headed toward the abandoned logging camp where she planned to park her vehicle. On her way, she stopped at the Lodge. Hank was on the back porch smoking his pipe.

"Making an early start to Jim's place, I see."

"I'm making a forced detour by the waterworks." Janet explained to Hank what she intended to do.

"That just may solve the problem. It's worth a try. You're in for some heavy work. Would you like for me to come along and help?"

"Thanks, but I think I can manage. The main reason I stopped by was to ask if it would be reasonably easy for me to go from the waterworks over the mountain and down to Jim's cabin."

"No reason not to cross over if you've a mind to. It's certainly closer than coming back and going by the trail. Go on up to the old sawmill. From there you can see a big outcropping of rock near the summit of the mountain. Keep just below the outcropping and follow it around to the south. The north way looks shorter but the going gets mighty rough that way. By the time you turn back to the west, you need to start looking for the great grandpa of all the fir trees. It's been lightning struck near the base and burned out some. It's hard to miss. Jim's place is about a mile and a half straight down the mountain from there."

"Thank you, Hank. It looks like a great day for a walk in the mountains."

"That it does. Never hurts to keep an eye out this time of year, though. Could be something building up behind the mountains where we can't see it right now. If it does start looking bad, just come on back and have lunch with me and Maggie."

"Okay, I will. Thanks."

Janet parked her 4 x 4 next to Jim's Jeep, slipped her pack on, and headed southwest around the lower slope of the mountain toward the creek.

She thought it was a marvelous day to be outdoors and it seemed that a large number of the forest creatures agreed with her. The woods were full of squirrels dashing madly from tree to tree, pausing momentarily to chatter disapproval of Janet's presence in their territory. A startled rabbit jumped from almost under her feet and went streaking through the forest. It was a bright, wonderful, clean world and Janet felt very contented to be where she was.

It didn't take Janet long to find the creek and follow it up to what she was beginning to think of as the Manning Waterworks. As she had suspected, there was a mass of leaves and pine needles collected around the end of the hose.

She put her pack on a nearby log and laid her jacket, hat, and gloves beside it. She used her tin cup for a refreshing drink and then sat back against the log to munch an apple and survey the scene of her soon-to-be-constructed marvel of engineering.

An hour later, she was beginning to wish that she had a stronger back and a weaker mind. She had propped the end of the hose out of the water so that it wouldn't fill with mud and debris, and then had collected every rock she could move. She built a rock barrier dividing the channel of the creek from a couple of feet below the end of the hose to about ten feet above it. Then she built a rock dam to act as a filter across the channel where the hose would be anchored. She slanted the dam into the other channel so that collected debris would tend to wash away, making it a self-cleaning filter, she hoped. It would also divert the full force of the water during heavy rains and allow the anchor rocks to stay in place.

It was 11:30 by the time she was satisfied with the stability of the structure. She was wet, cold, muddy, and proud of her accomplishment. She washed her face and hands and attempted to remove a few of the mud stains from her clothing. She finally gave up, gathered her belongings, and set off to keep her lunch date. She could shower and change clothes at Jim's cabin.

It wasn't until she reached the base of the rock outcropping that she noticed a change in the atmosphere. She had been so intent on moving quickly that she hadn't kept an eye on the weather. The normal forest sounds had disappeared, and the air was still and humid. What little she could see of the western sky was filled with dark and angry clouds that were moving rapidly in her direction.

She didn't have time to be angry with herself for being careless. She searched quickly along the outcropping for a place to take shelter, but there was nothing which would offer any protection. She stopped long enough to don her poncho. She was already wet from her dam-building, but it would help conserve what little body heat she had left. She prayed that the lightning-struck fir tree was nearby. Her best bet for shelter was Jim's house, but she knew that she was in trouble.

The wind rose suddenly and with great force. It became difficult to keep her footing on the steep slope. The temperature dropped rapidly and an icy rain started. Within minutes, the wind-whipped rain was so fierce and the sky so dark that Janet could barely see.

Lightning ripped through the sky and thunder vibrated the ground underfoot. Janet wanted to move further away from the tall trees where the lightning was most likely to strike, but she couldn't risk missing the burned-out tree which would point her to shelter and safety.

The temperature continued to drop and the rain changed to sleet. Janet tried to protect her face from the stinging ice pellets without much success. An icy coating began to form on the ground. Janet was tired and tried to move too quickly for the conditions. Her feet slid out from under her and she fell backward into the jagged branches of a deadfall. In the struggle to free herself from the branches and regain her feet, she cut her cheek and a sharp snag ripped the back of her poncho from shoulder to hem.

Janet felt her first moment of real fear when she realized she had lost the protective barrier between her and the icy wind. Her wet pantlegs had already begun to freeze and she knew it wouldn't be long before the remainder of her damp clothing did the same. The danger of hypothermia was very real if she didn't find shelter soon. She knew that the mental confusion which accompanied hypothermia could cause her to use poor judgment and make potentially fatal decisions.

Moving as quickly as she dared, it took Janet ten minutes to find her landmark. She crouched in the huge burned-out hollow in the tree. It gave her a momentary respite from the wind and sleet, but with more than a mile to go directly into the face of the storm, she dared not linger.

Wind whipped the sleet, now mixed with snow, into a blinding assault. She lowered her head against the wind and began to pick her way down the mountain, praying that her sense of direction wouldn't desert her. She felt fairly safe as long as the downward slope was obvious, but she had no way to make certain that she wasn't walking in circles as she crossed a series of small, level meadows which were open to the full force of the storm. At this point, even a few minutes could make the difference between life and death.

The intensity of the storm increased, enveloping her in a white fury. She couldn't see, could barely breathe. Her efforts to peer through the swirling sleet and snow left her disoriented. But she had to see. She had to!

Janet stopped and began to struggle with her ice-covered pack. Then she was terrified by her irrational behavior. My god! A flashlight would be useless. She had wasted precious minutes trying to get her flashlight!

Janet knew that she was as close to dying as she had ever been. But, damn it, she was going to live — and she had to save herself. No rescue team, however experienced, would venture out in a storm of this intensity. She had to stay in control. Panic could kill.

She forced herself to continue, cautiously putting one foot in front of the other. She felt a surge of hope when the steep downward slope resumed, and she gained the minimal shelter of the forest. She continued down for another ten minutes, then hesitated. She was certain that she had walked over a mile from the lightning-struck tree. She should be able to see or hear some sign of Jim's cabin.

There was a momentary lull in the storm. Janet listened carefully for the telltale thump of Jim's generator. Nothing. The storm seemed to be easing but at the same time she knew she was in deep trouble. There was little feeling in her feet and she could barely keep her balance. The numbing cold permeated her whole body and she found it hard to resist the desire to lie down and go to sleep.

"The trail, Janet. Just a few more steps. Find the trail. Don't give up now." The voice in her head was urgent, insistent.

In a moment of mental clarity she realized that her mind had drifted and she thought she had heard David's voice. Whatever the source of the idea, Janet knew that the trail could save her life. If she had missed the cabin, she should cross the trail leading up from the old logging camp.

Each step was an effort of will, but finally she stumbled onto the narrow trail. Within a few steps she could hear the faint sound of Jim's generator. Another hundred feet and she could see a gleam of light through the trees.

She struggled onto the porch and fumbled at the door just as the full fury of the storm was renewed. The door blew open and Jim caught her as she fell.

"Janet, my god, you're all right! We were organizing a search party to hunt for you. I was just on my way out."

"I'm so cold, so tired." She shook uncontrollably.

Jim slammed the door and stripped away her wet clothing. He slipped out of his parka, wrapped it around her, and carried her to a chair in front of the fireplace. He took a quick look at her hands and feet.

"Don't move. I'll be right back."

Jim returned in a minute, picked Janet up, and carried her into the bathroom. Water was running full force into the bathtub. He carefully lowered Janet into the tub. The water felt deliciously warm to her.

"Don't want to warm you up too fast. You don't appear to have any frostbite, but you are headed toward serious hypothermia. Now just lean back and relax and I'll take care of you."

Janet couldn't have done anything else. She had expended the last of her energy getting through the door to safety. She leaned back, closed her eyes, and enjoyed the warmth with the fervent hope that it wasn't her imagination. She could feel Jim making a more thorough examination of her hands and feet and gently cleaning the cut on her cheek. She was vaguely aware when he left the room, then drifted into sleep.

"Wake up, Janet. Come on now, open your eyes and drink this."

Janet opened her eyes and sat up, suddenly aware of her nudity. Jim laughed and handed her a towel.

"You're going to be all right if you can blush like that. Stay in the tub for a while and drink this hot tea. It's loaded with sugar, which should help. Lord, but you had us frightened."

"I was a little frightened myself," Janet answered as she tucked the bath towel around her. "It all happened so suddenly. It was my fault for getting caught by it, though. I didn't watch the weather like Hank told me to do. In Texas we'd call this a 'blue norther,' but I didn't know you had them here."

"It is unusual. The fury of it caught us all by surprise. I must confess that I didn't notice anything until the wind hit. By then I expected you any minute, so I didn't worry. Then Hank buzzed to find out if you were here and told me that you were coming over the mountain."

"Hank and Maggie — do they know I'm all right?"

"Yes. Hank and a couple of neighbors were just leaving to search up toward the old sawmill and on up that side of the mountain when I buzzed them a few minutes ago."

"That's crazy. All of you could have died out there."

"We knew the danger, but the storm seemed to be letting up, and we all know the terrain. And we would have been dressed for the weather. Hank was afraid that you didn't have anything with you but the clothes you were wearing and he knew you wouldn't last long dressed like that. He hoped that you had taken shelter in the old sawmill. Enough of that. How do you feel?"

"Tired, hungry, and a little shaky. Otherwise I can't complain."

"Can you manage to dry off and dress on your own?"

"Oh, yes."

Jim laughed at Janet's quick answer and she knew that she was blushing again.

"Good. I'll hand in some thermal underwear and a robe. While you dress, I'll fix you a tray so that you can eat in front of the fire. You can't risk getting chilled again."

Janet found that she was surprisingly weak as she dried off and bundled up in the thermals and robe. She was too lightheaded to manage the wool socks.

Jim knocked an the door. "Dressed yet?"

"Almost. I need a little help."

Jim opened the door, took one look, scooped Janet up in his arms, and carried her to a chair in front of the fireplace. He slipped the socks on her feet, then tucked a blanket around her and went to get her tray.

The food looked and smelled delicious. but Janet could barely force herself to eat. Her body's resources were so depleted that she felt weak and just wanted to sleep.

After she had eaten enough to satisfy Jim, he carried her into one of the bedrooms. She was almost asleep as he tucked her into bed. She dozed for a few minutes, then woke up in a panic until she reassured herself that she was safely inside, away from the storm.

She lay awake for a while, enjoying the beauty of the room. There was a lovely Navajo blanket displayed on one wall, its age evident from the clear, natural colors, and the extraordinarily dense weave of the handspun wool thread.

On a table in a corner were several pieces of black-on-white pottery which she immediately recognized from the designs and quality as Mimbres from southwestern New Mexico. What startled her most were a footed pipe, a willow leaf-shaped stone knife, and a pointed-bottomed pot, artifacts usually found in the Gallina area of northern New Mexico. A packing crate under the table seemed to be filled with similar items.

These were artifacts which belonged in a museum. Something wasn't right about them being in Jim's house. Janet was troubled as she drifted into sleep.

She slept until early evening. She felt a little weak, but over-all surprisingly well, as she sat on the side of the bed. Her freshly laundered clothes were neatly folded on a nearby chair. Her boots had been cleaned and were on the floor beside her pack.

Janet found that everything in her pack had escaped damage. She slipped out of the thermals and into her bra and panties, the grey wool pants, and the red cashmere sweater she had packed for her lunch date. As she stood in front of the dresser mirror to brush her hair and apply lipstick, she noticed the reflection of the empty table. All of the artifacts and the crate were gone. Only the Navajo rug remained.

A sudden knot formed in the pit of her stomach. It was possible that Jim had acquired those pieces by legitimate means. But if he had, why hide them?

Her first impulse was to confront Jim and demand an explanation. Her second thought was that he could claim that she had hallucinated the artifacts.

Janet sat on the side of the bed and thought about the situation. It occurred to her that she had stumbled into the middle of Jim's secret.

She and David had been aware for several years of the growing traffic in stolen Indian artifacts. They had seen the work of pot hunters more than once in remote areas of the southwestern wilderness — gaping holes in the earth where valuable artifacts and archeological information had been destroyed in the greedy search for a pot which would bring a big price from a private collector. Mimbres bowls like those she'd seen on the table could bring from $10,000 to $60,000 on the black market.

David and Janet had become even more disturbed on their backpacking trips during the past couple of years because it appeared that someone who could detect ruins invisible to the untrained eye, someone with an archeological background, had been directing operations in some of the more remote areas. Jim had that kind of expertise.

Another unsettling thought crossed Janet's mind. *The note. Not only had David written on the slip of paper, he had drawn pictures of Indian pottery — Mimbres pottery!* Janet hadn't thought the pictures were important. David had often doodled Indian designs and artifacts.

Janet was numbed by the thought that whatever Jim was doing might somehow be connected with David's murder.

I can't condemn him without evidence, Janet thought. *That's what everyone did to David. There might be a perfectly innocent explanation for all of this. I'll just wait and watch and keep an open mind.*

Chapter 7

Jim was busily preparing supper. The kitchen was filled with tempting odors. Janet was famished.

"Hi. Anything I can do to help?"

"Well, look at you. I expected a waif in a woolly robe. Do you usually carry a wardrobe with you?"

"Only when I have a date for lunch after dam building. Something smells wonderful."

"Sit down. It's almost ready. How do you feel?"

"Fine. No lasting damage done, especially to my appetite. I think I could eat a buffalo."

"Sorry, I ate the last buffalo yesterday. You'll have to settle for beef stew, hot biscuits, fresh butter, and wild blackberry jam."

"Don't stand there talking, man. Bring it on. I'm drooling all over my sweater."

Thank god, Jim thought. *She evidently didn't notice those things in the bedroom or she would be bombarding me with questions by now.*

Janet and Jim didn't talk much while they ate, but what conversation there was between them was light-hearted and humorous.

This Jim couldn't be involved in something as nasty as pot hunting and the black market, Janet thought. *Not*

with those evil men who would even kill an unwary back-
packer to keep from being detected. Not Jim.

They lingered at the table over coffee and cigarettes.

"That was superb, Jim. If you ever need job references I'll give you one for cooking, laundry, and nursing. By the way, thank you very much for all of it."

"Don't mention it. A huckleberry pie will be thanks enough."

"It's a deal. As much of that stuff as you eat, I don't understand why you aren't fat and blue."

Jim laughed. "I seem to remember saying something similar to you years ago, with the addition of fins and gills."

"I'll try to forget you said that. Say, how much longer do you think this storm will last?"

"With any luck it'll be clear by morning. The trail should be open sometime after lunch. By Tuesday, we'll have sunshine and beautiful weather again."

"Looks like you'll have me on your hands for at least two more meals. At the rate I'm putting it away, I'll have to pack out and replace your supplies. I know the road has to be closed for the winter after this storm."

"Jan, you've made statements twice now as if we were going to be stuck in here until spring. How did you get in here, anyway?"

"The old logging road, of course. How else?"

"You are joking, aren't you?"

Janet shook her head.

"My lord, didn't anyone tell you about the good road up from Gold Beach? It's been there for several years, on the far side of the ridge across the river."

"I had no idea. I didn't even look at a map. Hank said that nothing had changed and I assumed he meant the road, too. You mean that I expended all of that adrenalin and blood, sweat, and tears unnecessarily?"

"Yep. I'm surprised that Hank or Maggie didn't say something when you arrived."

"I didn't mention the trip in to them. I know how commonplace it always was to everyone but me. Now that you mention it, I did notice a new bridge across the Illinois the day I captured the grapes. Is that the road?"

"Yes. It runs north a short way and there's a bridge across the Rogue. A road of sorts goes on from here to Grants Pass, but it's more for a 4 x 4 in good weather. Another fifteen years will probably bring a superslab all the way up the river and a pair of golden arches in downtown Agness."

"Lord, I hope not. Unfortunately, 'civilization' is making inroads almost everywhere these days. When David and I bought our place on Lake Lewisville, south of Denton, we were practically in the wilderness. Now there are housing developments and people everywhere you look.

"I do know a couple of places in New Mexico where I can still go and not find ring tabs and beer cans. Ever done any digging in New Mexico?" Janet asked as she watched Jim's face over the rim of her coffee cup.

"No!" Jim said, sharply. "Just passed through once or twice."

"You should spend some time there," Janet said, baiting him. "If you know where to look, there are hundreds of almost unexcavated ruins.'"

"Oh, you know   a hole here, a hole there. If you know where to dig, you can make a lot of money pot hunting."

Jim rose abruptly and started clearing the table.

"Here, let me help."

"No, it won't take but a minute. Refill your coffee and go on in by the fire."

Janet was disturbed by Jim's reaction. His voice was controlled and emotionless, but his hands were trembling and his movements were awkward. *Oh god,* Janet thought, *is it guilt?* She found it difficult to reconcile his involvement in something criminal with the integrity and ideals of the teenaged Jim she remembered. He had always expressed such reverence for the remains of past civilizations and what they could tell people about themselves. People changed, but did they change that drastically?

Don't convict him on circumstantial evidence, Janet chided herself again as she stared into the flames in the fireplace. *There may be a perfectly simple explanation. Perhaps he is doing some cataloging or authentication of artifacts for a museum or university. Give him the benefit of the doubt. Don't do to Jim what has been done to David.*

"See, that didn't take long."

Janet felt guilty when she saw the tension lines on Jim's face. "Thanks again for the marvelous meal, Jim. You have been a super host."

"Think nothing of it."

"Say, I was just sitting here wondering about your professional status at the moment. Are you connected with any university or museum?"

Jim hesitated, then settled into an overstuffed chair before he answered. "No, no connections at all. I'm footloose and fancy free, as the saying goes. Why?"

"No reason. Just idle curiosity."

The two of them sat in silence for several minutes. There was a growing awkwardness as each pretended to be entranced by the dancing flames of the fire.

Jim swallowed hard, trying to rid himself of the sudden lump in his throat. *Not Janet,* he thought. *Maybe her husband, but not Janet.*

Janet was trying to think of some way to break the silence and dissipate the strained atmosphere when she thought of the manuscript in her pack.

"Dr. Scott, sir. Please, do you feel up to playing literary critic?" she asked in a pleading tone with clasped hands.

"Now that's what I like, a properly respectful attitude." A grin spread across his face and he heaved a tremendous sigh. "Just name the time and place."

"How about here and now? I just happen to have a couple of chapters of a novel in my pack."

"Terrific, bring them on."

While Jim read, Janet wandered around the room and found a stack of archeological and historical journals. As she thumbed through one, she considered the possibilities raised by the road from Gold Beach to Agness. That meant that it probably had not been someone from Agness who had searched her house. It also meant that she wasn't as safe from the men in the black Lincoln as she had thought. They didn't have to make themselves conspicuous by coming upriver on the mailboat, or leave a trail by hiring a private boat.

Janet turned the pages of the journal without attention to the contents until a title caught her eye: "Historical and Archeological Anomalies of the

Southwest." This was the subject of her personal research project at the university.

She scanned the article. It appeared to be well-written, from good research. She didn't recognize the name of the author, Mark Jamison, but his credentials were impressive. She felt just a little smug when she noted that her research had provided a couple of answers he hadn't found. She flipped through to find the pictures and biographical sketches of the journal's authors.

Janet was barely able to stifle her gasp. The face was familiar. The man in the crystal ball was real. He had a name — Mark Jamison.

Janet lit a cigarette with trembling hands and paced the floor. Jim glanced up from his reading.

"Are you okay? Not getting chilled, are you?"

"No. No, I'm fine. Just a little nervous about your coming critique of my writing," Janet stammered.

Jim smiled. "Don't be." With that, he resumed reading.

Oh, I'm perfectly fine, Jim. I may beat my head against the wall or hang by my fingernails any minute, Janet shrieked in her mind, *but I'm fine. Hey, Jim, a funny thing happened to me on the way to insanity. I've been seeing a man named Mark Jamison in my crystal ball. Cross my palm with silver. Maybe I can tell your fortune.*

Whoa. Wait a minute, Janet. Get a hold on yourself. Just calm down. Don't go off the deep end. The only thing that's changed is that the friendly face in the crystal ball has a name. Now let's see what you can find out about him.

Janet went into the kitchen and poured herself another cup of coffee. She sat down at the kitchen table and tried to reread the article, but she couldn't stop looking at the picture. Mark Jamison. She was certain she had never heard the name. She was equally certain that she had never seen his face except in the crystal ball. How could it be possible?

"Janet, have you got documentation for all of this or is the main storyline fiction?"

Janet jumped, startled to find Jim standing beside her.

"What? I'm sorry, I was reading. What did you say?"

"You're certainly jumpy tonight. I asked how much of this material on Marcus de Niza is fiction and how much you can document."

"I can document at least ninety-five percent, and I think I can more than justify the conclusions I've drawn in the other five percent."

"How dependable are your sources?"

"The best available. Prime source material."

"Why hasn't someone else come up with this slant on de Niza before now?"

"Well, you know the prejudice historians have had about de Niza — calling him a liar when they haven't bothered to quote him correctly or read his journals, and have ignored his work in Peru and other parts of South and Central America."

"That's true. What else?"

"Some of the records have just recently been found and translated. My god, Jim, those old Spaniards were obsessive record keepers."

"I know," Jim agreed. "They took sworn depositions from everyone in sight if someone burped."

"Just about," Janet laughed. "The secular and religious archives in Mexico and Spain are enormous. It makes it damned difficult to find anything. And, it's maddening because I want to read all of it."

"It sounds like it takes lots of good luck as well as time and patience to find everything on a particular subject."

"Yeah," Janet agreed. "The problem is that you're never certain that you have found it all."

"What got you started researching the Spanish Conquest?"

"Several years ago I started running into stories about lost Spanish silver mines in North Central Texas. Then I met an old farmer who had found some Spanish armor and an old silver mine. There were a few silver bars with markings which dated them, and placed the Spanish in the area far earlier than commonly believed. Seeing that armor and the silver bars, I was completely hooked on the history and archeology of the Southwest. But, enough of that. What do you think of the Marcus de Niza story so far?"

"I think that I am very unhappy because I have to wait to read the rest of the story. From the viewpoint of a history buff and archeologist, and an adventure story addict, it's damned fine writing."

"Wow. Thank you. If I ever get it finished, maybe a publisher and several hundred thousand other people will feel the same way. I won't hold my breath, though."

"I think you have a winner. Now, how about some dessert and another cup of coffee?"

"Sounds good. What's for dessert?"

"What else? Huckleberry pie with fresh cream so thick you have to dip it with a spoon — both compliments of Maggie."

Janet groaned. "I'm going to have to jog ten miles a day and chop a cord of wood to keep from becoming a blimp."

They took their dessert and coffee to the chairs in front of the fireplace. Janet was excited by Jim's reaction to her writing, but Mark Jamison and the crystal ball were foremost in her mind.

"Jim, I was reading an intriguing article in one of your magazines by a man who graduated from the same university you attended, a Mark Jamison. Do you know anything about him?"

"A little. We shared an apartment for three years in college and he was best man at my wedding. What do you want to know about him?"

"You're serious? You really know him?"

"Mark and I have been friends for about fourteen years."

"Where is he and what is he doing now?" *And why did I see him in the crystal ball?* Janet added to herself.

"He travels a great deal but he's living in Albuquerque right now. He did some excellent work in Africa but his main interest has always been in the Southwest."

"Do you know what he is working on now?"

"He's gone off on some wild tangent about pre-Columbian Romans in the Southwest. He's really gone haywire over it."

"Has he found anything?"

"How could he find what isn't there?"

"What makes you think it's such an impossibility?"

"Well, anyone who knows their history and archeology knows — "

"Oh, Jim, don't pull that on me," Janet interrupted.

"Anyone who relies on most of the standard textbooks on those subjects has about as much chance of getting complete and accurate information as ... as ... well, damn little chance!"

"Hey, don't get angry."

"It does make me angry. Sloppy research, armchair historians who never get off their butts to see the places they write about, scholars who ignore, or hide, or ridicule anything which doesn't fit their pet theories, people who hide behind a bunch of letters trailing after their names instead of paying attention to available facts and evidence and trying to discover the truth of our history — they all make me angry."

Janet knew she was overreacting. What she had said was true, but most of the emotion was generated by too many unanswered questions in too many areas of her own life.

"*You* don't have a PhD., Janet," Jim said icily, "and the facts have been recorded by professionals after careful research. No doubt you believe in visitors from outer space and the lost continent of Atlantis."

Janet ignored Jim's reference to her lack of a PhD. and stifled her sudden desire to laugh at his injured dignity.

"No, Jim. Nothing so romantic. And, you must understand that I'm not indicting all scholars, only those who are narrowminded and careless."

"Well," Jim said, somewhat mollified, "I'll be the first to admit that some of my colleagues can be stuffy and stubborn when it comes to dealing with information or evidence which doesn't seem to fit the accepted pattern, but I'd like to believe that they are the exceptions. I'm interested in knowing why you feel so strongly about Mark's theories. After all, how many dead Romans have been dug up in the Southwest?"

"The question might be, how many have been improperly identified?"

"Oh, oh. Methinks I am about to receive a learned lecture on Romans of the Old West."

"Laugh if you want to, *Dr*. Scott, but Mark Jamison may have the last laugh. There is more evidence than you might suppose, but I wouldn't want to bore you."

"On the contrary, you've rather piqued my interest. Your head seems to be packed full of bits and pieces of odd information. Just what evidence is there?"

"I'll be happy to tell you, but I'm beginning to feel a little chilly. I think I'd like to change back into those thermals and wrap up in your woolly robe, if I may."

"Sure. The temperature is still dropping. I'll put on a fresh pot of coffee while you are changing. There are a couple of things I need to check on outside, and it wouldn't hurt to bring in some more wood. It may take a few minutes."

"Is there anything I can do to help?"

"No. I just want to check on the pump and the generator to make certain we don't end up without water and electricity in the morning. You go get warm. You've already had enough excitement today."

Janet hurried into the bedroom and changed clothes at top speed. She intended to take advantage of Jim's absence to do some snooping. She checked the kitchen and saw that the coffee pot was perking. She could see Jim's silhouette against the light in the small shed which housed the generator.

There were two bedrooms in addition to the one Janet was using. The first bedroom was Jim's. The light from the hall allowed Janet to see that there was nothing of particular interest there. The second room was full of crates and boxes. A fast search revealed that several of the boxes contained some of Ginny's things and odds and ends of camping gear. The closet was a different matter. The items which had been removed from Janet's room were piled into the crate which had been under the table. There were two other crates which appeared to be filled with artifacts.

Janet had time to look quickly at a Mimbres bowl and see that it was indeed authentic before she heard the back door open. She closed the closet door and fled quietly out of the room and into the bathroom. She flushed the toilet as she heard Jim enter the living room.

She stopped for a moment to look at herself in the mirror. Her cheeks were flushed, her eyes too big and bright, her expression too tense. She had to get herself under control. *I have to put what I have seen out of my mind for now,* Janet told herself, *and let my enthusiasm for the subjects we're discussing take over and help me play my role.*

What she wanted to do was confront Jim and make him answer her questions. There was no doubt in her mind that the artifacts she had seen in the bedroom closet would bring several hundred thousand dollars from illicit sales. This had to be the "'mess" Hank McVey had referred to during his argument with Jim. Janet couldn't understand how Hank and Maggie could allow themselves to play even the smallest part in such activity.

Janet took a deep breath and opened the bathroom door.

Chapter 8

"Oh good, you're back," Janet said as she breezed into the living room. "How does it look out there?"

"Cold. There's a thin coating of ice over everything, but the sleet and snow have stopped, and the wind is dying down. The sky is beginning to clear to the west and I could see a star or two."

"If it clears off, it will get a lot colder tonight, won't it?"

"Yes, but it'll warm up fairly early tomorrow. Now, let's get on with your story of the 'Gladiators of the Golden West.' Say, that would make a good book title."

"All right, skeptic. I'll tell you a little over another cup of coffee and then I'm going to bed."

They sat at the kitchen table with the pot of coffee between them. Jim ate another piece of pie while Janet talked.

"For a good scholarly work from someone you'd respect, you might try reading *Before Columbus —
Links Between the Old World and Ancient America* by Cyrus H. Gordon. He was head of the Mediterranean studies at Brandeis. He compiled the archeological, ethnographic, and linguistic evidence which was known by 1970."

"1970? Isn't there anything more current?" Jim asked.

"Just stuff your face with pie and don't interrupt."

"Yes, ma'am."

"Now, to hit a few high points. In the '50s, a young couple exploring caves on Cook's Peak in New Mexico found a bag of ancient Roman coins."

"They could have been put there anytime," Jim said.

"True," Janet agreed, "but that was just one of several caches of Roman coins found in North America. Now explain this to me, Dr. Scott. About eighteen miles from Los Lunas, New Mexico, up a gully eroded into the cone of an ancient volcano, is a large basalt stone which has the Ten Commandments in Paleo-Hebrew chiseled on it. Paleo-Hebrew went out of use about 200 A.D."

"Damn, Janet," Jim interrupted, shaking his head. "Again, that could have been done any time. The Paleo-Hebrew alphabet has been available to scholars since the 1890s."

"Gotcha, Dr. Scott!" Janet grinned as she continued, "The first recorded sighting of the stone in modern times happened in the 1830s. It was covered with slow-growing lichen then.

"Now, would you please try to shut your mouth and open your mind and let me finish?"

"Okay," Jim nodded.

"Okay. Coronado saw an Indian village which had been demolished by large round stones launched by catapults, according to the descriptions of Indians living nearby. That event is hard to date. It seems to have been part of their oral history and was passed down for many generations.

"Coronado examined and described some of the round stones. They sound very much like the ballast stones from ancient Roman or Phoenician ships.

"And that, Dr. Scott, ties in with the Tucson artifacts. I'm assuming that you know that the Rio Grande was navigable up into the area of Los Lunas until comparatively recent times. Now, the Tucson artifacts — "

"Hey, wait a minute," Jim interrupted. "Don't I even get to ask questions?"

"Nope. Not tonight. We have all winter to fight about this. I just want to give you a little idea of what might have started Mark Jamison working on his theory and why I'm more than a little convinced that there is a great deal of truth to it. I have scads of material about these things which you can read the next time you're by the house. Then we can fight about it."

"Okay, if you insist. Now, you were saying ..."

"Yes, the Tucson artifacts, found embedded in a layer of caliche along with other items which could be dated back to approximately 800 A.D. There were thirty-seven objects which appeared to be of Roman origin. One was a large double cross made of lead. When opened, it contained, inscribed in Latin, the story of a city, Terra Calalus, its generations of rulers, and its problems with the Indians."

"Where are these artifacts now?"

"The last time I heard, they were in boxes in the basement of the Amerind Museum in Dragoon, Arizona. That story is too long to go into tonight. There is supporting evidence in a story that the Apache chief, Esconalea, told in the 1850s to an Overland Stage employee named Tevis. Personally, I think there's a good chance that Terra Calalus provided a pattern for the Chaeo Canyon culture — but that's another argument for another time."

Jim was almost imperceptibly shaking his head, his arms folded across his chest. Janet ignored his skepticism. She was determined to make him think.

"Jim, Coronado and his men went into present-day Kansas searching for the lost cities of gold. The story that the Indian, El Turko, told sent them there. Have you ever thought about that story? How could a sixteenth-century Pueblo Indian, living in New Mexico, describe ships with shields of gold attached to the sides and men in golden armor? El Turko either had an extraordinary imagination, or his story was based on verbal history, passed down for generations, about the Roman ship that is be-lieved to have come up the Rio Grande into the Los Lunas area."

Janet stopped to catch her breath. She felt the wave of excitement which always accompanied her thoughts on this subject.

"Have you ever looked at some of the Zuni customs and dietary restrictions in the light of possible Judeo-Roman influence? They even have household gods similar to the Lares and Penates. Even the Mimbres may have had something similar."

"Now, wait a minute, Janet. I've heard of the stone statues presented to Zuni couples when they marry, but I've never heard of anything like that being found on a Mimbres dig. I know about the five stone figures that were found in one Mimbres kiva, but they appeared to be representations of captives. And those five are the only ones which have been found."

"No, they aren't. I know the statues you are referring to, and I'm talking about something entirely different. The statues I'm talking about may not have been household gods, or the custom may not have been widespread. That idea is purely speculation on my part, but I know of several pairs of stone statues that have been found, and I know the specific Mimbres ruin where they were found by pot hunters."

Jim seemed disturbed, looking at Janet with a peculiarly intense expression. Janet wished that she hadn't allowed herself to get carried away enough to mention the statues when Jim began to press her for more information.

"What type of statues? Describe them. Where were they found? Are there more?"

"Hey, what is this, the Inquisition?"

"Sorry. It's just such an exciting idea. The thought of pot hunters getting them makes me angry."

Janet wondered if it was only the thought of someone else getting to them first that bothered Jim. She knew that a value of $75,000 had been placed on the five statues found in the kiva. She saw no harm in describing the statues to Jim now that she had mentioned them, but she was determined keep the location of the ruin to herself.

"I saw the head of one statue. The rest I know only from the description given to me by the man who found them. The pairs were life-sized male and female figures carved from native stone. The work was expertly done, like something you would expect to find in a Greek or Roman ruin.

"The features on the head I saw were definitely non-Indian. It was exquisite and if it had been done in marble and found somewhere else, I think any expert would have identified it as Greco-Roman." Janet paused for a sip of coffee.

"Where did you see it and where are the statues now?" Jim demanded. "More important, where were the statues found?"

Jim became extremely agitated, jumped to his feet, and pounded on the table in front of Janet.

"You have to tell me! I have to know!" Jim shouted.

Janet was frightened. This wasn't the Jim she knew. Fear turned to anger as Jim continued to glare at her. She stood up and shook her finger in his face.

"James Scott, don't you yell at me. I don't have to tell you a damn thing. I'm forced to be a guest in your house, but if you push me too far I'll walk down the mountain tonight!"

They stood and glared at each other. Inexplicably, the corners of Jim's mouth started to twitch and he began to laugh. "I'll just bet you would. You look like a Valkyrie ready for battle, though I don't think they wore thermal underwear and woolly robes."

He reached out and pulled Janet into his arms. She tried to break away, but he held her head against his shoulder and stroked her hair.

"I'm sorry, Jan. Maybe some day you'll understand and forgive my vile temper. For so long after Ginny died I didn't feel anything. Now my emotions swing from one extreme to another."

For an instant Janet took pity on him. She tilted her head back to tell him that she did understand. Before she could speak, he kissed her.

Her body betrayed her in a sudden wave of desire to be held close and loved. Jim's hands slipped under her robe and moved over her body as she answered his kiss. Then, she realized what they were doing and pulled away from him.

"I think we'd better go to bed. I mean, I ... uh ..." she stammered with embarrassment over her verbal blunder.

"I know what you mean. Goodnight, Janet."

Janet fled down the hall to her bedroom. Inside, she leaned against the door, legs weak, her body trembling.

She lay awake for a long time listening to Jim pace the floor. She knew that he was as emotionally shaky as she was. Whatever Jim might be involved in, he was also a man in intense pain. Twice, when she heard a stifled sob, she almost went to him, but she knew that she would be no more than a surrogate for Ginny. Later they would both despise themselves and each other.

Perhaps someday, when the ghosts of Ginny and David didn't stand between them and all the nagging questions had been satisfactorily answered, their friendship might grow into a deeper relationship, Janet told herself. For now, the desire she felt for the comforting feel of Jim's body next to hers had its roots in her loneliness for David.

Janet was up early after a restless night of troubled dreams. The sun was shining and nature's icy overcoat was already changing to drips and trickles. She dressed as quietly as possible and gathered her belongings. Jim's door was partially open as she tiptoed past. He was stretched across the bed, fully dressed, in a deep sleep. She was glad because that made her plans easier to carry out.

Janet located her manuscript, wrapped it in plastic, and put it in her pack. She also took the magazine containing the article written by Mark Jamison.

In the kitchen she discovered that the almost-full coffee pot was still warm. Jim must have been up most of the night. She lit the burner under the pot. She found an English muffin in the breadbox and popped it in the toaster. She sat at the kitchen table with a sheet of paper and a pencil she had taken from Jim's desk and wrote him a note while she ate.

Dear Friend,

Thank you for your hospitality and critique of my writing. It's a bright, beautiful day and you look as if you will sleep awhile longer, so I have helped myself to breakfast and will go home now.

Jim, what happened last night happened between two emotionally tattered, lonely people who have not become reconciled to their losses. Let's accept it as that and forget it and be wise enough not to put ourselves into a situation where it might happen again.

I won't be embarrassed around you, so please don't be ill-at-ease with me. We are in a unique position to understand each other's emotions. Let it be a bridge, rather than a barrier between us.

If you will come for dinner on Thursday, I'll have another installment of the de Niza story for you to read and a huckleberry pie to pay my bill.

See you then,

Janet

She reread the note and was pleased with it. She had struck the right note — candid, yet light. And, she had been able to claim a few days of privacy without being rude. She had a great deal of thinking to do about Jim and just how far she could trust the McVeys, and she didn't want any intrusions.

Janet propped the note in the middle of the kitchen table and looked around to see if she had forgotten anything. She located her hat, somewhat the worse for wear, and her walking stick, and slipped out the front door.

It was cold and damp, but there was no wind and the sun was beginning to warm the air. Janet made it to the old logging camp within an hour and stowed her pack in the Toyota. She stopped at the Lodge briefly when she saw lights on in the kitchen and let Maggie know that she was none the worse for her experience with the storm.

"You're out mighty early," Maggie said, eyeing Janet closely. "Is everything all right?"

"Everything is fine. I woke up early and decided that I had imposed on Jim long enough. He had a restless night and was sleeping so soundly that I didn't want to disturb him."

"Ginny?"

"Yes, I think so. I'm rather afraid that some of our conversation opened some old wounds. I left a note, but would you buzz him later and let him know I made the hike just fine?"

Maggie said that she would, so Janet headed for the log house.

The house was cold and uninviting when she walked in the door. She built fires in both stoves and was relieved to see that the water line was in working order when she turned on the tap to fill the tea kettle.

The house was toasty warm within a short while. Janet curled up in JBG with a cup of tea to think and sort through the previous evening's conversation with Jim. She couldn't concentrate. The idea of writing didn't appeal to her. Nothing did. She finally acknowledged to herself that she was mentally, physically, and emotionally exhausted. It seemed terrible to waste what was turning into a beautiful day, but Janet changed into her flannel gown and went to bed.

She slept until early afternoon and awoke full of energy and at peace with herself. The house needed attention, so she swept, dusted, and washed dishes. The woodbox was almost empty, so she slipped into her windbreaker and headed for the woodshed.

It was a little cool but very pleasant outdoors. Janet looked at the clear sky and bright sunshine, and found it difficult to believe that she had been caught in the fury of a storm just the day before. She sat on a stump and lit a cigarette, contemplating the happenings of the preceding day and night as she watched the changing patterns of sunlight on the surface of the river.

Life is like that river, she thought philosophically. *You can see the constantly changing surface and be totally unaware of the undercurrents and snags beneath which cause the bright, sparkling eddies and the dark, still pools. Jim's like that. I can see the surface patterns of his life shaped by Ginny's death. I wonder if he blames himself? That might explain his violent mood swings and a grief that is fresh and untempered by time. What I can't see about Jim is what lies beneath the surface that would make him become involved in the black market in artifacts. If Jim has lost his personal integrity, something terrible other than Ginny's death caused it to happen. I have to believe that.*

Janet stubbed out her cigarette and, out of habit, dug a hole with the heel of her boot and buried the butt. She paced up and down the river bank, attempting to put events and feelings into some sort of order. There didn't seem to be much logic or order to most of it. She decided it was kind of like being on the back of a runaway horse in the woods. A tree branch could come from out of nowhere and scoop you out of the saddle when you least expected it. And that's what events had been doing, coming out of nowhere to add confusion just as she thought she was beginning to make some progress.

Janet gathered an armload of firewood and went inside to heat a can of soup. She reread Mark Jamison's article while she ate. She was amazed by how closely his research had paralleled hers.

She stared at his picture for a long time and found that she liked what she saw in his face. There was character and strength, and just a hint of humor. She was deeply puzzled about the reason for his appearance in the crystal ball — mystified that she had seen anything there. Mark Jamison did seem to be a person with whom she had a great deal in common and she wanted to get to know him.

Now that the mysterious face in the crystal ball had an identity, she wondered if the phenomenon would be repeated. She went upstairs to the window seat. She cupped the ball in both hands and peered into it. At first all she saw were reflections of the surrounding room. Gradually a scene began to take shape. Mark Jamison was seated at his desk, reading a tattered, yellowed manuscript and taking notes.

"What are you searching for, Mark Jamison?" Janet whispered.

She was shocked when the figure in the ball turned abruptly and looked over his shoulder. He got up and went to the door and looked out. He returned to his desk, shaking his head in puzzlement.

Janet couldn't believe what she had seen. Mark had reacted as if he had heard her whisper. How could that be? Perhaps it was a coincidence. *Mark, Mark Jamison*, she thought urgently. He jumped and looked around.

"Damn it! What's going on? Who's calling my name?"

Janet almost dropped the crystal ball as the sound of his voice came clearly into her mind. The image faded and she shakily replaced the crystal ball on the table.

"Okay, David. You told me to use the crystal ball and not to be afraid," she said to the empty room. "I've used it and I'm only slightly freaked out. Why, David? What's the purpose. Does this man have the key to something I want or need?"

Janet mentally listed the things she needed and wanted: the answer to why David had been killed and who had done it, to know what Jim was doing and stop him if he was stealing and selling artifacts, and to someday find an ancient Roman settlement in the Southwest. Did Mark Jamison hold the key to one or all of these things?

Chapter 9

Janet found herself at a standstill during the next two days. No matter how much she thought and tried to put the pieces of her puzzle together, the picture didn't become any more complete. She didn't see or hear from Jim or the McVeys and she was content to leave it that way for now.

By Wednesday morning she had retreated into the world of Marcus de Niza. *At least writing accomplished something constructive*, she told herself. A little after noon she went downstairs to put a fresh pot of coffee on the stove. She heard a strange sound on her front porch. She peeked through the curtains at the figure sitting on one of the rickety chairs which passed for porch furniture. She could see a dilapidated hat and a gnarled hand holding a meerschaum pipe, and a beautiful but ancient Collie dog. She let out a cry of joy.

"Sam! Dan'l! I don't believe it!"

Old Sam nodded and rose as Janet ran out the door to embrace him.

"Howdy do, Miss Janet. Dan'l and me thought we might sit a spell and visit, if you be of a mind to join us."

"I am, I am," Janet said happily. "But wouldn't you like to come inside?"

"No thanky. Old Dan'l and me likes to be out-doors jist as much as we kin before winter sets in." Sam grinned through his mustache and seated himself again. "If you be a coffee drinker though, Dan'l and me wouldn't say no to a cup to warm our old bones. If it be no bother to ye, that is."

"No bother at all. I just put a fresh pot on. Sam, you have no idea how glad I am to see you. Is that really the same Dan'l?"

"Yep. Hard to believe, ain't it? She's nigh onto twenty years old now, but she still gets around like a pup."

Janet went inside to get coffee for the three of them. She was jubilant. It had never crossed her mind that Sam and his coffee-drinking dog were still alive.

Samuel Donnelly and his dog were a legend in southwestern Oregon. Sam was at least eighty years old, and despite his quaint manner of speech was a well-educated man. He had lived in a little cabin upriver for over forty years, but no one seemed to know where he had originally come from.

Sarah Peale had told Janet that he had just appeared one day and, after a short negotiation with an Indian family, had gone upriver and built his cabin. To her knowledge, and Janet's, no one had ever seen the inside of the cabin. He hunted and fished and gathered what grew wild, and occasionally brought in a few gold nuggets with a modest list of supplies to be bought by the next person going to town. He did a brisk business with the mail boat, receiving many bulky packages which Sarah was certain contained books.

According to the postmistress, Sam had left the mountains only one time. A "Special Delivery" letter had come addressed to Dr. Samuel Donnelly, post-marked San Francisco. He had left that afternoon on the mail boat. Two weeks later he had returned, dressed in an expensive suit, with a tiny puppy — Dan'l — nestled in his arms. He had looked sad and defeated, and no one had seen him for about three months after his return. After that, he had taken up his life as before.

During Janet's summers in Agness, she and Jim had often prowled the mountains with Sam and Dan'l. Sam had proved to be an excellent teacher, wise in the ways of the mountains and wise about life. He had taught Janet how to see and understand what she saw. He had patiently educated both Jim and Janet about which wild plants were good for food and medicine, and how to use them. He had taught them how to track game or humans and how to live in harmony with their surroundings. Janet's approach to life had been greatly influenced by Sam.

Janet laughed as she prepared the tray with cups for herself and Sam and a bowl for Dan'l. She stirred sugar and cream into the bowl, remembering that Dan'l didn't like black coffee. Both Sam and Dan'l were notorious for having a sweet tooth. She added a plate of cookies and two bars of candy to the tray.

Dan'l sat up and wagged her tail in anticipation as Janet stepped out with the tray. Janet placed the bowl and two cookies in front of Dan'l. The dog nuzzled her hand in thanks and began to lap her coffee daintily.

Sam's face lit up like a child's when he saw the cookies and candy bars.

"You haven't changed a bit. Still addicted to sweets."

"Yep. All this good healthy food I eat leaves me with a hankerin' for store-bought sweets," Sam said as he gleefully unwrapped a candy bar. Dan'l padded over and rested her head on Sam's knee, eyeing the candy intently.

"Worse than a couple of kids," Janet laughed.

Sam solemnly divided the candy bar and placed half in front of Dan'l. Janet would have sworn that the dog smiled just before she took the treat delicately between her teeth and carried it to a place beside her two cookies. Then, Dan'l began to lick the candy slowly, as if savoring every subtlety of flavor.

"What have you been up to the past fifteen years, Sam?"

"Bout the same. Hunt a little, fish a little, gather food for the winter, pan a little gold now and then. Dan'l and me, we roam the mountains in summer and do a sight of readin' and rockin' and thinkin' during the winter.

"Don't have to ask what you've been doin'. I kinda kept up with you through Maggie. Always knew you'd make a fine woman, and you did."

"Thank you, Sam. That means a lot, coming from you. I've thought of you many times through the years. I meant to write you regularly after I left here, but somehow I never did. I wanted to tell you how much you had influenced my life, and still do. I never looked at the world in quite the same way after those two summers."

Janet paused and stroked Dan'l's silky fur for a minute before she continued. "Jim taught me to love history and archeology, but you taught me to look beyond the obvious and see what most people missed.

You taught me to think and use my mind to understand and interpret what I see. That has had a strong influence on me whether I was dealing with people, or nature, or research. It helped me to know right away when I met David that he was a very special person, and that I wanted to spend my life with him. It has even helped me in some ways to deal with his death, I think."

Sam stealthily wiped his eyes on his shirt sleeve.

"Janet," he said, his eyes again filling with tears, "pardon the foolishness of an old man. I've so often thought that my life has been void of any worthwhile achievement. But, if anything that I have done or said has enriched your life in any way, then perhaps I've accomplished more than I thought."

Janet was deeply moved by his emotional words and by the fact that he had dropped his mountain dialect.

"Oh, Sam, you've lived a rich life. Don't you know that? I know that Jim and I weren't the only kids you taught. No one could take a walk through the woods with you and not come away with a different perspective on life. You are a very wise and brilliant man, but you're a very poor judge of the wonderful influence you have had on countless lives."

Sam gazed across the river to the far mountains as he absently stroked Dan'l's head.

"I'd like to believe you, Janet. How very much I'd like to believe you. An old man gets to thinking and wondering sometimes if he's going to have anything worthwhile in his account when he faces his Maker. Perhaps neither of you will judge me too harshly when the time comes. I'm glad to see that you are not making the same mistakes I did."

"What do you mean?"

"I came here in my grief to hide from life. I wanted to make certain that you hadn't done the same. You see, Janet, I subscribe to newspapers from several large cities. Dallas is one. I know what you have been through since your husband was killed. When I heard that you were coming here, I was afraid that you had given up the battle. I wasn't going to let that happen. I can tell just by looking at you that you haven't given up. That is one of the reasons I came to see you."

"Don't worry about me, Sam. I miss David and I still hurt at times more than I ever thought possible, but I won't quit until I know the who and why of David's death. I know, also, that I have a life to live, even if it's alone."

Sam nodded his approval and patted Janet's hand. They sat in companionable silence until Dan'l went to Janet and rested her head on Janet's knee and whined softly.

"What do you want, old girl?" Janet asked, stroking her silky fur. Dan'l immediately got up and picked up the empty bowl with her teeth and held it out. Janet looked at Sam and he was holding his cup out with a twinkle in his faded blue eyes.

"What a couple of characters," Janet laughed.

Sam chuckled and Dan'l looked very pleased with herself as Janet gave them refills.

"Sam, you indicated that you had another reason for coming to see me."

"Yes. It's Jim. Something is not right with that boy."

"Not right? What exactly do you mean?"

"Jim is mixed up in something that isn't good. I don't know what it is. I know that the past couple of years there have been some strangers in and out of here whose looks I don't like."

"Have you tried to talk with Jim about it?"

"He won't talk. Avoids me. Treats me as if I were senile. But I know what I've seen. There are two men who come and bring crates. After a week or two, there are sometimes two, sometimes three men who come in a big black Lincoln and take the crates away. Occasionally Jim will load the crates in his Jeep and be gone for a few days. He always gets uneasy when he sees me around. Janet, it's just not like that boy to be doing something underhanded. I think he is in some sort of trouble."

At the mention of the black Lincoln, Janet felt a thrill somewhere between fear and excitement.

"I think I know what Jim is doing, and I'm not at all happy about it, either." Janet described the things she had seen in Jim's cabin and his actions during her stay. Sam's expression grew more troubled. "Sam, I hate to think the worst of Jim, but the facts all seem to point in that direction."

"That they do," Sam said sadly. "I've known that boy all his life. Maggie and I helped bring him into the world when his folks got stranded in here by an early snowstorm. Never known a straighter young man. Always seemed to have a strong sense of right and wrong, right up until about six months before Ginny got killed."

"You mean this was going on before Ginny died?"

"Yes. He and Ginny spent part of the winter here. There were two men, Fischer and Ross, who came and stayed at the Lodge on two different occasions. I thought it was strange, them coming during the winter like that. I didn't like the feel of it, so I kept my eye on them. I happened on them out in the woods one day having an argument with Jim. "

"What were they arguing about?"

"I couldn't hear the words, only the sounds, but they were angry. I didn't want to get close enough for them to see me. Later that evening I invited myself to the Lodge and played 'local character' for them. I rambled on until I could bring up Jim's name without being obvious. Both of the fellows denied knowing him.

"Well, that made me mighty suspicious of those two, so I made it my business to keep an eye on them. I was afraid that Jim had gotten himself into some kind of serious trouble."

"Did you see them together again?"

"Yes, several times. I never could get close enough to hear anything. I even went so far as to ask Jim about Fischer and Ross, and he claimed he hadn't met them."

"What did Hank and Maggie have to say?"

"Nothing. You know how adept both of them are at avoiding a question they don't want to answer. But it was obvious that they were worried about something and it wasn't too long after that when they stopped taking guests at the Lodge."

"This Fischer and Ross, are they the men who bring the crates?"

"No. I don't quite know where they fit in. There was another young fellow who showed up a couple of days before Fischer and Ross left the last time — Mark something."

"Mark Jamison?"

"Yes. That's the name. Nice looking young fellow. He was a friend of Jim's and Ginny's. He visited a couple of times while Jim was in college."

"What about him?" Janet asked, uncertain that she really wanted to know.

"Well, he stayed up at Jim's place, but one day I saw him and Fischer and Ross with Jim up at the old sawmill. The three of them were ganged up on Jim, trying to convince him of something.

"Jim finally agreed to whatever it was and Jamison threw his arm around Jim's shoulders as if he was quite pleased. The four of them shook hands all around, then Fischer gave Jim some papers and money. Jamison left with them the next day. The next time I saw him, he came in with the men who brought the first load of crates. I haven't seen him since."

"Sam, I need to tell you about my David and why I'm here. There has to be some connection, but I can't see what it is."

Janet told Sam the whole story of David's note and being followed by the Lincoln, the ransacking of her home and office and the search of the log house. On impulse, she brought out the picture of Roscoe Carrac.

"That's the third man," Sam said, taking the picture from her hand and studying it thoughtfully. "He's the one who sometimes comes with the other two in the Lincoln to pick up the crates."

Janet hadn't expected that. She was stunned by the possibility of Jim's involvement with David's murder.

"Janet, listen to me. Whatever else Jim may be involved in, I cannot believe that he would knowingly be involved in murder. Perhaps whoever he is working for is, but not Jim."

"I want to believe that, but I have to know for certain. And Mark ... " Janet couldn't go on.

She wanted to cry. Somehow Mark Jamison had already gained a place in her thoughts as someone who would someday be a friend she could depend on, someone who was meant to be a part of her future. And it had even seemed that David had put his stamp of approval on it. Now she was having second thoughts about the whole experience with the crystal ball.

"What is it, honey? What's wrong?"

"Sam, please tell me. You are a doctor, aren't you?"

"I was," he said sadly. "I gave up medicine a long time ago except for an emergency now and then. Honey, if you're sick, you need to see a real doctor, not old Sam."

"I'm not physically sick, but I wonder if I'm losing my mind. You're a wise man and I suspect you have kept up with modern medicine more than you are willing to admit. I have to tell you something, and you must be completely honest with me about your opinion."

As Janet told Sam about her dream and the experiences with the crystal ball, and the discovery that the face belonged to Mark Jamison, the worry lines smoothed from his face and were replaced by a gentle smile.

"Child, put your fears to rest. There are some who might disagree with me, but I guarantee that you are not losing your mind. I've heard stranger stories than yours. In fact, your experiences, or variations of them, are not at all uncommon. You are a very creative person and I'll bet you use your intuition and have strong hunches from time to time."

"That's true, especially when I'm doing research and come to a dead end. I'll get a hunch to look at some off-beat source no one has thought of consulting and usually find what I'm looking for. But what does that have to do with this?"

"It's simply another manifestation of the creative part of your mind. It's too involved to discuss thoroughly now, but I have some excellent books I'll be happy to lend to you.

"Now, as to this Jamison fellow. Trust your feelings and trust David. We don't know the whole story of what is going on up here and things are not always what they appear to be. We may have drawn some conclusions that are not valid. We'll find the answers. I have no doubt of that. And don't do any more worrying about your mind. There's nothing wrong with it. You're just learning to use another part of it."

"Thank you, Sam. I hope you're right about things not being what they seem to be."

"Me, too, child. Now, us two old codgers have a mite of a walk ahead of us before dark, so we'll be thanking you for your hospitality and heading on toward home. You are every bit the intelligent, courageous woman I expected you to be. Together I think we can find some answers and maybe got Jim out of the mess he's in and solve your David's murder."

"I hope so. I'll try to live up to your expectations. It's so good to know that I have an ally. About the books ..."

"Why don't you walk over in the morning?"

"That's fine with me. Jim is coming for dinner tomorrow. Perhaps we can put our heads together and formulate a plan to get some information out of him."

Janet watched as Sam and Dan'l started upriver toward the trail to his secluded cabin. She had a sudden thought and rushed inside, then ran after them.

"Sam, wait up a minute. Take this box of candy bars. Maggie included them in my supplies and I don't care much for sweets."

"Thanky, Miss Janet. Dan'l and me, we'd be right proud to take 'em off your hands," Sam said with a big grin.

"Off with you," Janet laughed, "and no more of that hillbilly talk with me, you hear?"

"Yes'um, whatever you say, ma'am," Sam chortled back at Janet as he tipped his hat.

Janet watched until they were out of sight, thinking how much she would love to know the old man's history. He looked for all the world like some old desert prospector with his droopy mustache, dilapidated hat, faded jeans, and flannel shirt; that is, until you thought about what you were seeing. Sam's clothing was of the finest quality available. From his expensive, well-polished boots to his carefully-manicured fingernails, he was scrupulously clean. Even Dan'l always had a freshly groomed appearance. Janet knew that Sam had the table manners and social graces of a gentleman who was at ease in any social strata. Well, perhaps that was another mystery she would solve.

Janet's mind was only half on her writing after Sam left.

She finally put it aside and planned the dinner menu for the next night. Whatever was going on with Jim, Janet thought, at least there had been one positive result. With the Lodge closed, and no fishermen to cook for, Maggie had all those lovely jars of huckleberries to share with her. She baked two pies while she prepared a meal for herself.

Chapter 10

Thursday dawned clear and cold. Janet awakened in time to see the sunrise. It looked like an ideal day for her hike to Sam's cabin. She was excited. As far as she knew, not even Jim had ever been invited inside Sam's home.

Janet hurried through breakfast. With the outcome of her last hike still fresh in her mind, she propped a note in the middle of the kitchen table saying that she had gone to visit Sam and would return about three o'clock. As an extra precaution, she ran upstairs and looked out the windows to check the weather. There wasn't a cloud in sight.

Armed with her walking stick and her day pack to carry Sam's books in, she left the house in high spirits. Within fifteen minutes she had located the trail made by forty years of Sam's travels. It wasn't the easiest trail to Sam's cabin, but it was the most scenic. She and Jim had hiked both paths upriver many times and looked at Sam's cabin from a grove of trees, speculating on the reasons for Sam's secrecy about the way he lived.

Just for fun, and because it was Sam who had taught her how, she decided to read his and Dan'l's tracks and tell him about his homeward journey. Perhaps she could detect how many candy bars they had consumed on the way. The wrappers would go into Sam's pocket, but if their tracks indicated that they had paused and turned toward each other, that would give them away.

Janet was confused by the tracks. There were tracks of the outward journey but no fresh tracks showing Sam's return. She wondered if Sam had returned by a different route or had decided to spend the night at the Lodge.

A quarter of a mile down the trail, Sam's and Dan'l's tracks suddenly emerged from the woods. Janet studied the foot and paw prints. They were recent — no older than the previous afternoon — but partially obliterated by two sets of overlaying tracks which led in both directions.

Janet stepped off the trail and walked beside it for a long way, trying to make sense out of what she saw. It appeared that Sam and Dan'l had been in a hurry but had stopped at one point to look back. The superimposed tracks, because of size and depth, appeared to be those of two men who had been moving quickly as they followed Sam and Dan'l, and then running when they came back up the trail.

Janet felt a growing sense of uneasiness. She began to walk faster, reading sign as she went. For almost a mile the scenario remained unchanged. Then the trail led across the top of a small bluff. At that point, the two men had stepped from the trail while Sam and Dan'l had continued. Janet followed the tracks left by the two men. They continued only a few steps to the base of a small tree. One man had made several sets of tracks near a low limb, then both had returned to the trail and retraced their steps at a run.

Janet carefully planted her feet on either side of the tracks beneath the tree limb and attempted to see what had been of interest to the man. The limb blocked her field of vision until she stood on tiptoe. She noticed scratches on the limb, then saw the object of their interest.

"Oh, god! Oh no, not Sam!"

She was crying as she ran down the trail toward the huddled figures. There was nothing she could do for either of them.

It was a stark and bloody scene. It was also a scene of deepest love and loyalty.

Sam had been shot twice in the back with a high-powered rifle. There was no mark on Dan'l. Her tracks, by the hundreds, circled her beloved companion. She had kept watch over his body throughout the night, then had settled down beside him, her head on his shoulder, and had followed him down the last long trail. Her body was still warm.

Janet shook with a cold, hard anger. Dirt still clung to Sam's finger where he had traced a "J" in the moist earth.

"Damn you, Jim. Damn you." In that moment Janet came face to face with the knowledge that she could kill another human being.

Janet saw the scattered candy bars, most of them blood-soaked, and the tears came.

"Oh, Sam, you didn't deserve this. I swear I'll get whoever did this to you."

Janet turned away from the bodies and sat down on a rock several yards away. She lit a cigarette to calm her nerves. There was nothing she could do for Sam and Dan'l here, but if she used what Sam had taught her, she might be able to help the police a great deal.

She was careful not to obliterate any tracks as she made her way back to the place where the four sets of footprints had joined the trail. It was much more difficult to read sign in the woods. The ground was covered with a thick carpet of dead leaves and pine needles.

Sam and Dan'l had not left any trail which she could distinguish as theirs, but once her mind became alert to what to look for, the paths of the two men were obvious. There were broken branches where they had forced their way through a huckleberry thicket in a manner Sam would never have done.

Following broken twigs and scuffed leaves, Janet finally emerged on the old logging road. There were tire tracks of a large, heavy car. The vehicle had been pulled to the side of the road and parked. She had no doubt that it had been a big, black Lincoln with heavily tinted windows, though there was nothing to tell her that.

She backtracked the car, growing angrier by the minute. The trail led to the old logging camp and to the beginning of the trail to Jim's cabin. The car had been parked next to Jim's Jeep.

Janet couldn't distinguish one footprint from another on the heavily trampled ground. There seemed to be four different sets of prints, but she couldn't be certain. Then she saw the one bit of evidence she needed to tell her that Sam had been there and why he had been killed. There was one clear paw print next to where the car had been parked.

Something had drawn Sam's attention to the logging camp. He had decided to do some detective work and had been killed for his effort.

Janet ran toward the Lodge, a plan taking shape in her mind. She hoped that she could get Maggie and Hank to cooperate. When she burst through the kitchen door, she was stunned for a moment to see Maggie kneading dough. *My god! It had only been a week since she had sat here talking about David while Maggie did her weekly baking.*

"Janet, what's wrong?"

"Is Hank here?"

"Yes, he's in his office."

"Please get him so I only have to say it once."

Maggie hurried from the kitchen and returned momentarily with Hank.

"What is it, Janet?" Hank asked.

"It's Sam Donnelly. He's been murdered."

The shock and immediate grief was plain on both their faces as Janet explained where she had found Sam. She didn't mention the tracks.

"I'll call the sheriff in Gold Beach," Hank said, rising.

"No, not yet. Please, if you care at all about Sam or me, do what I ask. I think I know who killed Sam and why. Give me one hour, just one hour. Then call the sheriff and buzz Jim. Please, I don't want to accuse someone falsely, but I'm not going to let the murderer get away, either."

"Janet, you could be putting yourself in danger. Besides, how could you know who killed him?" Maggie asked.

"I can't explain it all right now, but Sam was killed on the way home from my place. I think our last conversation holds the key. Please, just trust me and do as I ask. And please, don't let anyone, even Jim, go near the trail until I return."

"Does this have something to do with Jim?" Hank asked.

"I don't know. I hope not. Will you do as I ask?"

Hank and Maggie looked at each other. Maggie nodded.

"All right, Janet," Hank agreed, "but only an hour, and be careful."

Janet glanced at the clock, then left the Lodge at a run, heading for the southern edge of the logging camp. From there she cut cross-country in the general direction of the old sawmill until she caught her first glimpse of the rock outcropping near the summit of the mountain. She continued to run as much as the terrain would allow.

The answer to the question in her mind might not seem like evidence to any one but her, but she was determined to have that answer. It would take only a minute in Jim's cabin to confirm her suspicion, and then she should be able to be back at the Lodge before Jim and the sheriff arrived.

Janet paused in a grove of trees above the cabin. It was a matter of seconds until she saw Jim hurry out the front door and take the trail down the mountain. She left her hiding place and entered through the kitchen door.

One glance into the closet of the middle bedroom was enough to tell her that the artifacts had been removed. She made a quick search through the rest of the cabin and the outbuildings. There was no trace of the artifacts. She had her answer. The men Jim had been dealing with were Sam's killers. That made Jim an accomplice at the very least. How any of this might tie in to David's murder still eluded her, but she felt one step nearer to that answer. She felt a mixture of anger and sorrow over Jim's involvement.

Janet started down the trail at a trot, trying to decide what to do with the information. There was only her word that the crates of artifacts had ever been in Jim's cabin. There was only her word for the subject of her last conversation with Sam. She was certain that Jim wouldn't volunteer any information. She didn't know what to expect from Hank and Maggie. The only person she could fully trust was herself.

Janet decided to point out the tracks to the sheriff and his men and hope that they were woodsmen enough to read them correctly. The "J" which Sam had drawn in the dirt, together with the evidence of the killers' car having been parked at the foot of Jim's trail, should point them in the right direction. She wouldn't make any accusations for the moment.

Janet left the trail at the halfway point between the cabin and the logging camp, and traveled directly down the steep slope, hoping to beat Jim to the bottom. When she arrived at the logging camp, Jim's Jeep was already gone. She cut across the clearing toward the Lodge but was brought to a standstill by the sight of two uniformed men leaning against their vehicle, deep in conversation with Jim and the McVeys.

"Damn it! They couldn't have gotten here that quickly from Gold Beach," Janet muttered. "Hank broke his promise and called them immediately."

She couldn't think of a good excuse for her absence, so she didn't offer one as she joined the group.

"I'm Janet Manning. I found Sam and Dan'l. You certainly didn't waste any time in getting here."

The two young deputies introduced themselves as Nichols and Owen. Janet couldn't help but remember the night when two other young deputies had come to her door with the news of David's murder and suspicions of her guilt. She hoped that nothing showed on her face, but she noted that Hank and Maggie were looking at her with strange expressions and Jim, flushed and nervous, refused to look at her at all.

"Mrs. Manning, I know this must be extremely upsetting for you. Dr. Scott has told us of the recent murder of your husband and your near death on the mountain during the storm," Deputy Nichols said. "Perhaps you would like to sit down and have a cup of coffee and take time to pull yourself together before you tell us how you happened to find Old Sam."

"I don't know what Jim has said to you, but I'm quite in control, ready to show you where I found Sam, and point out the tracks which tell clearly what happened."

"That's fine, ma'am, but we need to wait for the sheriff and the coroner," Nichols said. "Perhaps it would be best if we all had some coffee while we wait."

Janet couldn't believe what was happening. The deputies seemed completely uninterested in Sam's murder. Hank and Maggie looked at her with guarded expressions, while Jim's face was a mask devoid of emotion. Janet felt as if they all wished she would just disappear.

Maggie ushered the group onto the front veranda and supplied everyone with coffee and fresh cinnamon rolls. During the flurry of being seated and served, Janet noticed that Jim and Hank managed to exchange a few secretive words.

The thought of eating nauseated Janet. She lit a cigarette and sat for a few minutes in utter disbelief as the five calmly discussed the weather and the prospects for a good hunting season.

"Damn it!" she erupted. "Doesn't anyone care that Samuel Donnelly has been murdered?"

There was a moment of frozen silence. Before anyone could respond, a 4 x 4 with a sheriff's department emblem on the door pulled up in front of the Lodge. Nichols and Owen jumped to their feet and rushed to meet Sheriff Gates and the two men accompanying him. There was a hurried conference, then Sheriff Gates called to Jim.

"Dr. Scott, will you show us the way?"

Janet was furious as she pushed Jim aside and walked rapidly toward the group.

"Sheriff Gates, I'm Janet Manning. I found Sam. I'll show you where."

"No need, Mrs. Manning. Dr. Scott will show us."

"But — "

"No! You stay at the Lodge. I don't have time to deal with a hysterical woman," the sheriff said sharply as he turned away.

Janet grabbed his arm. "Damn it, I don't know what is going on here, but I'm not hysterical. I'm furious. I don't know what games *Mister* Scott is trying to play, but I can make a pretty good guess."

Sheriff Gates looked coldly at Janet. "And what is that?"

"He wants to make certain that he doesn't have to answer any embarrassing questions about his involvement with the men who killed Sam. I saw the proof."

"Now Janet, please don't allow yourself to get overwrought and say things you'll regret later," Jim said, putting his arm around Janet and pulling her close. "For god's sake, Janet, shut up," he said in a vicious tone no one else could hear.

Janet jerked away, only to have the sheriff grab her by both arms.

"Mrs. Manning, you're wasting valuable time with this nonsense. You shut up and stay here at the Lodge until we get back. I'll have some things to say to you then. Do you understand?"

"No. I don't understand. And I won't be at the Lodge. I'll be at the log house if you want me."

"See that you are."

Janet was livid as she turned toward the track leading to her house. The McVeys blocked the way.

"Janet, dear, you shouldn't be alone when you're upset like this. After what Jim has told us — "

"Just what in hell did Jim tell you?"

"Dear, there's no need to talk about that now," Maggie said soothingly.

"Oh yes there is. We damn well are going to talk about it right now!"

"Well, he told us how you lost control and got hysterical while you were stranded at his cabin," Maggie said, hesitantly. "He said he had to force a sedative on you to calm you down. He said it wasn't the first time he had seen you like that, raving and imagining all sorts of things."

"Maggie. Hank. Did it ever occur to you that your precious Jim might be lying? God knows that I am about as angry as I have ever been in my life, but I am in control. I was cold and exhausted the day of the storm, but I wasn't hysterical then and I'm not now- Jim didn't give me any sedative. And to set the record completely straight, Jim has never seen me in the state he described."

"Hank and I were surprised by what Jim told us. It seemed out of character for you. I just don't know what to think."

"Well, while you decide, I'm going home."

"At least allow Hank to drive you, dear."

Janet started to refuse, but she had a sudden idea which made her accept. Every minute could count. She nodded and climbed into the pickup.

As they started down the rough track, Hank glanced at Janet's impassive face. "Did you find what you were looking for at Jim's cabin?" he asked quietly.

"Yes, Hank. I'm afraid I did." Janet wasn't surprised that he knew where she had been.

"You believe that it implicates Jim in Sam's murder, don't you?"

"That and more, at least indirectly. You know something, don't you?"

"I know enough to tell you that things are not always what they seem. Janet, give Jim the benefit of the doubt. You can trust him. If and when he can, he will tell you what is going on."

"That's rather hard to do under the circumstances. I know what I have seen, and I know that what Sam saw got him killed. Besides, I'm not too sure how far I can trust you and Maggie anymore."

They were silent during the remainder of the short drive.

Janet dropped her empty day-pack just inside the door. She was worn out emotionally and physically, but there was something which she owed both to herself and to Sam and Dan'l, and just possibly to David.

She used the electric hot-pot to make herself a quick cup of tea, heavily laced with brown sugar. She drank it while she changed her blue plaid shirt and jeans for khaki pants and shirt. She grabbed her camera and left the house at a run.

Chapter 11

Janet cut through the woods and worked her way around the Lodge until she could cross the road into the logging camp without being seen. She found the clearest set of tire tracks and placed her pack of cigarettes beside them for a reference point. Then she took a picture of the general area to identify the location before she took closeup pictures of the tire tracks and Dan'l's paw print.

She followed the tracks back to the logging road, taking pictures at intervals so that they could later be put together to show the route the car had followed.

There weren't any clear footprints through the woods toward the trail, but Janet took a frame or two of places where the brush had been trampled. Where the footprints emerged onto the trail, Janet was surprised to see that the sheriff's party had stepped off the trail to avoid disturbing them.

Janet followed the tracks, taking pictures, as far as she dared without running the risk of being seen by the sheriff and his men. Then, she crossed the trail and cut toward the river until she could work her way around the murder scene and come out on a bluff on the far side.

Janet lay in deep shadow, watching the activity below her. A deputy was taking pictures under the direction of the man Janet assumed was the coroner. The coroner was taking notes or sketching the area. Nichols and Owen were on the bluff across from her where the killers had stood. They seemed to be making a thorough search of the area.

There was no sign of Jim and Sheriff Gates. Janet began to grow uneasy until she spotted them coming up the trail from Sam's cabin. They were engaged in a heated argument. As Janet watched through the zoom lens of her camera, Jim gestured toward two envelopes in Gates' hand. The sheriff shook his head. Jim pulled Gates off the trail and handed him something which he had taken from his billfold.

Janet recorded the whole scenario with her camera as Gates studied the paper and Jim continued to talk with an air of urgency. After a few minutes Gates nodded, handed the paper back to Jim, and shook hands with him. They continued their conversation for a few minutes. From their manner and the expression on their faces, Janet got the distinct feeling that a conspiracy was under way.

The scene had been so engrossing that she hadn't paid any attention to the other four men. Now she saw that Nichols and Owen had joined the two below her and were scanning the area. She saw Owen say something to the others and make just the slightest gesture in her direction with his head. She knew that she had either been sighted, or a flash of sunlight on her camera lens had given her away.

She didn't linger. Tired as she was, she summoned the strength to run down the river trail at top speed, bouncing from rock to rock, keeping her balance with a good deal of luck. Her mind was racing as she ran. If her luck continued, she would have perhaps as long as five minutes at the log house before any of them arrived. She had to make those minutes count. Her very life might depend on her ability to convince them that she hadn't left the house. In the event they didn't believe her, she had to make certain her film was hidden somewhere safe. Maybe she could convince someone of the truth with her pictures.

She rewound the film and removed it from the camera as she came in sight of the house. She stopped in the kitchen just long enough to fill the hot pot with water and plug it in and grab a plastic film container from her camera bag on the table. She shoved the roll of film into it and pushed it deep into the flour canister with a spoon.

She grabbed the camera bag, ran into the bedroom and slid the bag under the bed. She changed back into her jeans and blue plaid shirt and hid the khaki pants and shirt under a pile of laundry.

She raced into the living room, unscrewed the top of a kerosene lamp, and poured the contents over several sticks of wood in the pot-bellied stove and stuck a match to it. She hid the lamp in a kitchen cabinet and unplugged the hot pot. She poured a little of the hot water into the remainder of the tea in the cup she had used earlier, then poured the rest into the kettle on the stove. She hid the hot pot in a drawer.

Janet carried the teacup to the stool beside JBG. She retreated into the giant rocking chair, hugging her legs, chin resting on her knees. Every muscle in her body ached.

She cleared her mind and took a deep breath, held it for a moment, then exhaled slowly. She didn't dare allow herself to think about Sam and Dan'l or what the future might hold for her. She reached deep inside herself, as her *sensei* had taught her, and tapped the inner core of her being to dredge up whatever last reserves of calm strength were there to see her through the coming hours. A fragile peace had begun to seep through her when the kitchen door flew open.

"Damn you, Janet! What have you been up to?" Jim shouted.

"Dear me, aren't you afraid you'll make me hysterical bursting in this way?" Janet said sarcastically as Jim entered the living room.

"I know it was you that Owen saw on the bluff. What the hell were you up to?"

Before Janet could answer, they heard the sound of a vehicle outside.

"I seem to be very popular all of a sudden. You will excuse me while I answer the door?"

Jim looked as if he could choke Janet. As she opened the door for Deputy Nichols, Janet saw Jim surreptitiously test the temperature of the liquid in her tea cup and the kettle. He looked perplexed and suddenly uncertain of his ground.

"Come in, Deputy Nichols. One more and we'll have a fourth for bridge."

"Mrs. Manning, let's dispense with the foolishness. Murder is a serious business."

"I'm glad you realize that. I wasn't sure that any of you did, judging from your actions. I have made every attempt to offer my assistance in pointing out the evidence I saw both before and after I found Sam, and have been ignored and then treated as if I were brain-damaged. Sam's death is a very serious matter to me."

"Then you won't mind answering some questions," said the red-faced young deputy.

"Not as long as you treat me like a rational human being. *Doctor* Scott's psychological evaluation of me has no basis in fact."

Jim's face turned a deep red as Janet looked him straight in the eyes.

"I only wanted to protect you, Janet."

"From what? I don't need your protection. Your efforts would be better used in your own behalf."

Jim shrugged and turned away to stare out of the window.

"Now, deputy, what would you like to know?"

"Where have you been since you left the Lodge?"

"Right here."

"You didn't leave the house at all?"

"No. What is this all about? Didn't you find Sam and the tracks?"

"Yes, we did. However, someone was spying on us. The trail seemed to lead here. If it wasn't you, it could have been the killer. We need to know. Would you mind if I look around?"

"I see, my word isn't good enough."

"Let's just say, ma'am, that we'd like to be certain. You don't have to let me look, but it would save a lot of time and effort for all of us."

"Please look wherever you want. The bedroom on the left is only used for storage. I use the upstairs for writing and some of my camping gear."

Nichols nodded and left the room.

Janet stared at Jim until he turned from the window.

"Jim, please don't let them just leave Dan'l there. You will see that she is properly buried, won't you? She and Sam ..." She was suddenly choked with tears and unable to continue.

"Of course. I loved Sam and Dan'l, too." Jim's eyes were bright with unshed tears.

"Jim, you know who killed Sam. Please tell the sheriff. You can't let those men get away with it."

"Please trust me, Janet. There is so much more involved than I can tell you right now. Whatever happens during the next few days, you have to trust me. There are good reasons why the truth must not come out right now. I promise you that Sam's killer will be punished."

"I wish I could believe you."

"Then remember what Sam taught you. Things are not always what they appear to be." Jim's voice suddenly became harsh. "You should be an expert on that subject."

Janet stared at him as he abruptly left the room to have a word with the deputy, then stormed out the kitchen door. She was confused by his last words. The deputy interrupted her thoughts.

"Ma'am, Sheriff Gates asked me to stay here for your protection. I'll wait outside if you prefer."

"No need. I'll make us some coffee. Did you find what you were looking for?"

"No ma'am. It appears you were telling the truth. My apologies. I'll just take a quick look around outside while you take care of the coffee."

A short while later, Janet and the deputy were seated at the kitchen table.

"Thank you, Mrs. Manning. This sure tastes good."

Janet wondered if a little informality might encourage the deputy to tell her something about the investigation into Sam's death.

"Why don't you call me Janet, Deputy Nichols? Then maybe this won't all seem so cold and unfriendly. I've lost two dear friends today, you know."

"Yes'um. And, you can call me Ted." He looked thoughtfully at Janet as he sipped his coffee. "This is pretty rough on you, isn't it, coming so soon after your husband's death?"

Janet realized that Ted Nichols was neither as young or as ingenuous as he appeared. She sensed that he wanted her to talk about David so that he could judge for himself just how emotionally stable she was. She calmly told him about the circumstances of David's murder.

"And the police haven't found a clue as to who killed him or why?"

"No. They haven't really tried. They've been too busy trying to prove that he was a criminal."

Ted Nichols considered that for several seconds before he spoke. "So you have lived here before." It was a statement rather than a question.

"Yes, for two summers fifteen years ago. My parents lived here for two years, but I went to high school in Portland and then back to Texas to college."

"Dr. Scott was here then?"

"Yes. Jim and I were good friends."

"It was during those two summers, then, that you got to know Samuel Donnelly."

"Yes. Sam and Dan'l were a big part of our lives. I don't know how well you knew Sam, but he was one of the finest and wisest men I've ever known. I was at an age when my vision of life was limited to what directly affected me. Sam taught me to see a much larger world and to believe that I didn't have to accept any limitations because of age, sex, or circumstances. He had a profound and lasting effect on my life. I loved and respected him."

"Then why did you kill him?" Sheriff Gates said from the doorway.

Chapter 12

" You must be insane!" Janet shouted as she started to her feet.

"Just stay right there. Don't move."

Gates' hand was on the butt of his gun. Jim and Deputy Owen flanked him.

"You can't be serious about this."

"You were just too clever for your own good," Jim said, enigmatically.

"Jim, you can't believe I'd hurt Sam. You know I didn't."

"Mrs. Manning, before this goes any further, so that there will be no misunderstandings later, you will be informed of your rights. Nichols, read Mrs. Manning her rights."

Janet felt as if she were playing a role in a third-rate detective drama as she stood looking from face to face. Ted appeared to be mystified as he stumbled through the phrases Janet was hearing for the second time in a matter of months. Jim was silently mouthing, "Trust me," which was the last thing she felt like doing. Sheriff Gates was expressionless. Deputy Owen was smiling.

When Ted finished, Sheriff Gates asked Janet if she understood her rights.

"Yes, I do. What comes next — handcuffs and a body search?"

"Body search, yes. No handcuffs for now. Dr. Scott, will you get Mrs. McVey down here?"

"Oh, no you don't. You've cooked up this charade, now do your own dirty work. Here, I'll make it easy for you."

Janet was furious as she peeled out of her shirt and jeans. "There, do you see any concealed weapons, or do you want me to take the rest of it off?" Janet shouted, indicating her red lace half-bra and bikini panties.

Ted stared with his mouth open, his face a fiery red. Owen leered.

"I see nothing which is currently classified as an illegal weapon," Sheriff Gates commented drily. "Please cover yourself."

Janet glanced at Jim. He was biting his lip to keep from laughing. "I hope you are thoroughly enjoying yourself, Jim. One of these days you won't be able to find anything funny. That's a promise."

Janet pulled her jeans on and buttoned her shirt. "Now, sheriff, I give up my right to remain silent. What do you want to know and whatever gave you the insane idea that I killed Sam Donnelly?"

"Mrs. Manning, when did you first learn that you were Samuel Donnelly's sole heir?"

"What? But I'm not. Besides, Sam didn't have anything. What gave you such a ridiculous idea?"

"This."

Sheriff Gates handed Janet an envelope marked: "TO BE OPENED IMMEDIATELY UPON MY DEATH."

Janet's hands trembled as she removed several sheets of paper from the large envelope. She scanned the first sheet and saw that it contained instructions for Sam's burial and for Dan'l's care, should she outlive him. The remaining pages were a copy of Sam's will.

Janet was stunned as she read the words. Sam had left her everything he owned, and it was a staggering amount. There was a country estate in northern California and its contents, stocks, bonds, over $750,000 in cash, and his cabin and its contents.

Janet looked at the date of the will. It had been originally drawn up almost ten years before with a few changes made the week after David's death.

"You don't think I knew about this? I hadn't seen or heard from Sam in fifteen years until yesterday. I didn't even know he was still alive until I saw him on the porch. I certainly had no idea he was a wealthy man."

"You want us to believe that this old man left an estate worth millions to someone he hadn't seen or talked to in fifteen years? That's a little more than I can make myself believe."

"I don't care how hard it is to believe, sheriff. It's the truth. I can't imagine why he left everything to me. Even if I had known about it, that wouldn't prove I killed him."

"We only have your word that you didn't know. It's possible that you didn't know until he told you yesterday. Under the circumstances, I imagine that you haven't been allowed to collect on your husband's insurance and may be desperate for cash."

"That's ridiculous," Janet said, but a little knot of fear was growing. She hadn't been allowed to settle David's estate yet, and she had very little money at the moment.

The sheriff shook his head. "You're a quick-thinking, clever young woman who thought she was smarter than a backwater sheriff. Where is your rifle? You do own one?"

"Yes. I have a 30-06 and a .22. They are both upstairs."

"Owen, bring the 30-06 down. Take a good look around while you're up there. Nichols, you search the downstairs again, and do it thoroughly this time."

Janet hated the thought of anyone pawing through her things, but she felt certain the sheriff didn't really have enough evidence to charge her with murder. As long as they didn't search her pickup, she didn't think they could charge her with anything. The rifles were legal. She didn't know what the Oregon law was on well-concealed handguns. David had created a compartment that looked like a normal part of the driver's seat in her Toyota 4 x 4. By dropping her hand and putting pressure on one particular spot, a palm-sized .38 Special would fall into her hand. She was afraid that if the sheriff found anything to justify arresting her, she would never get out of jail alive.

Janet was engrossed in her thoughts and didn't notice that Owen and Nichols had left the room until Sheriff Gates bent over and quickly whispered in her ear.

"I know you didn't kill Sam. Don't trust anyone but Dr. Scott or me. We'll explain later."

Jim touched her on the shoulder. "Please, Janet. Please, for Sam and Dan'l, play along with us."

Janet stared at them, speechless. *Trust them?* she thought. *They are setting me up for Sam's murder and they want me to trust them?*

"All right, Mrs. Manning, I have a few questions," the sheriff said in loud voice. "When was the last time your rifle was fired?"

Janet lit a cigarette with trembling hands before she answered. "Several months ago. Not since David died."

"There was a 30-06 shell casing on the bluff where the killer stood."

"Certainly you don't think I have the only 30-06 in Oregon? You might question the two men who made the tracks. You had to have seen the tracks."

"Oh yes, the tracks. Well, a clever little lady like you wouldn't have found it too difficult to lay a false set of tracks. It has been done before. Or, maybe you had a couple of hired guns if you didn't have the stomach for pulling the trigger yourself."

"Wait a damn — "

"Nothing up there but some camping gear and this 30-06 and a box of ammo," Owen interrupted as he entered the room. "Same brand as the casing we found. Looks like this pretty well wraps it up. She had a motive and her tracks put her on the scene. The old man scratched her initial in the dirt. Here's the murder weapon. Shall I handcuff her?"

"Now just a damn minute! Nobody has proved anything. That 'J' could just as easily have meant Jim, and a test of that rifle will prove it hasn't been fired in months. You don't have anything that will stand up in court. I don't think you even have enough to arrest me. You're trying to set me up and I'm not — "

"Feisty little bitch," Owen laughed. "Anyone ever check on where you were when your old man was shot?"

"You dirty, vicious, bastard!" Janet erupted.

"That will be enough from both of you," Sheriff Gates shouted. "Mrs. Manning, sit down and shut up. Owen, you shut up and write a receipt for the rifle and then check around outside.

"Nichols, what the hell is taking you so long?"

Ted Nichols entered the room carrying Janet's khaki shirt and pants and her binoculars. "I'm sorry, sir. I found these under a pile of dirty laundry. They've been worn recently. The binoculars were at the back of a shelf in the closet."

"Seems like you didn't do your job the first time. Now check out the kitchen."

"Yes, sir."

The embarrassed deputy laid Janet's possessions on the couch and made a rapid exit into the kitchen. Janet wavered between relief that he either hadn't found the camera bag or didn't think it was important, and anxiety over how thorough he would be in his search of the kitchen.

She turned defiantly to the sheriff. "Are you going to arrest me?"

"Not exactly."

"How can you 'not exactly' arrest someone? I've had enough of this farce. I want some answers now."

Jim raised a warning finger as Owen opened the front door.

"Mrs. Manning, we will have some tests run on your rifle," the sheriff said. "It will take several days to get the results. Until then, don't make any attempt to leave the area. I'm putting you in the custody of Dr. Scott. If you must go into town for any reason, either Dr. Scott or Hank McVey will accompany you. Make it easy on yourself."

"Don't worry, sheriff. I'll see that she stays put," Jim said.

Janet flashed him an angry look. "I don't need a keeper. I just want to be left alone. I'm not going anywhere. My rifle didn't kill Sam and neither did I. And I didn't kill my husband! Now, if you're finished, get the hell out of here. All of you!"

Janet was confused, exhausted, and on the verge of tears. She didn't want any of them to have the satisfaction of seeing her cry. She ran into her bedroom, slammed the door, and fell across the bed. She heard the front door open and close and cars drive away. She cried until she fell asleep.

A hand gently shaking Janet's shoulder awakened her to a dark room.

"Who is it? What do you want?" Janet asked in alarm.

"It's all right, Janet. It's Jim. Just a minute and I'll turn on the light."

"What are you doing here? What do you want?"

"Take it easy, Janet. I didn't want to leave you alone tonight. I know you need a good night's sleep, but you deserve some answers, and a hot shower and some food won't hurt you, either. I've heated plenty of water for a shower and supper is in the oven. Let's call a truce until you've had that shower and something to eat."

Janet was too tired to do battle. "At the moment, that sounds so good that all I can say is 'Thank you,' but I'll have plenty to say later."

"I can just bet that you will. Now off to the shower with you. I'll have supper on the table by the time you finish."

Janet sat on the edge of the bed for a few minutes to clear her mind, then gathered up her gown and robe and headed for the shower. As the soothing, steamy water began to relax her, her thoughts turned to the bizarre and tragic events of the day. *Jim, you'd better have some damn good answers,* she thought. *And if this ties in with David's murder ...*

She found Jim in the kitchen.

"Feeling better?"

"Yes. Now, let's talk."

"Not yet. I know you have a hundred questions, and I promise to answer all of them after we eat. We've both had a grueling day and we'll be in much better shape if we take time to have a peaceful meal. Just for half an hour, Janet, let's put everything aside."

Janet agreed reluctantly. She knew she was going to need all of her wits and stamina to do battle with Jim. As they sat down at the kitchen table, she marveled at the cozy normality of the scene after the harrowing events of the day.

"Jim, you may have all kinds of ulterior motives for your concern and kindness, but I'm going to take them at face value for now. I'm that frantic for some semblance of sanity. But that doesn't mean that I trust you or will believe a word of what you have to say later."

"That's fair enough. I can't say that I blame you."

When the meal was finished they lingered over coffee, reluctant to disturb the peace of the moment, yet knowing that it couldn't be avoided for long. Jim leaned across the table to light Janet's cigarette, then lit his own. He leaned back and grinned.

"What's funny?"

"'I see nothing which is currently classified as illegal.' My god, you should have been arrested on the spot for carrying concealed weapons."

"I'm glad you enjoyed it," Janet replied coldly. "I saw very little humor in being accused of murder, and I saw no reason to make Maggie a party to it."

"I'm sorry, Janet. You have every right to be angry. Sometimes, a person's mind can just take so much before it reaches out for a little humor in the name of self-preservation. At the same time, little lady, you more than earned everything that happened to you," Jim continued with a note of anger creeping into his voice. "You can't be involved in any part of a dirty business and not have some moral responsibility for all of it. Your friends play a vicious game and — "

"My friends?" Janet interrupted. "What in hell are you talking about? You're the one whose friends play dirty. Are you going to deny that the men who killed Sam had come to pick up a shipment of illegal artifacts from you?"

Janet felt such rage that she grabbed her coffee and cigarettes and retreated to the living room to JBG to buy herself a moment to regain control. Jim followed.

"How is it that you know about the men and what they were doing if you aren't involved? What you said up at my place about pot hunting and your knowledge of obscure ruins which had been looted certainly made it sound as if you are involved. Or was it just your husband?"

"Neither. I was baiting you, and you fell for it. I wanted to know just how deeply involved you are."

"Who told you that I am? I know it wasn't Hank or Maggie."

"You did."

"I did?"

"Yes, when you removed the artifacts from the bedroom and hid them. That got my attention and made me suspicious. While you were outside, I snooped around and found the other crates in the closet in the middle bedroom."

"Are you telling me that you are not involved in the black market in artifacts?"

"That's exactly what I'm telling you. David and I despised pot hunters and did our best to stop them. What I know about your activities comes from my own observations and some things Sam told me. Jim, how on earth could you let yourself become involved in something so despicable?"

"I'm not, at least not in the way you think. The plain truth is that I'm working undercover as a government agent to put an end to the black market."

"Oh really? I'd love to believe you. Got any proof?"

Jim reached for his billfold and extracted a folded sheet of paper from an inner compartment.

"This is all I can offer you at the moment."

Janet looked at the letterhead and read the terse statement of Jim's authorization as a special agent. It was signed by the heads of three government agencies and stated that it could be verified through the nearest FBI office.

"It's an interesting paper," Janet remarked as she handed it back to Jim. "I didn't realize there were three government agencies capable of cooperating with each other. Is this how you conned Sheriff Gates into framing me for murder?"

Chapter 13

Jim walked into the kitchen and returned with the coffee pot. He maintained his silence until he had refilled their cups.

"Whatever you choose to believe, Janet, I had been trying to protect you."

"Is that why you told the deputies and the McVeys that wild story about my mental and emotional instability and why you made certain that I'm the prime suspect in Sam's murder — to protect me? Be serious. You were protecting yourself."

"Some of both. When Hank told me you had found Sam, he said that you had gone off somewhere saying that you thought you knew who killed Sam and why. We were both concerned about you. I was also concerned about salvaging what I could of two years of hard work put into trying to identify all the people involved in the black market setup.

"I didn't have any idea of how you were involved or what danger you might put us all in by what you would say to the deputies. The best thing I could think of was to make your mental state suspect."

"I see. You were so concerned about protecting me that you made it appear that I was mentally incompetent and then framed me for murder. Gee, if you weren't my friend I might be facing a firing squad for treason."

"Now wait a minute, Janet. At least try to understand how it appeared from my viewpoint."

"I don't want to hear what you thought. I want some real answers and a reason to believe you."

"The letter ..."

"All that your letter tells me is that someone acquired an impressive letterhead, typed a letter, and signed it. Since I don't correspond with any of these three men, I don't happen to have samples of their signatures at hand."

"I'll take you to the Lodge now and let you phone the FBI office in Portland."

"I intend to do just that, but not from the Lodge. I can't be certain that you haven't tampered with the phone line. You can drive me to Gold Beach tomorrow."

"If that's what you want."

"It is. Now, why don't you go ahead and tell me your version of what you are doing, and why you and the sheriff want people to believe that I killed Sam."

Jim nodded, but remained silent while Janet put more wood into the stove and moved the Jolly Brown Giant where she could directly face Jim. She looked at him and felt a sudden rush of pity at his bleak and beaten appearance. A flash of intuition made her blurt a question.

"Jim, what does all of this have to do with Ginny?"

"How could you know? I never told anyone."

"Somehow the expression on your face made me ask."

"Janet, you have to understand something about Ginny. She wasn't bad. She was a child who never grew up. It was my fault. She had spent all of her life in logging camps until we married. I showed her a new, exciting world — one that money could buy — and she wasn't ready to deal with it. She was like a child seeing a toy store for the first time, overwhelmed with the magic of it, but afraid it would all suddenly disappear.

"Mark Jamison had already recruited me for the government when I discovered that Ginny was hiding choice artifacts and selling them."

"How did you find out?"

"We were excavating a room block. Ginny was working alone when she discovered a burial under the floor of one room. She didn't tell anyone until she had the skeleton fully exposed. I was disturbed by her secrecy and the absence of burial goods. We had routinely found pots, tools, and other artifacts with every burial.

"I finally decided it was just an anomaly. Then, it happened again, and I became suspicious."

"I can see why you would be suspicious," Janet said. "What was her explanation?"

"I didn't question her right then. I decided to watch her. A couple of nights after she found the second burial, I woke up just as she was leaving our tent. I followed her. She had hidden the artifacts in some brush not far from the ruin. I stopped her when she began to load them into the trunk of her car.

"She was upset that I had caught her. She brushed aside the illegal aspects of her actions, and didn't seem to understand that she was playing a deadly serious game. She only saw that she had found a way to make a lot of money. I never did find out who her contact was or how they got together."

Janet felt that Jim was finally being honest with her. She rejoiced at the knowledge that Mark Jamison was one of the "good guys," but her heart went out to Jim in his obvious pain.

"I spent too much time away from the dig in Arizona. I thought I had convinced Ginny to stop selling artifacts. She had no idea what I was doing. She thought that my absences were partly because of problems with our relationship and partly related to business involving the dig. There was an area which had begun to show a lot of promise, but I had ordered the crew to stop digging there until I returned. There was too much danger of a rock slide from the cliff above them. I was gone for four days and when I returned, I found Ginny seriously injured and two others dead. The cliff had collapsed and crushed Ginny's legs and pelvis. A broken rib had punctured her lung.

"Before Ginny died, she told me that she had continued to dig and had taken some choice artifacts to sell so that she could surprise me with a lot of money. She thought that then I would love her again and take her traveling like I had before."

Jim swallowed hard, took a sip of coffee and lit another cigarette. "She never understood that I worked because I enjoyed what I did, not from necessity. I tried to love her, Janet. I really did try."

"I'm sorry, Jim. Having known Ginny, I understand. You don't need to say anymore."

"It's a relief to talk about it. I've never told even Hank and Maggie what she did. I've felt so responsible for her death and such hatred for the people who took advantage of her. Then, when it seemed that you were involved, I ... I ..."

"But I'm not, Jim. At least I wasn't until today."

"I believe that, but now you are involved, and I have to tell you the rest of it because I need your help. I know there is a well-organized group dealing in the illicit sale of artifacts and antiquities on an international scale. The U.S. suppliers seem to be predominately in the Southwest and they are also funneling artifacts from northern Mexico across the border into the States. Money from the sales buys drugs and weapons and god only knows what else. This bunch has left a trail of death and misery behind them that is difficult to believe. The many 'accidental' deaths and mysterious disappearances of campers, hunters, and backpackers over the last few years are the least of it."

"How did you find out about the organization?"

"Mark Jamison stumbled onto part of the setup when he was in Europe, and he managed to infiltrate it as a supplier when he returned to the States. He had to pull out when some of his professional colleagues began to get too interested in what he was doing and were about to compromise him."

"That's when he got you involved?"

"Yes. He sent word up the pipeline that he had to lay low for a while and he also cast doubt on the authenticity of some of the artifacts which were passing through his hands. Mark's message convinced the head man that he needed someone to authenticate the artifacts or his market could dry up if it became known that he sometimes sold fake artifacts. He offered to recruit an expert and was given the go-ahead. Then he sent the government agents who were his contacts to see me, and finally came himself when I refused to get involved."

"The agents — Fischer and Ross?"

"Yes, but how — "

"Sam told me that he saw at least two of the meetings. I'll tell you about that later. Go on with what you were saying."

"Mark convinced me to cooperate. Between the two of us, we have identified everyone in the pipeline from the suppliers to the two men who pick up the shipments from me. They work directly for the big boss, but their trail stops in Gold Beach. We suspect that there is someone in the sheriff's office who always makes things happen so that they aren't followed beyond that point. That's where you come in."

"I think I'm beginning to get the picture. If those two men are publicized as murder suspects, then your line of contact may be broken. If, on the other hand, you seem to cover for them and set me up instead, it strengthens your position and allows business to continue an usual. As a bonus, you may be able to uncover the contact in Gold Beach."

Jim rose and started pacing. "That's pretty much how we have it figured. I hated to do this to you, but everything fell into place so fast and so perfectly."

"Jim," Janet interrupted. "There is one thing that worries me. Are you certain you can trust Sheriff Gates?"

"Yes. He was thoroughly checked out by the FBI and his name was given to me as someone I could trust if I ever got in a tight bind."

"That's a relief. What about Nichols and Owen?"

"I can't vouch for them."

Janet got up and stretched. She felt strangely exhilarated by the danger and adventure, now that she knew what was involved. She believed that she was several steps closer to understanding why David had been killed and finding his killer, even though she still couldn't see the threads which made the connection.

She knew she could add to Jim's store of facts about the two men and their probable destination, but she wasn't quite ready to completely abandon caution where he was concerned. She believed his story about Ginny, but she still wanted verification of his undercover status, and she wasn't comfortable with his tendency to act on impulse.

"I still have quite a few questions, but you can answer them later. Right now, I'm curious about something else. How did you and Sheriff Gates fabricate Sam's will so quickly?"

"We didn't. We found it when we searched his cabin. You, my dear, are a very wealthy young woman, and it gave us the perfect motive to use in building the case against you."

"But where did all of Sam's money come from and why did he leave it to me? Why not you or the McVeys? Surely he has family somewhere."

"I may have the answer to your questions out in my Jeep. By the way, Janet, I hope you aren't going to make a fuss about me spending the night here."

"I don't see why you should. You know that I'm not going anywhere."

"It isn't a whim. You need the protection."

"From what? Damn it, Jim. What else haven't you told me? It's my life you're playing fast and loose with, and I want to know it all. Now!"

"Well, hell! I had to make some quick decisions around here today and they may not have been the best ones," Jim said defensively. "You aren't the only one with feelings. You seem to forget that I lost someone today whom I loved dearly, too. Damn it, Janet, I loved Sam. He brought me into the world and he has been my teacher and closest companion all my life." Jim's voice broke and he could scarcely choke out the words. "If I had just told him what was going on. If I hadn't shut him out. Janet, I killed him just as surely as if I had pulled the trigger."

Janet ran to Jim and put her arms around him, ashamed that she had been insensitive to his pain. He buried his face in her hair as hard, dry sobs wracked his body. She was frightened by the depth of his grief. He barely seemed aware of Janet as she led him to the couch. She held him for a long time, stroking his hair and crooning words of comfort until they both fell into an exhausted sleep.

Jim roused an hour later and carried the sleeping Janet into her bedroom. He slipped off her robe, tucked her under the covers, and stood looking down at her.

"I tried to love Ginny," he murmured, "but there was always you."

Jim stripped to his briefs, slipped into the bed and encircled Janet with his arms. She unconsciously moved closer and put her head on his chest and one arm around his waist.

Forgive me, love, Jim thought. *This may be the only chance I ever have to hold you like this.*

Chapter 14

It was still dark when Janet awoke in Jim's arms, his hand cupping one breast. She slipped from under the covers and slid her pillow into the vacancy as Jim stirred and then settled back into a deep sleep. She found her robe and slippers, and tiptoed into the living room.

Janet stirred the fire, added wood and poured a cup of the still-warm coffee. Her mind was crowded with thoughts and questions. So much remained unanswered about Sam and Jim, and how it all connected with David. There was even more unanswered about what was happening to her as unfamiliar facets of herself continued to surface.

She was distressed over awakening in bed with Jim. She knew that nothing had happened between them, though she didn't remember how they had gotten there. She was disturbed because she had accepted, even in the seconds before being fully awake, that it was Jim beside her and not David.

Almost every night since David's death she had reached out sometime during the night expecting to find him beside her, or had felt a sense of his presence. Tonight there had been only Jim, and in some strange way that made her feel unfaithful.

Janet thought about David for a long time and explored her feelings. The two of them had been considered morally old-fashioned by contemporary standards. Both had been virgins on their wedding night and there had never been any question about either of them becoming involved with anyone else. Why should she feel guilty now over nothing?

Janet, she thought, *you have to face and accept the fact that David is dead. You are alive. You no longer have a husband or a marriage to be faithful to. It is only with yourself that you must keep faith.*

She got up and idly pulled the curtain aside to look out of the window as she contemplated what keeping faith with herself meant. The bright moonlight showed large, wet flakes of falling snow. It had been snowing heavily for several hours, and a thick blanket of white covered the scene.

The falling snow had a hypnotic effect on her.

> *Janet lost awareness of her physical surroundings as her mind reached out for the tranquility of the scene. Peace became a tangible entity which she could touch and taste and smell. For that moment there was no now, no yesterday, no tomorrow. She was not Janet Manning. She was a falling snowflake — unique, yet part of the whole. She was a shaft of moonlight shining through a break in the clouds. She was the mountain across the river, shrouded in snow, yet unmistakable in its identity as a mountain, whatever cloak it might wear. She was a towering fir tree, branches laden with snow, patiently awaiting the change of seasons for another century. She was Janet Manning.*

Whatever happened in that moment changed Janet. As she turned away from the window, she knew that the person who had first looked out upon that scene and the person she was now were two different people. She didn't feel moved to analyze the experience. She was a whole person as she had never been whole prior to that moment. She felt freed from an old captivity, not having been aware that she was captive.

Janet didn't attempt to articulate these thoughts to herself. They were facts that she knew. For some inexplicable reason, she had been given a glimpse of that state of being sought by mystics. She had no idea if the change in her would last. She knew now that she could face whatever life might hold for her without fear. And that was enough.

The growing chill of the room pulled her attention toward more mundane subjects. Only a few coals remained in the stove and the woodbox was empty. Jim was asleep when she tiptoed into the bedroom for her clothes. She retreated to the living room to dress. She had left her jacket in the bedroom, so she slipped into Jim's and pulled on the gloves she found in the pocket. She quietly opened the kitchen door and stepped out into a pristine world of white.

It was an enchanted world. There was no sound and the only movement was that of the falling snowflakes. She took a deep breath and felt a thrill of excitement at the almost fragrant lack of fragrance which accompanies a snowfall — clean, crisp, cold. She stepped off of the porch into the knee-deep snow and headed for the woodshed. She stacked a day's supply of wood on the porch and carried an armload inside.

The fire in the cookstove had warmed the kitchen by the time she had changed out of her damp boots and hung Jim's jacket and gloves to dry. She was enormously hungry, so she opened a can of bacon and put a dozen strips in an iron skillet. She mixed a generous batch of biscuits and by the time she had them rolled out and cut, there were hot bacon drippings to grease the pan. She heard Jim stirring as she put the biscuits in the oven. She blotted the bacon on a paper towel and put it on the warming shelf.

"Eggs?" she called toward the bedroom. The only answer she heard was muffled and indistinct from the direction of the bathroom, but it had a negative sound to it. She poured herself a cup of coffee, lit a cigarette, and sat down at the kitchen table.

She knew that the first few minutes with Jim were going to be awkward for both of them. She felt a bond with Jim, but she was afraid that he wanted more from her than she was ready to give. Or perhaps he would be afraid that having shared her bed, for whatever reason, she would have expectations that he wasn't ready to fulfill.

"Good morning, bright eyes." She looked up to see Jim grinning in the doorway.

"The biscuits!" She jumped for the oven, looking around frantically for a potholder. Jim grabbed a towel from the counter.

"Here. Caught you daydreaming, didn't I?"

"Yes," Janet laughed. "But there's no damage done. See?" She held the pan of golden-brown biscuits toward him.

"Nothing wrong with those except that they need to be eaten," Jim agreed.

The only sounds for the next few minutes were those of enjoyment as they consumed the bacon, and biscuits dripping with butter and jam.

"Um, that was superb," Jim said as he leaned back in his chair and lit a cigarette to accompany his second cup of coffee.

"It's still good," Janet said, trying to be dainty about licking butter and wild raspberry jam from her fingers. She gave up and rinsed her hands at the sink. "Need a refill on coffee?"

"Not yet."

Jim was silent and thoughtful as she refilled her cup. Janet knew that the conversation was about to become serious and she wanted to say what was on her mind to spare Jim any later embarrassment.

"Jim, about last night. The only way I know to do this is to just say what's on my mind."

"Please, Janet, let me say what's on *my* mind, since I was the one who created the situation. Maybe someday there will be something beautiful between us, and maybe there won't. I will always cherish the memory of holding you in my arms last night, but for now I'm satisfied with friendship and the memory of a moment when two emotionally tattered friends reached out to each other for comfort. 'Nuf said?"

" 'Nuf said," Janet answered, choosing not to even mentally acknowledge the deep emotion behind Jim's words. "Now, I still have several unanswered questions. You said that you had something which might explain why Sam made me his heir. There was also something which made you feel that I needed protection."

"Come here, Janet."

She followed as he led the way to the spare bedroom. Empty boxes were piled in the corner where she had put them after unpacking. Jim pushed the empty cartons aside to reveal two small, carefully taped boxes underneath.

"Richards and Lacey carried the last shipment of artifacts down from my place, except for these two boxes. When I got to the logging camp with them, Richards and Lacey were gone. That must have been when they found Sam snooping around and followed him. If only ..."

"No, none of that," Janet said firmly. "What is done, is done. Now, why are the boxes here?"

"I left them in the Jeep, thinking that Richards and Lacey had been scared off by someone nosing around and would come back later to pick them up. When I found out about Sam the next morning and saw that the boxes were still in the Jeep, I had no idea what might happen. I didn't want to be forced into answering awkward questions in front of the wrong person.

"So, while I was rushing up the mountain to see if the artifacts had been removed from your cabin, you were hiding some of them here. Why not leave them at the Lodge?"

"Two reasons. Nichols and Owen were already at the Lodge by the time I got there. They were just a few miles down the road when Hank called the sheriff. When you weren't at the Lodge, I offered to come down here and get you. That gave me an opportunity to stash the boxes. Which brings me to the second reason. I've been using this house as a secondary pick-up point for some time now. If too many people were around or the weather was bad and a pick-up from the logging camp wasn't safe, I would put the stuff here and they would come by boat and get it. No one has stayed here in over a year, so it worked out fine. I didn't have the opportunity to tell them that the house is occupied now."

"So you think that this Richards and Lacey will come here for the boxes?"

"I'll bet on it. I expected them last night, as soon as they had a chance to hear that you have been accused of Sam's murder. Evidently they haven't heard or they got snowed in. Chances are that they're holed up in one of the summer cabins on up the river."

"But why are you so certain they will come back instead of leaving these boxes until the next time? Under the circumstances I would think that this is the last place they would want to be for a while."

Jim didn't answer as he cut the tape on one box with his pocketknife. There were several small boxes packed inside. Jim reached for a hinged case. Janet gasped as he opened the lid.

She carefully lifted the necklace from the case. It was the most exquisite thing she had ever seen. It appeared to be of Indian origin, yet not typical of any group she knew. There were eighteen strands of tiny gold beads which had been cast rather than individually shaped by hand. Each bead had a faint pattern of vines and leaves. Interspersed randomly among the beads were beautifully detailed pottery birds in flight. They appeared to be incredibly old, yet were finished with a fine azure glaze and had tiny, roughly shaped red stones inset for eyes. At the center of the shortest strand, one bird sat on a turquoise nest. Hand-polished pieces of irregularly shaped turquoise were scattered through the strands.

"This is gorgeous. Except for the cast beads and the azure glaze, I would say that it is very old and possibly of Indian origin. Where on earth did this come from? You can't let them have it."

"Hold on, Janet. You're right. We couldn't let them have the original. This is a copy."

"Oh." She felt a real sense of disappointment. "That explains the cast beads and the lovely azure glaze."

"No, it doesn't. It is identical to the original. But, the original is about 900 years old while this is only a few months old."

"But who made the original? I don't recognize the style."

"It came out of a Gallina pithouse."

"That can't be. Nothing like this has ever been found there. A few crude beads are about the only jewelry which has ever been attributed to them."

"There is another anomaly for you to ponder. I've seen the exact spot where it was found, and during our investigation we found three more pieces in the same pithouse which appeared to be the work of the same person. Unfortunately, those pieces were stolen and are probably in some private collection. But there was no doubt that they were from the same time period as the Gallina people."

"Damn! Those pieces might have been proof of some type of pre-Columbian European influence on the Gallina culture. How did you get the original necklace?"

"It was in a private collection. The man who owned it had shown it to a few people and word got around. He refused several offers to buy it. Somehow, the big boss of our setup either saw it or heard about it. He passed orders down the pipeline to get the necklace by any means necessary. I was able to contact the owner through one of our agents. In short, he allowed us to have a copy made in exchange for us allowing him to donate the original to a museum when all of this is finished and have the copy returned to him."

"That sounds like a little gentle blackmail was involved."

"There was. However, he didn't mind the copy being 'stolen' nearly so much as he would have minded the original being taken. The bottom line is that I have reason to believe that the big man wants this necklace for his own personal collection, and we want him to have it. Because it is unique, it will be easier to trace than any of the other artifacts. We're banking on him not being able to resist showing it off, and people do talk. It's a long shot, but it's the best we have at the moment."

"I see. He will probably believe that the person it was stolen from won't say anything because the necklace was obtained illegally in the first place. He will be a little more careless about showing it off than he would be with another artifact."

"Right. But there is something else which is more important right now. Let me put this away and then we need to talk."

Ten minutes later Jim and Janet were seated at the kitchen table with cups of coffee.

"I swear, Jim, I've had more coffee in the last two weeks than I normally drink in a year. I hope my nerves and kidneys survive."

Jim laughed, then became serious. "I want all of you to survive. I'm afraid that Sheriff Gates and I didn't think things through very well when we framed you for Sam's murder."

"What do you mean? Just tell me straight out."

"I may be seeing trouble where there isn't any, but I do know a little about how Richards' and Lacey's minds work. They are a strange pair. Stupid in some ways, shrewd in others. I'm trying to look at things the way I think they will. If you were really as emotionally and mentally unstable as I described, then it wouldn't be too farfetched for you to commit suicide. They could easily arrange that and it would take them off the hook permanently. It wouldn't be the first time they have arranged a murder to look like suicide. They would assume that it would be accepted as your admission of guilt for Sam's murder."

"That's just great. Not only do you frame me for Sam's murder, you set me up to be murdered."

"I'm sorry. I know that doesn't help, but I am sorry. We just didn't think things through well enough in the time we had. The reality is that that's the way things are. As I see it, until this is settled, we need to stick together like glue. I can't give those two a chance to get you alone. If I can get those boxes to them and get them on their way, then maybe their boss will talk some sense to them. At least it will give us some time to decide what to do next."

Janet got up and started to pace the floor. She glanced out of the window. "It's quit snowing. It's going to be a beautiful day somewhere for somebody. Damn!"

"Janet." Jim started toward her with concern.

"No, it's okay. I'm all right. For some insane reason I'm not afraid. I just feel as if I'm in some third-rate gangster movie. It makes me feel a little embarrassed and ashamed, somehow soiled, by being mixed up in this, though it isn't of my own doing. Does that make any sense?"

"Yeah. Yeah, it does. I know the feeling. It's like you bought a ticket to see *Snow White and the Seven Dwarfs* and it turns out to be the X-rated version. You feel self-conscious and embarrassed to be seen there."

"Exactly. It helps to know that someone else understands. Now, I think I'd better tell you something. First, answer a question for me. Do Richards and Lacey drive a big black Lincoln with heavily tinted windows?"

"They did until this last trip. They had a grey Lincoln this time and were really grousing about getting even with, in their words, some bitch who made them wreck their car. But how ... oh, no. You?"

"'Fraid so." Janet told him how the men had followed her from Texas and how she had lured them into the treacherous curve.

"Oh, shit!" Jim exploded. "But why were they following you?"

"I don't know. The third guy who sometimes comes with them is Roscoe Carrac, the one who trashed my house and office. There has to be some connection between them and the black market and David's murder, but I can't put it together. I guess I'd better tell you the rest of it. The real reason I came to Agness was because of that note you found in my billfold when you were snooping in here that first day."

Jim turned red. "I'm sorry about that. It's a bad habit I've developed since I got into this business. That note really bothered me. Did David write it?"

"Yes, the night before he was killed. I've followed every lead and clue that I could find looking for the reason for his murder and his killer. Everything led to dead ends. Then, just a few weeks ago, I was thumbing through the book David had been reading in bed that last night and I found the note stuck between its pages. Now that I know who Richards and Lacey are, I know that I'm on the right track."

"You're also in a hell of a lot more danger than I thought, and so am I."

"Do you have a gun with you?"

"No."

"I still have that .22 magnum rifle upstairs, and there's also a .38 Special hidden in my Toyota. Maybe we had better keep them handy until your friends have come and gone."

"I think you're right."

Janet explained where the .38 Special was hidden and where to find the extra shells.

"David must have been some guy."

"Yes, he was. One very special guy."

Janet began to gather the dirty dishes and pile them in the dishpan, grinning to herself. No doubt David would have come up with some wild, but totally workable, plan for solving this whole mess. Damn, she missed him.

Jim stepped to the kitchen door, pulling on his jacket, just as Janet glanced out of the window.

"Jim, two men in a boat are heading into the landing just below the house."

Jim pushed her away from the window and looked out. "It's them." He glanced around the kitchen. "Quick, hand me the cup and plate off the table."

Janet shoved the dishes toward him as he crammed the loaded dishpan into the cabinet under the sink. He grabbed the leftovers from their breakfast and put them in the oven.

"Janet, go in the bedroom and get into bed. Now! No argument. It's just possible that they won't recognize your Toyota underneath all that snow, but no matter what happens, you pretend to be asleep. I don't want them to see you if we can avoid it. I particularly don't want them to know you have seen them. Now go!"

Janet threw her shirt, pants, and boots into the closet and ran for the bed. She assumed what she hoped was a look of natural sleep with the covers pulled partially over her face. She heard Jim open the front door. After a few seconds there was a low murmur of voices, the words indistinguishable. Then she heard footsteps in the living room. The murmur took on an intensity which made it clear that an argument was underway. Janet prayed that Jim knew what he was doing and wouldn't get them both killed.

Janet was trying to formulate a possible course of action should things get out of hand when she had a sudden hysterical urge to laugh. She had thought of sneaking out through the window to retrieve her .38 from the Toyota, when she had a mental flash of herself in her lavender lace panties and bra, knee deep in snow, shooting it out with the bad guys in the best "James Bond" tradition.

The sound of voices ceased. Footsteps came toward the hall between the two bedrooms. Someone entered the opposite room, but Janet had the eerie feeling that someone else had opened her bedroom door and was staring at the back of her head. She knew it wasn't Jim.

She tried to breathe slowly and evenly. She knew she was getting enough oxygen, but felt as if she was suffocating. She had to move, to do something. She shifted position, cuddled up to the pillow, murmured "Jim," and then pretended to settle into a deep sleep. A few seconds later, she heard the door close softly.

There was another round of intense whispering, then the front door closed and the house was quiet. She waited for a couple of minutes, then got up and quickly dressed. She tiptoed into the living room and peeked through a gap in the curtain. Jim was on the landing beside the boat, in violent argument with one man while the other man stowed the boxes.

The risk of being seen was too great to justify trying to get her .38 from the pickup. The range was too far for it to be effective, anyway. She knew that she had to do something when she saw the second man join in the argument and move threateningly toward Jim.

Janet raced upstairs. Her .22 magnum rifle was in its case, fully loaded. The head of the brass bed was against the curtainless front windows. She knelt on the floor beside the bed and edged around until she could reach the window sash. Luck was with her. The window opened easily and quietly. She slid it open about halfway and then eased onto the bed, rifle ready. She wanted everything in her favor if she had to shoot. No awkward shooting through window panes, no second or two of warning if she broke one out.

The argument was still raging when Jim turned and started to walk away. One of the men grabbed his arm and swung him around. Jim side-stepped as he threw a punch. Then all hell broke loose. As engrossing as the savage fist fight was, Janet kept her attention on the second man. He ran to the boat and picked up a large billy club and started toward the fighting men.

Janet took aim a little ahead and above him as he raised the club to hit Jim from behind. She held her breath, squeezed the trigger, and hoped for the best. When he dropped the club and cradled his hand against his chest, Janet knew that she would never admit to anyone that the shot had been pure luck rather than skill. Jim knocked the other man down with a solid right and started toward the house.

From the second floor window, Janet could see what was hidden from Jim by some bushes. The man on the ground raised up, shook his head, and produced a gun from under his jacket. As he started to follow Jim, Janet laid down a barrage of carefully placed shots between them. She systematically tried to herd both men toward their boat, away from Jim. They seemed to get the idea right away, because they ran for the boat.

The wounded man huddled in the bow while the other one started the motor. He turned the boat up river and they were soon out of sight. Janet ran downstairs and met Jim on the front porch.

"Jim, are you all right?"

"A little bruised, battered, and out of breath. Otherwise okay. I think you just saved my life and yours. Thanks."

Jim put his arms around Janet. They were both trembling.

"Jim, you get in the house. Here, take this." She handed him her rifle. "I'm going to get my .38, then I'll be in to administer some first aid."

It took a little time and a lot of effort to get the door of the 4 x 4 open. There was enough moisture in the snow that the door had frozen shut. Janet had the .38 and a couple of boxes of shells in her hand when she heard the sound of a vehicle struggling through the snow. She was about to run inside and barricade the door when she recognized the distinctive rattle of the McVeys' pickup. She watched as it came into sight, slipping, sliding, and bouncing through the snow.

Maggie, rifle in hand, was out of the pickup before it came to a complete stop. "Are you all right? Where's Jim? We heard shots. Is somebody hurt?"

"Goldurn, Maggie. Stop for a breath and let her answer," Hank growled as he crawled out of the pickup.

"We're both fine. Come in before I freeze to death."

"You planning to use that toy?" Hank pointed at the .38.

"If I have to. It's meaner than it looks," Janet said, shoving it into the rear pocket of her jeans.

Maggie came to an abrupt halt just inside the door when she saw Jim. She looked at him and then at Janet with a piercing look which said more than any words. Jim and Janet looked at each other and laughed.

"No, Maggie. I didn't do that to him. He was a perfect gentleman."

The corners of Hank's mouth twitched as Maggie turned a bright red and protested. "Why, I never thought anything else."

"Woman," Hank chuckled, "don't make it any worse by lying about it." He turned to Jim. "Maybe you'd better tell us what did happen. I saw the tracks outside."

Janet got her first aid kit while Jim began the story. Maggie tended to Jim's split lip, bruised cheeks, and scraped knuckles while Janet poured coffee and set the leftover biscuits and bacon on the table. Hank nodded his approval as she added butter and jam, and began to eat as he listened. The chaotic thoughts in Janet's mind blotted out Jim's voice until she heard his last sentence.

"So Janet shot Lacey through the hand and then laid down a barrage of shots that herded them to the boat while I got up to the house."

Janet jumped up. "That reminds me, I forgot to close the window upstairs."

She rushed out in spite of Hank's offer to do it. She didn't want to be congratulated for her marksmanship. This was her first act of violence toward another human being and the reaction had set in. She needed to be alone and think about it.

She closed the window and sat down on the bed and buried her face in her hands. *Well, Janet, you've really gotten yourself into a mess. Where do you go from here? You can't walk away and pretend that none of this ever happened. You're rich because a dear old man is dead. If you hang around and try to make that come out right, you may end up dead yourself, or having to kill someone. If you survive, you may finally find the answer to David's death, but is it worth more killing? Can you live with blood on your hands? Oh, damn it, David. Why did you leave me?*

"Janet." Hank was standing beside the bed. He dropped her cigarettes and lighter in her lap and sat down on the foot of the bed and began to fill his pipe. After he had it lit, he looked at Janet thoughtfully. "Can an old man give you some advice?"

"I'd welcome it. I'm feeling pretty shaky at the moment."

"So you should. A body shouldn't be comfortable with doing violence toward another person, however much that person may deserve it." Hank drew on his pipe and then watched the smoke for several seconds. "It would be nice to send you back to Texas to forget all this, but you wouldn't go if you could.

"That brings up a question. Tell me, do you trust me and Maggie now?"

"Yes."

"Do you trust Jim now, and can you be comfortable staying in the same house with him, knowing how he feels about you?"

"Yes, I do trust Jim. And yes, I can be comfortable staying with him. He has put whatever deeper feelings he has for me on the shelf for now. You don't miss much, do you?"

Hank grinned and shook his head. "Not much. Now, while you were sleeping yesterday afternoon, Jim told us what happened here with the sheriff and his men, and the stupid thing they did in framing you for Sam's murder. Of course, Maggie and I already knew about his work as an undercover agent. He also told us just now about your earlier run-in with Richards and Lacey. I have an idea and I want you to hear me out."

"Sure. I'm ready for some ideas."

"I think you and Jim need to disappear for a week or two. You both need to be somewhere where you not only feel safe but are safe. You need to be able to sit down and do some heavy thinking without having to wonder if someone is going to take a shot at you if you step out the door or look out the window."

"That sounds great, but — "

"Now just shush till I finish. You came here to find out who killed your David, and now there's Sam and Dan'l added to the list. It's going to be a long time and a lot of hard miles before this is over.

"Right now you are running on coffee and nerves and not much else. Jim isn't in much better shape. I have a little cabin up toward Iron Mountain that nobody knows about. It isn't much, but it's well-built and weather-tight, and nobody will know you are there. I can take you part way in Jim's Jeep and help you pack in the rest of the way."

"Whoa, wait a minute. I can't just run away."

"That isn't what I'm asking you to do, Janet. I know that you weren't listening to Jim downstairs. The fight was over you. Richards and Lacey were determined to take you with them. Frankly, Janet, there isn't any way that Jim or I can adequately protect you as long as you stay here. Someone would have to be on watch constantly. That just isn't realistic. I think those two are holed up in the Johnson's summer cabin a few miles up the river, and I'll bet money that they will be back. But, they can't stay around indefinitely. I figure a week will see them on their way."

"But the sheriff ..."

"I'll clear it with him. A week should give him time to clear up the murder charge against you. That was a bad move for Gates and Jim to make. Richards and Lacey aren't the only danger. There are a lot of people around here who owed Sam a great deal, and some of them might not be willing to wait for the wheels of justice to grind their slow way if they thought you had killed Sam. That's another reason you need to be somewhere safe."

"Now, that Lacey fellow may have to get medical treatment for his hand. Even if he doesn't, they can't stay around here forever. I'll see that Gates fixes up an inquest and stretches the rules enough so that Sam's murder is attributed to person or persons unknown or a hunting accident, and that you are cleared."

"Hank — "

"Just be quiet and let me finish. You and Jim both need some peace and quiet and a chance to do some serious thinking. You are going to have to be strong and at peace with yourself to survive this. To be blunt about it, I don't want you or me or Maggie or Jim, or anyone else, hurt or killed because you or Jim have to stop and make a decision about how far you are willing to go to see this thing through.

"If someone is shooting at you or any of the rest of us, that isn't the time to stop and have to think for even a split-second about whether or not you are willing to kill in defense of yourself or us. Nor, my dear, can you afford to be distracted by personal grief or problems. I've seen a lot of strange things in these mountains, and I know that you can't always depend on the laws and rules of polite society to survive."

"I'm beginning to see that."

"Good. Now, one more thing. You may think that I'm a crazy old coot, but I'm going to say it anyway. If you can open your heart and mind to the mountains and let yourself feel a part of them, in some sort of almost mystical way it's as if their strength and peace and eternalness become a part of you." Hank finished in a rush, uncomfortable with sharing such private feelings.

"I know what you mean, Hank. I experienced something of that last night while I was looking at the snow-covered landscape in the moonlight. It was as if I became a part of all that I saw and was filled with a peace which transcended anything I've ever experienced.

"As for the rest of what you've said, I understand and I know you are right. There is a time to stand and fight and there is a time to retreat for a while. When do we leave?"

"Good girl," Hank said gruffly, patting her hand. "We'll leave just as soon as we can get the necessary supplies together."

"Shouldn't I call Sheriff Gates, and what about Sam's funeral arrangements?"

"Maggie and I will take care of those things. Now, let's get things organized."

Janet let Hank look through her camping gear and advise her on what would be useful. They went downstairs with their arms loaded. Maggie had been busy. The dishes were washed and a small box of Janet's personal things were on the table.

"Hank, you take that box out to the pickup. I sent Jim ahead with a list of things to do at the Lodge. Janet, I took the liberty of sending your laundry with Jim. If you will pick out the other clothes you want to take, I'll put them in your pack while you get your writing materials and whatever else you may want." Maggie was breathless at that point.

"Slow down, woman. You sound like a sergeant with a new recruit. Give Janet a minute to get her breath," Hank growled good-naturedly.

"That's all right. I know we need to work quickly. But I need to know how far we'll have to pack in so I can judge how much weight I can carry. Jim and

I will have to leave enough room in our two packs for food."

"Three packs," Hank said.

"Four," Maggie said in a very firm, no-nonsense tone. Hank looked at her and started to say something. "Four," Maggie repeated with finality.

Hank shrugged and picked up the box, mumbling under his breath, "Stubborn woman."

"I don't understand," Janet said. "Are you going to stay with us for a while?"

"No. We'll pack food in for you and hike out this evening. The weather won't hold long. We'll probably get more snow tonight or early tomorrow. It'll cover our tracks," Hank said.

"We'll plan on you staying a week, but we'll take food for two weeks just in case something unforeseen happens and you have to stay longer and Hank and I can't get back. I want you to have room for your writing materials so you'll have something to keep you busy. Jim told me what a wonderful story you are writing and I want you to finish it. Jim can chop wood and cook and make himself useful and stay out of your way. That's why I'm going." Maggie looked at Hank as if daring him to contradict her.

Hank shook his head and shrugged his shoulders, conveying that it was useless to argue with her. He started out the door with the box, then turned back. "It's about five miles, Janet. The terrain is pretty rugged but there isn't much climbing."

"Thank you, Hank."

It took Maggie and Janet about fifteen minutes to assemble the items Janet wanted to take and place them properly in her pack. Janet filled the side pockets with extra ammo for her .22 and .38 and wished for the 30-06, which was in the sheriff's custody. She took one last look around. On impulse, she wrapped the crystal ball in a bandanna and slipped it into the pack.

At the Lodge, Janet prepared an early lunch while Maggie and Hank sorted out a generous supply of dried fruits and vegetables, smoked fish, beef and venison jerky, and miscellaneous other foodstuffs. Maggie explained to Janet that they kept a large supply of such things for emergencies. and that Jim kept an extra pack, survival equipment, and several changes of clothing at the Lodge for the same reason.

"We never know when an emergency might occur which would make it necessary for us to pack out to rescue someone in bad weather," Jim added.

After lunch, Janet sorted through her clean laundry and packed what she needed. They stowed everything in Jim's Jeep. She and Maggie climbed into the back seat.

Chapter 15

Janet had white knuckles and one rush of adrenalin after another for the first couple of miles. After that, she settled down to a more relaxed level of simple terror. They were traveling the same road she had driven two weeks earlier, but now the virgin snow made it difficult to detect the location of the road bed in many places, and drifts hid areas where sections of the road had disappeared into the river.

Hank directed Jim onto a side road where Janet would have sworn there wasn't one. It seemed as if they had been driving for hours when Hank told Jim to stop and let Janet and Maggie out, then turn the Jeep around and park it. Jim gave Hank a questioning glance, but followed the instructions without comment.

Janet was stiff and feeling the fatigue which follows a prolonged adrenalin high. It felt good to be out of the Jeep and in the cold air, but she surveyed the surrounding terrain with some anxiety. There was barely enough room for Jim to maneuver the Jeep back and forth, with Hank's direction, until he succeeded in turning it around. The slope was straight up on one side of the road, straight down on the other.

As she struggled into her pack, Janet wondered which direction Hank expected them to go — up or down. Neither looked to be a realistic possibility. Hank looked at the sky with a concern which did nothing to improve her peace of mind. Snow appeared imminent.

"Hank, are you sure?" Jim asked.

"Yes," he answered sharply. "We need to hurry, though. Janet, you follow me. Step exactly where I step. Maggie, you follow Janet. Jim, you bring up the rear."

With those terse instructions, Hank stepped over the edge of the cliff. Janet took a firm grip on her walking stick, swallowed hard, and followed. What had been hidden from her was a path no more than two feet wide which led down the face of the cliff to a creek about two hundred feet below.

Janet tried not to focus her eyes anywhere but on the next step ahead, but the sheer drop in her peripheral vision continued to draw her attention. She was thankful that they were in an area where the snowfall had been light. She unashamedly heaved an audible sigh of relief when she reached the creek bank and level ground.

Hank didn't pause or even look back as he continued a hundred yards upstream to a place where they could cross without wetting their feet. On the far side, he led them away from the creek toward a thick stand of trees. The ground began to rise steadily and Janet's pack got heavier by the minute.

Janet was determined not to call a halt for rest or slacken her pace until Hank did. None of them would be here if it wasn't for her, and the longer the trip in took, the more it would increase the danger of the return trip for the McVeys. Even now, she knew that they could not hope to get back to the Lodge before dark.

After a mile of steady walking, a tumble of boulders appeared to block the way. Hank didn't hesitate. He walked directly toward what appeared to be an impassable box canyon and disappeared. Janet couldn't hold back an exclamation of surprise as she followed him. She had no idea that such a geological formation existed in this part of Oregon.

Janet stepped into a large crack, almost a tunnel. It was deep and narrow. The bottom was cluttered with large rocks and a water seep which soon disappeared underground. Trees and brush provided a concealing canopy overhead.

As they scrambled from one precarious step to another, Janet was reminded of some of the rugged little canyons which she had explored in New Mexico. At times the crack narrowed until she barely had clearance for the width of her shoulders.

When she looked up and couldn't see the sky, she felt a twinge of claustrophobia.

After about two miles, the canyon widened and Hank called a halt. Janet was trembling with fatigue and Jim wasn't in much better shape. Hank and Maggie didn't appear to be affected. Jim and Janet drank from a spring and gratefully accepted candy bars from Maggie. No one seemed inclined to talk. It was cold, damp, and gloomy. Janet thought longingly of the dry heat and sunshine of a Southwestern summer.

Jim lit a cigarette and handed it to Janet, then lit one for himself. Hank lit his pipe and Maggie unwrapped a stick of chewing gum.

"How much farther?" Janet asked.

"Couple of miles. There is a mite of rough walking ahead, then it gets easy," Hank answered.

Janet wasn't happy over the prospect of Hank's "mite of rough walking," but decided that she could hold out for two more miles.

"Hank, this is a strange canyon," Jim said. "What do you suppose formed it?"

"I figure an earthquake. Must have been a doozie to split the earth like this. Most likely another one will come along one of these days and close it up again," Hank answered as he stood up and settled his pack more solidly on his lanky frame. As they joined Hank, Janet felt a chill of fear run up her spine at the mental picture of the grinding earth moving to close up this ragged wound. *Oh well,* she told herself, *it's been this way for centuries and with any luck will be this way for centuries more.*

As she climbed steadily for the next half-mile, Janet began to wonder if this wasn't a fool's errand. The more she thought about it, the more aggravated she became. She didn't like running away. It seemed to her that all they were doing was creating an extremely dangerous situation for Hank and Maggie on their homeward journey and making them the focus for Richards' and Lacey's ire. Besides, by what right had Jim put her in this dangerous situation?

She didn't care that she wasn't thinking logically. Her anger and resentment grew with every step and she was almost at the point of refusing to continue when something clicked in her mind.

The irritability and anger were part of an old habit pattern, a reaction to fatigue and stress which she thought she had conquered long ago. It had surfaced during her early years of backpacking. "Bitchiness" had been David's blunt term for it. She had put a lot of effort into changing that reaction, but here she was feeling bitchy again. *Maybe I need this week of seclusion more than I realized*, she thought.

An exclamation from Jim snapped her attention back to her surroundings. She was appalled at what confronted them.

Forty feet of packed earth barred the way. It appeared to be the result of an ancient landslide which had eroded into an almost vertical wall. Small slabs of rock protruded haphazardly from the exposed surface. There wasn't another way out.

"Is this your 'mite of rough walking'?" she asked Hank.

"No need to get excited," Hank growled. "It ain't as bad as it looks. Just watch me and then follow."

"Janet, pay attention," Hank said sharply. Numbly she watched as he negotiated the seemingly impossible climb. "All right, now come on up."

Janet took a deep breath and muttered a phrase which had seen her through many tight spots. "I can do anything I have to — once."

The trick to it, Janet found, was to move quickly, not allowing her weight to remain in one spot long enough to loosen the rocks, and keep her balance by judicious use of her walking stick. About fifteen feet from the top, a rather large slab of rock loosened and began to slide just as she reached for the next foothold.

"Look out below," she yelled and continued climbing without pause.

"Well done," Hank said as she made it over the top and leaned against the first available tree.

"Are Jim and Maggie okay?"

"Yep. You just made it easy for them."

The earth slide proved fortuitous in that it provided a rather gentle slope more than half way up the cliff.

"Is that the last of your 'mite of rough walking,' or is there more to come?"

Hank grinned as he gave Maggie a hand over the top. "That was it. It's just a stroll from here."

"For once he's telling the truth," Maggie said. "I've been expecting that wall to come down for years," she continued, peering over. "I always stay well away from it when Hank is climbing it. Otherwise, you'd be digging me and Jim out."

Janet saw that they were on top of a ridge which fell away sharply on either side. It was evident that their approach had been the best choice. Ascending either of the slopes with heavy packs would have been more of an ordeal than they had just experienced.

The walking was easy, though the ridge led steadily upward. The late afternoon sky was leaden, promising almost immediate rain or snow.

Maggie walked beside Janet, telling her about the cabin. "It's outfitted with most of the essentials. You'll find plenty of pots and pans and such. Actually, Hank and I have it fixed up pretty nice. That cabin has been the best-kept secret we've ever had," she said with a breathless little giggle.

"I think I detect romance in the air," Janet said teasingly.

"You'll probably think that we're a couple of old fools. Hank built that cabin for me almost forty years ago as a wedding present. We spent our honeymoon there, and we've spent our anniversary there every year since, and several weeks besides. It's our place to go when we want to get away from everyone and just be together. We've had so many wonderful times there. I've never told anyone about it." Maggie's eyes were aglow with memories.

"I think that is absolutely wonderful, Maggie. I've always believed that a good marriage never loses its romance and you and Hank are proof of that. No one will ever hear about your hideaway from me."

Maggie's description gave Janet assurance that she could expect a reasonable level of comfort. The fact that Maggie and Hank were sharing such a precious secret of forty years gave Janet some idea of the amount of danger which they believed existed for her and Jim. That wasn't reassuring.

Maggie interrupted her thoughts. "There are two other things I want to tell you about our place. There is a large waterfall close to the cabin. Behind it there is a little cave where a person could hide if they needed to. Actually, it's more of a crevice than a cave. It's about eight feet wide and tall and about twice that deep. I've been in it only twice, but it struck me as a good place to hide.

"The other thing is a back way out. If you follow the waterfall down to the floor of the valley, and that isn't easy, you'll see a little trickle of a creek coming in on your right. If you look sharp, you'll see a faint forest trail. It's hard to follow at best and almost impossible if there is snow. It strikes the river about two miles north of Sam's cabin. I don't expect you will need it, but it makes more sense if you should have to walk out. It's about twelve miles back to Agness by the trail. If you go back the way we came, and walk the road, it's over twenty."

Maggie laughed. "I guess I've read too many westerns, but I always like to have a back way out of wherever I am."

Janet understood how Maggie felt. Call it survival instinct or whatever, she never liked to be boxed in anywhere.

It wasn't long before Janet heard the sound of falling water and noticed a distinct difference in the terrain. The ground was level. As they emerged from the trees, she could see that they were on a huge rocky ledge, almost a hanging valley, and she caught a glimpse of a waterfall which took her breath away.

Hank led them toward a dense growth of pine and fir, away from the waterfall. Janet could see then that they were indeed in an oval-shaped hanging valley. The ridge they had traversed was at one end of the valley and the waterfall was at the opposite end. On the backside of the valley, rocky bluffs rose above the level of the trees. On the front side, the mountain fell away in what appeared to be an impassably steep slope. It was wild, beautiful, and somewhat overwhelming.

As they neared the base of the bluffs, Janet was instantly enchanted by the tiny cabin tucked under the trees. It was constructed from hand-shaped logs with a large stone chimney at one end. Wooden shutters covered the windows and there was a heavy Dutch-type door.

Hank opened the door and stepped back to allow Maggie and Janet to precede him. As he and Jim followed, he began to issue terse instructions. "Maggie, you and Janet get our packs emptied and build a fire. Fix us something quick to eat. I'll show Jim where the wood and water are. Then we'd best be on our way."

Maggie nodded and lit a kerosene lamp as Hank and Jim went out the door. Janet got a quick over-all impression of a neat, colorful, snug cabin as she began to empty the McVeys' backpacks and sort out the sandwiches, boiled eggs, and cookies which had been packed for a quick meal.

Maggie lit the fire which was already laid in the huge stone fireplace dominating one end of the cabin. She picked up a large, blackened coffee pot. "I'll just step out and get Hank to fill this at the spring."

Half an hour later, Janet and Jim bade Hank and Maggie goodbye just as a light rain began to fall. Janet knew that at the higher elevations it would be snowing. She shuddered at the thought of the arduous trip ahead of the McVeys and wished that they would stay until morning, but she said nothing. She knew they wouldn't stay, and insisting would only delay them.

Hank's parting words didn't relieve the tension. "If you don't hear from us by the end of two weeks, you'll know that something has happened to prevent our return. You'll have to use your own judgment about what to do. We should have it all sorted out within a week, though." With that, Hank and Maggie were out of the door and soon out of sight.

"How long until dark?"

"About thirty minutes. They have good flashlights and Hank said they have traveled the trail in the dark several times," Jim said sharply.

Janet didn't take offense at Jim's tone. They were both on the fine edge of exhaustion and Janet knew that Jim was very concerned for the McVeys' safety. He paced the room for a few minutes, then pulled on his jacket and cap.

"Got something to put water in?"

Janet handed him the two water buckets she had found while putting the supplies away.

While Jim was outside, Janet took a quick survey of the cabin. There were two rooms — the large kitchen-living room combination where the fireplace was, and a small bedroom. The interior was paneled with knotty pine. There were large cupboards in the kitchen area and most of one wall in the living area was taken up by book-filled shelves. The floor was covered by several brightly colored braided rugs. The windows, though tightly shuttered, were framed with attractive curtains.

The furniture was obviously Hank's handiwork. There was a large rocker to accommodate his tall, lanky frame, and a smaller one with a matching footstool for Maggie. In addition to the sturdy pine kitchen table with matching chairs, there was a small, graceful, myrtlewood desk and chair.

The fireplace was a work of art. For a pioneer woman, it would have been the modern equivalent of a microwave range with all the latest gadgets. There was a small metal oven built into the stonework. A large cast-iron hook swung out to hold pots over the fire, and there was an adjustable grill. A variety of longhandled pewter spoons, ladles, forks, and spatulas hung on nearby hooks.

Janet surveyed the sleeping arrangements with dismay. There was one large bed. She decided that she would spread her sleeping bag in front of the fireplace if she could find no other solution. There would be no more sharing a bed with Jim.

She was relieved to find two folding camp beds with foam pads in the large closet. It took her less than five minutes to set one up in a convenient corner of the living room near a couple of empty shelves and spread her sleeping bag on it. She took the extra pillow from the bed, arranged her clothes and cosmetics on the shelves, and had a very cozy corner.

By then, Janet had a pressing problem. She put on her jacket, got her flashlight, and stuffed some tissue in her pocket. Jim was just coming in the door with an armload of wood.

"Jim, is there a convenient log around here?"

"All the modern conveniences," he grinned. "Just follow the path behind the cabin past the woodpile."

It was dark and the temperature was dropping. The rain had stopped but an occasional snowflake drifted through the beam of her flashlight. She found the path and passed the woodpile which was protected by a heavy tarp. A few more steps and she saw the object of her search. She laughed as she hurried toward it. The structure showed evidence of Hank's sense of humor. It was a stereotypical outhouse, complete with crescent moon cut high in the door.

Jim was bringing in the buckets of water when Janet returned to the cabin. Snow was beginning to fall in earnest.

Neither of them voiced their concern for Hank and Maggie as they hung their jackets on the pegs beside the door.

Jim took in Janet's sleeping arrangements without comment and carried his pack into the bedroom. Janet moved the myrtlewood desk nearer to her corner and arranged her writing materials and tape recorder on it. She put the crystal ball on one corner.

As she surveyed the setup, she noted that it would be simple to string a cord across the corner and hang up a sheet or blanket to shield her bed from view. She rummaged in a small wooden chest where Hank kept an assortment of tools and rope, and found a ball of binder's twine and a couple of large tacks. When she had the twine in place, she went into the bedroom where Jim was unpacking.

"Seen any extra sheets or light blankets? Maggie said there were some stored in the bedroom."

Jim pointed toward a chest with a hinged lid which doubled as a window seat. Janet lifted the lid and found an East Indian cotton spread patterned in bronze, black, and peacock blue. As she fastened it to the cord with clothes pins, she was pleased to see that it harmonized with the room.

"There," she said as Jim came in, "now we both have privacy and either of us can use the living room at odd hours without disturbing the other."

Jim's answer was a grunt as he poured himself a cup of coffee, then opened the door a crack to peer out. A blizzard was in progress and the wind was rising. Jim slammed the door, flopped down in Hank's rocker, and lit a cigarette. Janet knew that he was afraid of a white-out — that vicious combination of snow and wind which can disorient the most capable woodsman.

Janet poured herself a cup of coffee and sat down at the desk. Her thoughts turned to the past few months, and the past few days in particular. As she watched the reflections of the firelight in the crystal ball, she thought about old Sam and Dan'l, and wondered what Jim had which would explain Sam's will. She didn't want to ask him about it right then.

She considered the situation she was in and wondered if she would manage to live through the next few weeks. She certainly intended to give it her best shot. She winced at the unintended pun and turned her thoughts to Hank and Maggie.

The dancing reflections in the crystal ball had taken on the appearance of falling snow. It took a moment for Janet to realize what she was seeing. There was a faint glow of light and two indistinct figures. As the image cleared, she could see Hank brushing snow from the windshield of the Jeep while Maggie stowed their empty packs in back and climbed into the front seat. Hank joined her and attempted to start the engine but there was only a momentary grinding noise and then silence.

"Damn!"

"What? What's wrong?"

"Oh, nothing. Sorry. Just thinking out loud."

Jim gave her a curious look and then returned to his brooding. Janet continued to watch the unfolding scene with increasing anxiety until she realized what Hank was doing. Maggie had moved to the driver's seat while Hank removed a case from the back of the Jeep and attached jumper cables from it to the battery. She saw that the case contained an extra battery. Hank gave a sign to Maggie and the Jeep's engine roared to life. After a few minutes, Janet breathed a sigh of relief as the headlights came on. Hank took Maggie's place behind the wheel and drove off in the direction of the Lodge.

"Jim, do you carry an extra battery in the Jeep for emergencies?"

"Yeah. Why?"

"Nothing. Just wondered."

Janet wandered around the room, wishing that she could say something to ease Jim's mind, but knowing that he would never believe her. She was more than a little amazed to find out that the crystal ball worked for something other than contact with Mark Jamison. How long ago that all seemed.

She browsed the book shelves and noted that there were several old Gene Stratton Porter novels among the many books.

She took one from the shelf and settled into Maggie's rocker. As she read, Jim paced the floor, stirred the fire, drank coffee, and chain-smoked.

After a couple of hours, Janet casually moved over to the desk and peered into the crystal ball. Snow. Faint headlights, then darkness. The Jeep parked in its usual place. And there, yes, Hank and Maggie walking arm-in-arm across the deserted logging camp toward the Lodge.

Janet heaved an audible sigh of relief and rose from the desk. She joined Jim where he was standing in front of the fireplace and slipped an arm around his waist.

"It's okay. They are home safely now."

"How can you possibly know that?" Jim snapped and jerked away from her touch.

"Just believe me, Jim. I know. I'm going to bed now and get some much needed sleep. I suggest that you do the same."

"How can you know they're safe?"

"Call it woman's intuition. I'm as sure as if I had seen it with my own eyes. Good night."

Chapter 16

Janet awoke to the third straight day of rain. The only cheering thought was that she didn't have to begin her day with a baptism of icy rain during a trip to "the necessary," as her grandmother had called it. *It's pretty bleak,* she thought, *when the greatest source of happiness in your life is a chamber pot.*

The previous two days had been hell. Jim was irritable and seemed to be getting a cold. Janet almost wished he would get pneumonia so that he would stay in bed and stop his infernal pacing. If she tried to ignore him and write, he paced and grumbled. If she tried to talk to him, he responded in brusque monosyllables.

Surely the rain would end soon. Even the snow had been preferable. Why couldn't Oregon have nice sensible rain like Texas and New Mexico — four inches in two hours and then sunshine? Here it could rain for six weeks before that much fell, but in the process everything got damp and clammy. She remembered being miserable during her senior year in Portland when it had done just that.

Oh, hell. I'm getting as grumpy as Jim. So much for the peace and solitude and constructive thinking. I haven't even been able to write a decent sentence. She struggled out of her sleeping bag and proceeded, with utmost haste, to stir up the coals in the fireplace and build a blazing fire.

Janet was very concerned about Jim's cold, so she put on her jacket and Jim's poncho and went out to bring in wood and water. She looked longingly at the big tin tub hanging on a nail on the back wall of the cabin and made herself a promise. Tomorrow, rain or shine, she was going to have a nice hot bath.

The sky seemed a bit lighter, the clouds less dense. Perhaps by afternoon the rain would stop and there would be some sunshine. She was anxious to do some exploring. She wanted to see the waterfall and the cave behind it and locate the trail Maggie had told her about. She also wanted to climb the bluffs behind the cabin and get some perspective on where they were.

She filled the buckets at the spring and carried them back to the cabin, only splashing one leg and foot. By the time she had carried in three loads of firewood, the rain had stopped and Jim was awake. She could hear his hard, dry cough.

"Jim, I'm coming in," she warned at the bedroom door.

The room was quite cool, but Jim was hot and feverish. A faint red rash peppered his cheeks. Janet pulled the blanket down to his waist, looked at his chest, and laughed until tears streamed down her cheeks. The more she tried to stop, the harder she laughed.

"What the hell's so funny?" Jim growled.

"... mm ... measles," she choked out with another explosion of laughter.

Jim sat up and looked at himself in disbelief. "Measles? You're out of your mind. No, damn it, you're not. But it's not funny, Janet. Now stop it!"

"I'm sorry, Jim," she said, giggling. "How on earth did you got the measles?"

He thought a moment. "The ranger station. I visited Roger and Marie a couple of weeks ago and their kids had the measles. Measles!" Jim groaned in disgust.

"Ah, gorgeous heroine and handsome hero in secluded cabin surrounded by danger and intrigue and ... and ... measles," Janet teased him.

Jim gave her a furious look, then in spite of all he could do, began to laugh.

"No wonder you've been such a bear for the past two days. I was about ready to throw you out into the rain and lock the door."

"I know. I've been so miserable I couldn't think straight and I didn't had any idea of what was wrong with me. Sorry I've been so ornery. What now?"

"I think you ought to stay in bed today and tomorrow if you still have a fever. Just relax and sleep. Then we'll see what you feel like doing later. You should feel a lot better when you finish breaking out."

"Janet," Jim said hesitantly. "This isn't like having mumps is it? I mean, there aren't any uh ... complications?"

Janet laughed. "No, your manhood is safe."

Janet took Jim a pan of warm water to wash his hands and face and, much to his chagrin, slipped the chamber pot under the edge of his bed. He ate only a small portion of the breakfast Janet prepared for him, but gratefully swallowed two aspirins.

By the time Janet had washed the breakfast dishes and put a pot of soup to simmer on the fire, the sun was shining brightly. She went outside and opened all the shutters, and felt considerably more cheerful when she checked on Jim.

"I really have a bad case of cabin fever. I think I'll take advantage of the sunshine and go exploring for a little while."

"I don't like the idea of you going out alone."

"Look, Jim, I understand the situation we are in and I'm not going to do anything dangerous. I just want to see the waterfall and a place or two that Maggie told me about. Then I want to sit on a rock in the sunshine and do some of the thinking I'm supposed to do while we're here. I may stay out a couple of hours, but I'll probably be within shouting distance the whole time."

"Okay," Jim said reluctantly. "I'll probably sleep, but I wish I could go with you."

"You'll feel better in a day or two. If you get hungry while I'm out, there's a pot of soup on the fire."

Jim was asleep by the time Janet was ready to leave. That was fine with her. She didn't want to explain to Jim why she was taking a loaded backpack. She didn't think it would ever prove necessary for them to hide in the cave behind the waterfall, but it never hurt to be prepared.

There weren't any clouds in the sky. Janet hoped that was a sign of good weather for a day or two. She walked to the edge of the valley and thrilled at the magnificent view of the surrounding mountains. There was a glint of snow on the higher peaks. She took a deep breath and felt alive and free.

The waterfall would have bean a tourist attraction if it had been more accessible. It was one of the most beautiful Janet had ever seen. It began about a hundred feet above her and fell into a deep rock basin about forty feet in diameter. As the water overflowed the basin, it fell for another two hundred feet in a misty veil, and disappeared among the trees below her.

If it had been warmer, nothing could have stopped her from skinny-dipping in the pool. *Hank and Maggie must have had some terrific times here*, she thought.

At first she couldn't see a way to get behind the waterfall without wading into the pool. That prospect didn't appeal to her at all. She climbed around on the rocks at the side of the falls and finally saw a place where it might be possible to squeeze through. She loosened the belt of her pack and freed one of the shoulder straps. She had no desire to be trapped in a crevice or underwater because she couldn't get out of her pack. She scrambled to the top of the boulder. A light breeze carried a fine icy spray into her face and made the rocky surface slippery.

She surveyed the descent. There was a crevice about eight feet below which was just large enough to accommodate her and her pack. Two feet up on the opposite side was a narrow ledge which looked as if it led around the outcropping and behind the waterfall. If it didn't, she was probably in for a very cold swim and some difficult explanations to Jim.

Janet had to descend facing away from the boulder because there would be no room to turn around once she got down. There was a small hole in the rock about halfway down where she wedged the tip of her walking stick. She used this to slow her seat-of-the-pants descent and reached the bottom of the crevice without incident.

The roar of the waterfall was deafening and the motion of the water in her peripheral vision was disorienting. Coupled with the restriction of movement, the assault on her senses produced a momentary panic. She took a deep breath and shut the sound and movement out of her consciousness. It took some maneuvering in the confined space to get one foot up on the ledge, but she managed it. She used her walking stick to help push herself up until the other foot was in position.

Janet was balanced on six inches of slippery ledge which angled up and around the outcropping. Her bottom and pack hung out over the pool. She edged one foot forward, and then the other, a few inches at a time, until she rounded the point of the outcropping. There the ledge widened and the rock face was concave so that she could step behind the sheet of falling water. There was a ledge about four feet wide, three feet above the surface of the pool.

The entrance to the crevice was in front of Janet. She slipped out of her pack and leaned it against the wall. With flashlight and walking stick, she cautiously stepped inside the opening. The caves of New Mexico had taught her not to take altitude, temperature, or location for granted where snakes were concerned.

The cave was as Maggie had described it and Janet neither saw, smelled, nor sensed the presence of any snakes. She retrieved her pack and reentered. She took the kerosene lantern from her backpack, filled and lit it, and placed it on the floor. Then she sat down and poured herself a cup of coffee from her Thermos.

She smiled with a feeling of smug satisfaction. She had just joined a very small, elite group. After all, how many people could there be at that precise moment who were sitting behind a waterfall on a secluded mountain? Talk about solitude. No one in the world knew where she was.

Janet reveled in the curiously muted sound of the waterfall and the sensation of being completely alone. It was good. In a strange way it was a reminder and a renewal of the feeling she had experienced looking out of her window at the snowstorm.

She hated to break the spell, but she needed to find a place to leave the supplies she had brought and finish her explorations before Jim woke up and started to worry about her.

The crevice narrowed abruptly at the rear and ended in a small tumble of rocks. Near the ceiling on one side there seemed to be a small ledge or niche. She didn't want to start poking things onto it until she knew how wide it was and made certain that she wouldn't lose anything down a crack or hole.

She balanced precariously on the loose rocks and set the lantern on the ledge, then scrambled up for a look. The ledge was much wider than it had appeared from below. What she saw beyond it electrified every cell in her body.

The lantern light revealed a cave approximately twenty by thirty feet with a tunnel leading out of the opposite end. Boxes filled the room. Some were intact, carefully wrapped in many layers of oiled paper. Others had rotted and broken open to spill their priceless contents across the floor. Jade, porcelain, bronze, pieces inlaid with gold and silver — an ancient Chinese treasure.

Janet's palms were sweaty, her mouth dry, her heart pounding, as she looked at the treasure. "Oh, damn, damn," she whispered. "Why now? Why did it have to be now?" Her hands ached to touch the treasure and open the intact boxes, but she knew what she had to do. Their lives were too complicated now to deal with this. It had waited for centuries. It could wait a few weeks more.

"Another time," she whispered to an exquisite golden Buddha. With centuries-old patience, it seemed to agree and she heard an echo in her mind, "Another time."

Janet almost cried with frustration as she wrestled enough rocks into place to seal the opening. She felt a profound sorrow for those who had lost such beauty. She felt burdened by the knowledge of its existence. It was one thing too much in her life right now and she couldn't share it with anyone.

Her task finished, she placed the blankets, dried food, and other supplies on the ledge in front of the rocks she had wedged into place. She extinguished the lantern and left it. She gathered her things by the light of her flashlight.

Getting out was much easier than getting in. Within five minutes she was standing on solid ground looking back at the waterfall. She ached to share her discovery with Jim, but this was the McVeys private place and they had the right to know first and make the decision about who would be told. None of them needed the distraction now. Their thoughts and energies needed to be directed toward staying alive and resolving the problems which already faced them. A find such as this should be dealt with properly and at one's leisure with undivided attention.

Janet hurried toward the cabin, suddenly anxious to be in touch with the commonplace realities of rocking chairs, wood fires, and braided rugs. She paused just before she opened the door and allowed herself to relive that first second of discovery. Then she mentally took the whole experience and placed it in a large box, tied it with a bright ribbon, and labeled it TO BE OPENED LATER — a mental exercise she used when she wanted to free her mind of some thought or worry.

Jim was asleep. Janet changed into dry jeans and shirt, added a log to the fire, and stirred the soup. The aroma awakened her appetite.

"Janet? Janet, are you there?" Jim's drowsy voice startled her.

"Yes, I'm back. How are you feeling?" Janet asked from the door of the bedroom.

"A little better, I think. See anything interesting on your walk?"

"The waterfall is magnificent. I think it's taller than Multnomah Falls. I don't know how it has escaped discovery all these years."

"What I saw of it the day we arrived was spectacular," Jim agreed. "Hank told me that it isn't visible from any place below, unless someone is standing right at its foot. The trees and the lay of the land tend to shield it and deaden the sound."

"How about some soup? I was just about to have a bowl when you called."

"That sounds good. I'd like to get up for a while. You put it on the table and I'll be there in a minute."

"Okay, but put on something warm. You can't afford to get a cold on top of the measles."

Janet had laid out cheese and crackers and ladled soup into two bowls when Jim made his appearance. Except for his size, he looked just like a little boy freshly awakened from a nap — a little boy with tousled hair and measles. He was dressed in thermal underwear bottoms, a long-tailed flannel shirt, and heavy wool socks. Janet put forth a mighty effort to keep from laughing and the effort didn't pass unnoticed.

"Don't you dare start laughing again."

"I'm trying very hard not to. Could I just smile a little?"

"Well, I have to admit that this is one of the most ludicrous situations imaginable. Go ahead and laugh. I can't blame you. But you have to make me a promise. Now Janet, stop giggling for a minute. I'm really serious about this."

"What?"

"You have to promise that you won't tell anyone I had the measles. Not Hank and Maggie, and particularly not Roger and Marie. They would never let me live it down. If any of them find out, Sarah Peale will eventually hear about it and then the whole state will know."

"All right. It will be our secret. That's a promise. But you'd better hope that the spots are gone before anyone sees you or I won't have to tell."

After they ate, Janet cleared the table, washed the dishes, and then decided to take a nap. She left Jim rocking in front of the fire, retreated to her corner, slept and dreamed of treasure caves filled with carved jade and golden Buddhas.

Chapter 17

The next few days were a strange mixture of lethargy and restlessness for Janet. Jim spent most of his time in bed, either reading or sleeping, and made few demands on Janet's time. When it rained, Janet paced the cabin and longed to be outside. When the weather was beautiful, she couldn't motivate herself to venture outside except to bring in wood and water. She finally had the opportunity to write and think and couldn't do either. Every time she forced herself to sit down with pencil and paper, her attention wandered until it focused on that damned crystal ball.

She knew she was wasting valuable time, but she seemed to be under a spell which compelled her. It was as if the crystal ball and Mark Jamison provided her with an escape into a world where David and Sam hadn't been murdered and evil men didn't exist. She soon found herself gazing into it for hours at a time.

Janet no longer questioned her ability to watch the daily life of Mark Jamison and elicit answers to occasional questions. Mark was preparing a paper about his early work in Africa. She found the subject interesting, but she wished he would return to the project he had been working on when she first started watching him.

At first, she did ask a few questions about Africa. Although he answered, Mark seemed increasingly distressed by the contact. When Janet realized that he believed her voice to be a bizarre mental aberration, she tried to be content with simply observing him. More and more, she found his world a temporary refuge from the chaos of her own life.

Gradually Janet began to neglect herself and the cabin. She allowed the fire to go out several times and didn't remember to prepare a meal unless her own hunger reminded her or Jim asked for something to eat. Then she would quickly throw a meal together and usually not bother to wash up afterward. She didn't even prepare the hot bath which had seemed so inviting a few days earlier. She felt comfortable only when she was staring into the crystal ball or immersed in making a written record of her observations.

They had been at the cabin a little over a week when Jim began to insist that Janet allow him to read what she had written and tell him what was going on in her mind. Janet was indignant. She considered his questions a rude intrusion into her private life with Mark.

"Damn it, Janet, get out of here. Go for a walk. Climb a mountain. Do something besides sitting here like a zombie for hours at a time," Jim demanded.

When Jim reached out and picked up the crystal ball, Janet doubled her fist and drew back to hit him. Her reaction slammed her back into the full reality of how obsessive she had become. That moment of uncontrolled rage showed her more than any words that she had to get out and away from the cabin and get some perspective on what was happening to her.

"Oh, god. Yes, you're right, Jim. I'm sorry. I do need to get out for a while."

"I don't like for you to go alone, but I don't feel well enough to go with you. Will you humor me and carry your .38 so that you can fire a signal if you get in a jam?"

Janet was willing to agree to almost anything.

The woods were cool and damp, so Janet chose to explore the bluffs behind the cabin. They proved to be an easy climb, in spite of their forbidding appearance. About halfway up she found a ledge which offered a comfortable seat in the sunshine and a panoramic view.

Her first thoughts were for Jim. She had pretty much ignored him the past couple of days, and she realized that he wasn't recovering from the measles the way he should. She was ashamed of herself and embarrassed by her neglect of him. She determined to check him out thoroughly when she returned to the cabin and find out what was wrong and do what she could about it.

An objective look at her activities and attitudes of the past few days didn't make her any prouder of herself. In one way, her actions seemed sick and obsessive, and yet she wasn't willing to write off the whole experience in that way. The unhealthy aspect was that she had allowed it to become the ruling factor in her life, inhibiting her normal day-to-day functioning, and that was sick. She knew that part of the reason she had allowed it to happen was that her mind and emotions had been overloaded to the breaking point. She also knew there were better ways to deal with it than a retreat into a dream world.

Janet gradually became aware that she had been hearing an alien sound for several minutes. Even as it penetrated her consciousness, it took several seconds for the significance to register.

She searched the sky until she saw it, almost invisible against the wispy white clouds. A Cessna 172, the familiar shape easily identified. It was flying circular patterns, banking low over the hills and valleys below her. A search pattern.

The prickles down her spine instantly convinced her that the plane boded no good for her and Jim. She watched the plane. Each pass brought it nearer to the hanging valley. From her own flying experience and work with aerial photography, she knew it wasn't easy to spot someone, or even a cabin, from the air in a wooded area. But she was in plain sight, clad in a gold-colored windbreaker.

Janet peeled out of the windbreaker and stuffed it under some rocks, thankful for the tan shirt covering her white sweater. She scrambled down the bluff until she found an overhang which formed a pocket just large enough for her to curl up and wedge herself into as the sound of the plane grew louder. It was beginning the near leg of its pattern.

It took all of Janet's self-control to remain where she was as the engine noise grew louder.

"Damn idiot!" she yelled as the plane banked and turned not over a hundred feet from the bluffs. "Are you that desperate to find us or are you just plain stupid?"

Her pulse was racing but she remained motionless for several minutes until the engine noise faded away in the direction of the old logging road. She waited another minute, straining to hear any sound of its return. She wriggled out of her hidey-hole and sat down, waiting for her legs to quit trembling.

Janet felt certain that neither she nor the cabin had been sighted. She couldn't see the cabin from her perch above it and it would be less visible from the plane. There wasn't even a telltale wisp of smoke to betray its presence.

She climbed up to retrieve her windbreaker, anxious to descend and find out what Jim thought about the plane. A flash of vivid blue on the ridge which gave access to the valley caught her eye. She froze and scanned the area. There it was again. Too large, too blue to be a bird.

Janet stuffed the windbreaker under her sweater and descended the bluff in half the time it had taken her to climb it. She dropped the windbreaker behind some rocks and hit level ground running. She dodged from tree to tree until she reached the entrance to the valley.

The underbrush was scanty and it was difficult to find cover. She squatted behind the thickest growth she could find, hoping that the unexpectedness of her presence would give her a cloak of invisibility. She made certain that there was no longer an empty chamber under the hammer of her .38 Special and waited.

Ten minutes passed and she was just about to change position when she heard movement and caught the sound of voices. She peered through the tangle of brush and saw a young blond man wearing a vivid blue jacket, followed by a lean, sharp-faced man dressed in brown. Both were armed, carrying light packs and moving warily. They stopped ten feet from where Janet was crouching.

Janet made herself look away and tried to do as she had been taught by an old Apache friend, and her *sensei*. "Never look directly at someone you are hiding from," the old Apache had told her. "Your eyes act like a magnet, drawing attention toward you. Imagine that you are a part of your surroundings. Be a part of them. In such a way did my ancestors make themselves invisible to those who hunted them."

Her *sensei* had taught her to draw in her *Ki* — that aura of one's being which can make another aware of one's presence without the use of sight or hearing.

She hoped to hell they both had known what they were talking about. She took a slow, deep breath and focused her awareness within herself and imagined that she was part of the underbrush. Something worked. In her peripheral vision she saw the man in brown make a visual sweep of the area and appear satisfied that he and his partner were alone.

"Ben, can't we take a breather?" Blue Jacket asked. "I'm beat."

"Five minutes," the one now identified as Ben replied. "The cabin has to be pretty close. I can see bluffs above those trees. It should be somewhere near the base of the bluffs."

The two men squatted on their haunches in silence. Blue Jacket lit a cigarette while Ben checked his gun.

"Think we'll have to go that far?" Blue Jacket asked, nodding toward the gun.

"Unless we find them together. If she's out wandering around and armed, she's liable to be pretty trigger-happy by now. I don't want that female taking pot-shots at me, not after what she did to Lacey. I intend to get out of here with my hide in one piece."

Blue Jacket nodded his agreement and stubbed his cigarette out in the pine needles.

"Don, when we locate the cabin, if there's no sign of her, you check the back and I'll take the front."

As Ben issued these instructions, he stood up and dug a hole in the damp earth with his boot heel and gestured toward the discarded cigarette butt. Don flipped the butt into the hole and started to stand up as Ben covered it. While their attention was directed toward that commendable activity and their minds full of plans for sneaking up on the cabin, Janet made her move.

"Freeze, gentlemen! Now slowly put your hands over your heads and lean on the nearest tree and spread your legs."

Seldom had two men ever been more surprised. They followed instructions immediately.

"Now look, Ms. Manning. You're making a mistake. We're — "

"Shut up and follow instructions. You, Ben, ease that gun out of the holster with two fingers and toss it gently in this direction. Slow and easy. Any quick movements and I'll pull this trigger."

Ben looked over his shoulder at Janet. She pulled the hammer back into full cock and took a stance with her legs slightly spread, one hand supporting the other, and aimed at his head. He slowly turned to face the tree and moved his hand toward the holster until he could grasp the butt of his gun with his forefinger and thumb. He tossed it several feet behind him and returned his hand above his head.

"Nicely done. Now you, Don, do the same."

Don hesitated. "Don't be stupid. Do what she says," Ben ordered. Don started to protest, then seemed to think better of it and eased his gun out, but deliberately dropped it at his feet.

"Don't be cute," Janet snapped. "It wouldn't bother me to shoot you. Now edge that gun back with your foot and give it a nice little nudge in this direction."

Don grudgingly obeyed.

"Don't move. Don't even take a deep breath." Janet stooped, picked up a dead branch, and used it to drag both guns to her feet. "Now open your jackets and your shirts. I want to see your armpits, waists, and backs." They complied without argument. "Now, one at a time, pull up your pant legs."

When Janet was satisfied that neither of them carried another weapon, she made them sit on the ground with their arms and legs around a tree.

"Look, lady, you have this all wrong," Don sputtered. "If you'll just let us explain."

"Shut up. I'll explain and you listen. One more word and I'll shoot you in the foot, then it'll be your knee, and I'll let your imagination take over from there. Give me your boot-laces and your belts."

When Janet had the requested items in hand, she allowed them to stand. "Now, drop your pants." She ignored the groans of protest. "You can hold them at arm's length with two fingers. Now, start walking toward that grove of trees in front of the bluffs."

Janet felt calm and cool and completely in control of the situation. She thoroughly enjoyed the two men's discomfort as they clomped along in their lace-less boots, hobbled by their lowered pants. Even as she laughed, she was no less wary.

When they reached the cabin, Janet ordered them to stop about fifteen feet away while she banged on Jim's window to get his attention.

"Get your gun, Jim. I caught these two bastards sneaking up on the cabin. Open the door and keep them covered."

Janet heard Jim stumbling toward the door, knocking something over on the way. He opened the door, looked at the two men, lowered his gun and began to laugh.

"Janet ... you ... they ... " He doubled over with merriment.

"Damn it, Jim. Tell her who we are before she shoots us," Ben snapped. "She's lethal!"

Janet had a very strange feeling in the pit of her stomach as Jim slapped Ben on the back and continued to laugh uproariously.

"They ... they ... you," Jim stopped and took a deep breath. "Janet, you've just captured two of the government's finest."

"What? What do you mean?"

Jim could hardly answer. "Put your gun away and meet Ben Fischer and Don Ross."

"I .... uh .... "

"Ma'am, if you'll just stop pointing that gun at me, I'd like to put my pants on," Ben Fischer said.

"Oh. Oh yes. I'm so sorry. I didn't know," Janet sputtered, turning the .38 away and carefully lowering the hammer from its cocked position. Then she remembered something which made her pause.

"Just a damn minute. You have a little explaining to do, Mr. Fischer. Out there in the woods when you were talking to your partner, it certainly sounded as if you intended to use this on me," Janet said, indicating his gun now encrusted with damp earth.

Ben winced as he looked at it. "I can understand how it might have sounded that way," he answered thoughtfully. "Our intent was to cover you so that we didn't get shot before Jim could identify us. We expected that you might be pretty edgy by now."

"Trigger-happy, I believe was the term you used."

"Yes, I did use that term, Ms. Manning. I had no way of knowing how you would react to the sudden appearance of two strangers. Hank McVey told us how you handled Richards and Lacey. I just try never to be caught unprepared in any situation."

Jim was snickering as Janet returned the boot-laces, belts, and guns. From the glint in his eye, Janet knew what was coming and, short of strangling him, there was no way to prevent it.

"Well, you sure got caught with your pants down this time," Jim snorted.

Janet and the two men looked at each other and refused to change expressions.

"Mr. Fischer, Mr Ross, you'll have to excuse Jim. Anyone who runs around in public covered with red spots can't be expected to have any couth."

"Janet, you promised," Jim protested.

"I didn't say anything which isn't perfectly evident to these gentlemen."

"Hm ... looks like the same kind of spots my sister's kid had last year," Don Ross mused. "Seems she said it was measles or some such kiddy ailment."

"All right, all right. So I've got the measles. Let's make a deal, guys. You don't tell anyone about my little indisposition and I won't tell anyone what happened here today. Okay?" There was quick agreement from the two government agents. "Now, fellows," Janet interrupted, "since you have the really important things taken care of, might I suggest that we go inside and get warm, and find out what prompted this little visit."

While Janet hastily restored a semblance of order to the cabin and prepared a meal, Ben and Don cleaned their guns and explained the purpose for their presence.

"Jim, we've got to get you back into circulation. I think the break we have been hoping for has happened," Ben said. "Ray Lawton flew a man into Agness a couple of days ago. The man has been inquiring about you. He claims to be an anthropologist named Brownell. He says he wants to consult you about some of your work in Africa."

"That's remotely possible," Jim interrupted. "It happens occasionally."

"Not this time," Don said. "I recognized Brownell from a case I worked on several years ago. His real name is Amos Yaeger. He's the front man for an import-export conglomerate which has offices in San Francisco, Houston, and New York. The top man in the firm is Frederick Bryce.

"Bryce, I know that name. He was involved in a Senate investigation. Something to do with illegal shipments of arms," Janet said.

"He's the one. Ben and I put in sixteen months trying to get evidence against him, but he had a friend or two in high places and the whole investigation was finally dropped."

"Do you think Bryce is 'Mr. Big' in the black market?" Jim asked.

"It's possible. Even if Bryce isn't directly involved, Yaeger is a sure bet. Hank McVey has been keeping an eye on him and saw him meet Richards and Lacey out in the woods."

"Oh, lord," Jim groaned. "Are they still around?"

"Yes," Ben answered. "They are holed up in the Johnson's summer cabin. Which brings me to another part of the story."

Ben paused to take a sip of coffee. Janet looked out of the window and saw that twilight was fast approaching.

"Fellows, I hate to interrupt a good story, but I need to get wood and water in before dark. Can you wait a few minutes?"

"Sure. Let us help. Don, I'll get the wood if you'll get the water."

"Sure thing."

"I think I'll lay down for a few minutes," Jim said. Janet looked at him in surprise and didn't care for what she saw. "You've got fever again." His forehead was hot and damp to the touch and he looked rather shaky. "Let me get you a couple of aspirins, and then it's bed for you."

"Yeah. I really don't feel very well. I think I'll sleep for a while." Jim swallowed the aspirins and headed for the bedroom.

Janet put on her jacket and collected the water buckets. She glanced in at Jim before she went out. He appeared to be asleep. She wished for a doctor, or at least some antibiotics. His breathing sounded raspy.

She joined Ben and Don outside. She pointed Ben toward the woodpile and she and Don headed for the spring.

"Don, who is Ray Lawton? Is he involved in all of this?"

"Not really. Ray is a bush pilot. Flew for years in Canada and Alaska. He's had a few minor brushes with the law, but he's a pretty good guy. He and his planes just happen to be available to whoever is willing to pay his price. He's completely loyal to whoever happens to be signing his paycheck. He flies where he is told and keeps his mouth shut, but he does draw the line at flying drugs."

"I know you must have seen that Cessna when you were coming up the ridge. Was that him?"

"Yeah. I'm afraid we got suckered into that one. This hasn't exactly been our day."

"Were they following you or looking for us?"

"They were probably hoping to follow us to either you or Jim or both."

"Doesn't that mean Jim's cover is blown if Yaeger or Lawton know that you and Ben work for the government?"

"They don't know. Lawton may suspect something but he wouldn't say anything. As far as Yaeger knows, we're just friends of the McVeys. Ben and I keep a pretty low profile."

"What did you mean about getting suckered in this morning?"

"Ray flew Yaeger out this morning to refuel the plane and take care of some business. At least that's what they said. We thought it would be the perfect time to come up here. We had to use Jim's Jeep to get over that damned road. We were about ten miles out when they flew over and apparently recognized the Jeep. Ray tried to maintain the appearance of a sight-seeing jaunt, but he made every effort to keep us in sight."

"What did you do?"

"We waited until they were out of sight for a minute and ditched the Jeep in a grove of trees. They flew up and down the road several times and then started search patterns."

"Do you think they saw you? Could they find the trail?"

"No, to both questions. We drove over a mile past the trailhead and walked back after we ditched the Jeep. We were very careful not to be seen."

"We're probably safe then. I'm positive they didn't spot me or the cabin. That Lawton scared the hell out of me, though. He made his last pass within about a hundred feet of the bluffs. Bush pilot or not, that was pure stupidity."

By this time, Janet and Don had filled the buckets and were back at the cabin door. "Don, if you'll go ahead and take the water in, I'll get the windbreaker I dropped at the base of the bluffs."

Something nagged at the back of Janet's mind. something Ben or Don had said. The import-export company. That was it. There was an office in Houston. David's consulting job had been for an import-export company in Houston.

It got dark and cold in the few minutes it took Janet to locate her windbreaker and return to the cabin. Ben and Don were sitting at the kitchen table talking quietly.

"Did Hank tell you about my husband, David, and that Richards and Lacey followed me from Texas?"

"Yes," Ben answered.

"David's last assignment was a job for an import-export company in Houston. It's too much of a coincidence. There has to be some connection, but what?"

"Janet," Ben said softly, "people sometimes get drawn into things way over their heads. I don't know what the connection could be, but you need to be prepared — "

"To find out that David was doing something illegal?" Janet interrupted. "No. That is *not* a possibility. You didn't know David or you wouldn't suggest it."

Janet turned on her heel and went into the bedroom to check on Jim. He was sweating heavily and his breathing sounded as if there was some lung congestion. Sleep was the only medicine they had, so Janet didn't wake him.

Before she left the room, she stopped and confronted the shadow of a doubt which lurked in the farthest reaches of her mind. Had all of those other wives and mothers been just as sure of their men as she was of David? Was there a possibility that she hadn't known David as well as she thought she did? She searched her mind and heart and heaved a sigh of relief. No. She was sure of David. Nothing about David caused her a moment of doubt — only the constant doubts of others who hadn't known him.

"How is Jim?" Ben asked as she joined them. "Will he be able to travel tomorrow?"

"I don't know. I think his fever has broken. He's sweating, but I don't like the sound of his breathing. Couldn't we wait a couple of days?"

"Not really. Unless it is life-threatening, he has to go tomorrow. And you go tomorrow, even if he can't."

"You're going to have to be pretty convincing to make me leave him if he isn't well enough to travel."

Don stood up. "Why don't I wash up from supper while you two talk."

"Sure, if you want to."

Janet and Ben moved to the rocking chairs in front of the fireplace while Don got busy.

"The coroner's inquest into Sam's death is set for the day after tomorrow. Sheriff Gates has delayed as long as he can. You have to be there since you found Sam. The inquest will officially establish the cause of Sam's death. Unfortunately, feelings around Agness and Gold Beach are beginning to run pretty high against you. Gates agrees with us that it is imperative that you be officially and publicly cleared as soon as possible.

"We want you to go to Sam's cabin tomorrow and spend the night. We'll meet you and take you by boat to Gold Beach the following morning."

"Sneak me in, you mean. Hank was afraid this would happen."

"Sam Donnelly was loved by a lot of people. That brings me to the next step. Immediately after the inquest, we want to fly you to San Francisco for a few days. Sam's attorney will meet you and take this opportunity to discuss Sam's estate with you."

"Now wait. I understand that I have to attend the inquest, but why are you so anxious to get me out of the way afterward?"

"Well, this is not going to be a standard inquest. If everything goes according to plan, it will set any one of several possible scenarios into motion. We must be able to concentrate our attention on certain people without being concerned for your safety. We want you safely out of the way. It's just that simple."

"Okay. No problem."

Don turned from the dishpan and stared at Janet. "That's it? Okay?"

Janet nodded.

"Well I'll be damned."

"I don't understand."

"Sometimes the hardest part of our job is getting people out of the way to let us do it. From everything we have heard about you, we thought we might have a real battle on our hands to keep you out of the middle of everything."

"Sorry. Wrong gal. You two know a whole lot more about this situation and these people and how to deal with them than I do. I can usually take care of myself, but this isn't the time or place to make an issue of it. Besides, somewhere in all of this I'm finally going to know why my husband was killed and who did it, and the rest of the world is going to know that he was an innocent victim.

"Now, I'm curious to know what has been going on during our absence and what you expect to happen."

"I think you've earned the right to know everything we know, including our best guesses," Ben said. Don nodded in agreement. "Sheriff Gates has discovered who the contact is in Gold Beach — Lloyd Owen."

"That doesn't surprise me. He was quite eager to arrest me for Sam's murder and suggested that I killed David. How did the sheriff find out?"

"He had been watching Owen for a while because Owen lived a great deal better than his salary would allow. He wondered if Owen was involved in drugs but there was no evidence. When Jim told Gates about the black market, he began to pay even more attention to Owens activities. Last week Gates saw him leave on what was supposed to be a routine patrol, but he loaded a boat with supplies and headed up the Rogue. Gates called Hank McVey and asked him to keep an eye out for Owen in that area. Hank followed Owen to the Johnson cabin where he met Richards and Lacey and gave them the supplies.

"Hank took quite a chance, Janet. You really owe him one. He got close enough to the cabin to over-hear their conversation. Owen got Lacey's 30-06, intending to substitute it for yours in the ballistics test. Hank let Gates know, Gates took Ted Nichols into his confidence, and they substituted a third 30-06 for yours. When Owen made the switch, he got that one. They sent your rifle and Lacey's in for tests. Your rifle was okay, of course. Lacey's was the murder weapon.

Janet shivered. "Now that is frightening. Thank goodness for Hank and Sheriff Gates. I would have been in terrible trouble without them."

"That's true," Don said. "Owen altered the paper-work — changed the serial numbers — to make it appear that the murder weapon was the one they got from you."

"Has Owen been arrested?"

"Not yet. Not until after the inquest. He doesn't know that the sheriff is onto him. Aside from that, we suspect that Yaeger may have decided to throw Richards and Lacey to the wolves whether or not you are indicted for murder. We think this is why he wants to contact Jim, and we want to give him every opportunity before we make a move," Don said.

"Yaeger is interested in you, also," Ben adds. "In his pose as an anthropologist, he said that he had heard you were in Agness. He asked if you and Jim are working on a project together. It seems that he had read one of your articles. We told him that the only thing you and Jim are working on together is a hot and heavy affair."

"Well just for the record, Jim and I are friends and nothing more."

"We don't want Yaeger to know that," Ben said.

"I don't follow your thinking."

Don had finished the dishes and pulled up a chair to join Ben and Janet. "It's like this, Janet. If Jim's interest in you and yours in him appears to be purely romantic, we think Yaeger is less likely to see you as a threat. Jim is much more important to him right now than Richards and Lacey. They are just two errand boys who have gotten sloppy and caused him a lot of problems. They can be replaced. It would be difficult to find someone else with Jim's background. He not only authenticates and appraises the artifacts, he sometimes tips Yaeger's people to new sources of supply."

"Yaeger may think that you are potentially useful, but I think his main concern is how much you know about his setup. If you are right about the connection between this and your husband's murder, then he's probably even more worried. We have to tip the scales in your favor every way we can and make him think that either of you can be used as leverage to keep the other in line."

"Okay, I can see that. But what you don't know is that he may see more potential in me than you realize. I'll bet the article he read was the research material which was stolen from my office a few weeks ago. The subject was rare and unusual Indian artifacts. I'm somewhat of an authority on the subject. That should give Jim an additional talking point in my favor.

"In fact," Janet continued, "Jim could tell Yaeger that he was the one who encouraged me to come to Agness because he knew I would be a good source of information, and he is just stringing me along by getting me involved in an affair."

"That's an even better story than the one we concocted," Ben said.

"I only see one problem. How will Jim explain why I shot Lacey?"

"We'll think of something. I think Jim can handle Yaeger. That leaves us with Richards and Lacey. They are the type who want revenge. The fact that a woman got the best of them makes it even more important."

"So I'll still be a target even after I'm cleared of Sam's murder. Gee, it's nice to be popular," she quipped. "Sorry about the levity there. I understand what you want and I'll cooperate. What do you want me to say at the inquest?"

"Just tell the truth, only not all of it," Ben said. "Tell how you came to find Sam's body and followed the tracks back to the road. Let the trail end at the road. Don't mention Jim or the artifacts. Remember that the only purpose of the inquest is to establish the cause of death. In this case, however, we want to stretch the bounds a bit and give enough evidence to point in the right direction without giving away the whole show."

"That sounds simple enough. By the way, there is a roll of film in the flour canister in my kitchen. I took pictures of the tire tracks and footprints from the logging camp to the bluff. They may be useful. There are some other pictures of Jim and Sheriff Gates together which probably shouldn't be seen by anyone else. You'd better get the film tomorrow before someone else finds it."

Don shook his head. "You've been a busy little lady. Thank god we're on the same side."

Janet laughed and changed the subject. "I assume that you will take Jim back in the Jeep tomorrow. Does that mean that you want me to go alone by the trail?"

Ben stared into the fire for a moment before he answered. "Janet, I won't ask if you can make it alone, but do you mind going alone? It would certainly simplify things for us. We can't run the risk of you being seen with us in the Jeep, and it would be difficult to account for either Don or I being gone."

"I shouldn't have any problem. Maggie described the trail to me."

"There is some risk involved. The trail goes within a quarter of a mile of the Johnson cabin. Richards and Lacey might decide to take a stroll and cross your path."

"I doubt it. They don't strike me as nature lovers, but I'll be careful. How are you going to handle Jim's reappearance?"

"Ben and I were discussing that earlier. We think Jim's measles will take care of that nicely. We'll say that we found him hiding out at the ranger station to keep anyone from knowing that he had the measles.

Since the evidence is there for Yaeger to see, he should believe the story."

"Jim is going to hate that. But won't that pose a danger for the ranger and his family? Richards and Lacey might think I'm there and go looking for me."

"No. We'll have Jim say that Sheriff Gates has you in protective custody and he doesn't know where you are. And Don and I will have been doing a little out-of-season deer hunting. That will explain our evasiveness."

"You seem to have covered all the angles. Well, if we're going to leave here tomorrow there are several things I need to do."

Janet quietly checked on Jim. He was sleeping peacefully and his breathing seemed easier. She felt a great sense of relief. She didn't want to leave Jim behind.

She gathered her personal belongings and began to fill her pack. Ben and Don laid out food for breakfast and helped prepare the cabin to be closed.

When everything was done to Janet's satisfaction, she got her jacket and flashlight and made a trip to the "necessary." The sky was clear and crowded with stars. It was quiet and peaceful, but Janet sensed change in the air, as if this was the proverbial calm before the storm, and the storm she sensed had nothing to do with the weather.

When she returned to the cabin, Ben and Don had spread their sleeping bags on the rug in front of the fireplace and were preparing to settle in for the night. Ben stopped Janet as she started toward her corner.

"I have something for you. Hank McVey found it in Jim's Jeep and asked me to give it to you. I had forgotten until now."

"Thank you, Ben."

Janet's hands were shaking as she took the envelope which was addressed to her in Samuel Donnelly's handwriting. She carried a kerosene lamp behind her curtain and placed it on the shelf. She was both eager and reluctant to read this last message from Sam. There was a lump in her throat as she changed into her flannel gown. She sat cross-legged on her bed and stared at the envelope before she opened it.

There were several pages of Sam's beautiful, old-fashioned handwriting. The words unfolded the love, pain, and tragedy of Dr. Samuel Donnelly's life and solved the mystery of why he had made Janet his heir. Janet was sobbing by the time she read the last sentence, sobbing and remembering her last conversation with Sam, remembering the body of the dear old man and his faithful dog.

"Shhh, Janet. Don't cry. This will all be over soon," Jim whispered in her ear as he sat down beside her and put his arms around her. "It's all going to be okay."

"I know. It's not that. Oh, Jim, all those years and I never wrote Sam or had any idea how he felt about me," She held the letter out. "It's all here. The story of Sam's life."

Jim wiped the tears from her cheeks. "Will you tell me about it?"

So Janet told him the story of the young doctor who married a fragile society girl, and of the birth of a beautiful daughter delivered on a stormy night when they couldn't get to the hospital. The baby brain-damaged, the young mother blaming herself and her husband. Sam had watched helplessly as his young bride's love turned to hate and self-recrimination. Sam had blamed himself for her suicide. He had made arrangements for the child to be raised on his palatial estate with all that money could provide, while he withdrew to the life of a hermit.

Sam had seen his daughter, Julia, only once, after twenty years, when she had become seriously ill. She had died and Sam had returned to his self-imposed exile accompanied by her new puppy, Danielle.

Chapter 18

" So that explains the mystery of Sam Donnelly," Jim said. "But what does it have to do with you?"

"Here, read these last two pages."

Sam had written:

Janet, you cannot judge me more harshly than I judge myself, and yet, it seemed at the time that I did the best I could for Julia. She was cared for by loving people and lived the life of a fairy-tale princess who never grew up. She ruled over a small but adoring kingdom of children who came to play with her in the storybook land I created for her.

I could not play a role in the life I created for her, but I know that she never lacked for love or companionship or anything else it was possible to provide. She was happy every day of her life. How many people can say that about themselves or their children?

Looking back, my regrets are not for Julia, though some would say that I heartlessly abandoned her. My regrets are for the wasted years of my own life.

Perhaps it will count a little with my Maker that I loved His world and tried to awaken others to its wonders. The first summer that you came here and I saw the eagerness and joy with which you learned to see the world around you, you touched my life in a very special way and became the daughter I might have had, the daughter of my heart and mind.

Through the years, in your mother's letters to Maggie, I have watched you grow to womanhood. I have celebrated the joyous events of your life and have wept at your sorrows. I have seen that you are not afraid to live and think beyond the limits which confine most to mediocrity. For that reason, I have left to you all of my material possessions so that whatever you might wish to accomplish will not be hindered through the simple lack of money.

All of my familial and charitable obligations have long since been met, so you need feel no duties in those directions. What I leave you is yours to do with as you please. In my own somewhat prideful way, I would like to think that what I have left you is freedom.

Samuel Maxwell Donnelly, M. D.

Jim brushed a tear from his eye as he handed the pages back to Janet. "That's quite a letter."

"Yes, it is. It's an awesome thing to find that I have been that important to someone and didn't know it. I've got a lot of thinking to do when we get clear of this mess. Having complete financial independence is a totally new concept to me. It's not quite real yet. That sweet, dear old man."

"Yes, he was. I think that I have just found the source of the very generous trust fund I got when I turned twenty-one. Do you have any idea what you will do with the money?"

"I've always had dreams about what I would do if I had the money to do it. Now I don't know. I do know that I want the ranch in New Mexico that David and I had planned to buy. Anything past that is going to take a lot of thinking."

Jim and Janet talked a few minutes longer. Janet was relieved that Jim was feeling a great deal better. Soon they said goodnight and the only sounds to be heard were the crackling of the burning logs in the fireplace.

The morning was clear and cold. Everyone was up early, preparing breakfast, filling packs, and doing the last-minute chores to restore the cabin to its original order.

Jim looked and felt much better, although the measles rash was still prominent. They speculated that the high fever of the previous evening had probably been the peak of his illness and that he would show progressive improvement. Janet was a little uneasy about Jim hiking in the cold, damp air, but there didn't appear to be much choice.

Janet was on her way back from the "necessary" when she heard the airplane. The sporadic sound of the engine, suddenly followed by silence, turned her cold with fear. A brief glimpse of the plane through the trees told her that the pilot was preparing for a crash landing. He was heading toward the summit of the mountain above the bluffs.

Janet ran for the cabin and started giving instructions as she grabbed the first-aid kit and dumped everything out of Ben's small daypack.

"There's a plane going down on the mountain. Jim, get a clean sheet and put it in the pack. Don, put a couple of blankets and a hatchet in your pack. Ben, there's a canteen and some rope in the tool chest."

Janet stuck her .38 in her belt, shrugged into Ben's pack and grabbed her gloves and walking stick on the way out the door. "Up the bluffs," she shouted over her shoulder.

She was thankful that the bluffs were an easy climb. She paused at the top and scanned the mountain above her. She didn't see any sign of wreckage or smoke, but she had a pretty good idea of where the plane had gone down. At least she knew what she would have done under the same circumstances.

"Where do we go from here?" Jim asked as he caught up with her. "Did you see the crash?"

Ben and Don joined them before she could answer.

"Was it Ray Lawton in the same plane as yesterday?" Ben asked.

"It was a blue and white Cessna 172. The engine quit. Probably carburetor ice. From what I could see, the pilot bumped the starter to get the prop horizontal and put on full flaps. He headed for the summit, probably looking for a couple of trees to hang it between."

"I don't understand," Don said.

"He'd look for a place where the forest thinned out and hope for a couple of tall trees close enough together so he could go in low between them and shear the wings off as he landed. That's his best bet for walking away from a crash up here."

"Janet, I'll take the pack. You lead the way since you seem to know what you're doing," Ben said.

"Okay."

The slope was steep and slippery, with a thick covering of pine and fir needles. It made rough walking. They had been climbing for about twenty minutes when Janet called a break. Something was bothering her, but she couldn't quite put her finger on what it was. When Jim started to light a cigarette, she realized what it was and knocked the lighter from his hand.

"What the hell?"

"Gasoline. It's faint, but it's there."

"You're right," Don agreed, sniffing the air.

"The wreckage should be fairly close. Let's spread out and work our way toward the top," Janet said.

"Keep your guns handy," Ben said. "If it is Yaeger and that bunch and they aren't dead or hurt, they could be dangerous."

Janet nodded as they separated and slipped her .38 from her belt to the pocket of her jacket where she could keep her hand on it. The smell of gasoline grew stronger as the trees grew sparser and Janet knew that her guess had been correct. She caught a flash of metal through the trees and whistled to the others.

Lady Luck had ridden part way with Ray Lawton. He had found his trees, two Douglas firs on the edge of a clearing, but he hadn't been able to get low enough. He had hit them about fifty feet above the ground.

The wings had sheared off, but the control cables had opened one side of the plane like a string on a box of oatmeal. One of the wings was caught in the tree limbs, hanging like a giant Christmas tree ornament. The other wing had dragged behind the fuselage like a sea anchor. The fuselage had knocked down some smaller trees and had come to a sudden fatal stop against an outcropping of rock.

Janet felt the sting of tears in her eyes and angrily brushed them away. "Good try. Damned good try." She saluted the crumpled figure in the pilot's seat.

"He's dead," Janet said as the others joined her. "I think his neck is broken."

"That's Lawton," Don said, peering into what was left of the cockpit. "There's someone in the back seat. I think he's alive."

"Be careful," Janet warned as Don and Ben struggled to remove the man from the wreckage. "There's a lot of gasoline around."

Janet helped Jim spread a blanket on the ground. She knew that the man was Lacey when she saw the bandaged hand.

"His leg is broken just above the knee. There's blood all over him from somewhere," Ben said as they lowered Lacey onto the blanket.

"He's been shot in the chest."

"You're right, Janet. Don, take a look around," Ben ordered.

"Try not to disturb anything," Janet added. "There may be tracks Jim and I can follow."

Lacey was groaning and mumbling as Janet tried to staunch the flow of blood from his chest. His eyes flickered open. "You … here?"

"Shhh, don't talk. We'll try to help you."

"No use ... couldn't walk ... Richards shot me ... Yaeger's orders ... bastards."

Lacey gave a cry of pain. Blood gushed out of his mouth over Janet's hands. His breathing stopped.

Janet jumped up, ran a few steps, and was violently ill. She couldn't seem to stop retching. Every time she drew a breath, the smell of Lacey's blood filled her nostrils until she seemed to taste it. Suddenly it was all mixed up with seeing the gunshot wounds in David's body and old Sam shot in the back.

"Janet, give me your hands," Jim ordered. He used a strip torn from the sheet and water from the canteen to wash away the blood. As her heaving subsided, he led her farther away from the plane and bathed her face. "There, that's better. Come on and walk with me for a minute."

Jim guided her through the trees until they were well away from the plane and the air smelled fresh and sweet. He put his arms around her and hugged her briefly.

"Don't think about any of it for a minute. Just sit down and look at the trees and the sky and see the beauty."

"Thanks, Jim. I'm okay now. I'm sorry I let it get to me."

"Don't apologize. You weren't the only one to lose your breakfast."

Janet wasn't aware that she was crying until Jim touched her cheek.

"I'm sorry. I can't seem to stop. There has just been so much pointless death. Here are two more wasted lives. Lawton made such a damned good effort, yet he died while those other two scum walked away. Even Lacey deserved better than being shot like an injured animal. Do I sound ridiculous?"

Jim reached out and took Janet's hand. "No, hon. You sound like a mighty tough little gal who has had far too much death to deal with, and yet can still appreciate a gallant effort from a fellow pilot and have compassion for human frailty."

"Maybe. It just seems like a contradiction to shed tears over the death of the man who killed Sam and wanted to kill me."

"Janet, my dear, you ought to know by now that the whole human race is just one contradiction after another."

Janet gave a fleeting smile and sighed. "That's true. Why should I be any different?" She stood up and took a deep breath. "I'm all right now. Come on. I've got lots to do besides play philosopher on the mountain top."

Ben and Don had placed Lacey's blanket-wrapped body back into the plane and had covered Ray Lawton with another blanket. They were in the process of blocking up the openings with pieces from the plane and anything else they could find to give some protection from wild animals. They both looked a little pale.

"Jim, take a look at this box. Don found it about fifty yards down the other side of the mountain."

The only thing missing from the box, which Janet had last seen in her spare bedroom, was the jeweler's case containing the copy of the Gallina necklace.

"No reason to leave the rest of the artifacts here," Jim said, fitting the box into one pack. "What do we do now?"

Ben shrugged. "I don't think there is much to be gained by trying to follow Yaeger and Richards. Their tracks clearly head in the opposite direction from the cabin. They will either make it out or they won't. Realistically, we need more manpower to conduct any kind of a search."

"True," Janet agreed. "We're not equipped for hiking unfamiliar mountains in the cold. Jim doesn't need any more exertion than it takes to get back to the cabin."

The men agreed with Janet. They took one last look around, then headed down the mountain. The cabin was a welcome haven when they stumbled in the door.

Each one took a turn with plenty of soap and water, trying to scrub away the smell of blood and death. Later, with several cups of coffee under their belts, they ate cheese and crackers and shared pork and beans out of a can. Then the four of them stretched out on the rug in front of the fireplace.

"This changes things, doesn't it?" Janet asked. "In what way?" Ben said.

"It doesn't seem necessary for me to hike out to Sam's cabin. Can't we all go back together? I'd welcome a hot bath and a night in my own bed."

"Sounds all right to me," Ben answered. "I don't expect to see Richards or Yaeger for a long time. However, I do think that one of us should stay with you."

Everyone got quiet, either drowsing or lost in thought. Janet's mind was busy and she started a train of thought which prompted an unsuppressible giggle.

"Lord, lady, if there is anything funny about all of this, please tell me," Don said.

"I just got to thinking about the past few weeks from a writer's point of view. What a plot. Moments of high drama, danger, and intrigue separated by eating binges, punctuated with gallons of coffee and hundreds of cigarettes. A librarian wouldn't know whether to catalog it under food or fiction. Goodness knows, no one would ever mistake it for fact."

The three men laughed.

"One of the things which you have to get used to about Janet is that she has a weird sense of humor which surfaces at the most unexpected moments," Jim said.

"I seem to remember that you laugh at bizarre and inappropriate moments, dear," Janet countered.

Ben sat up. "Janet, you fascinate me. You have a strange assortment of skills and knowledge for a historian, or what ever you are. Would you care to enlighten me about your background?"

"No great mystery. I grew up in all kinds of out-of-the-way places. Old Sam taught me woodscraft and tracking. Jim got me interested in history and archaeology. From there it was a short trip into backpacking, mountain climbing, and survival training. David and I were interested in martial arts. We took judo and karate from an instructor who had also trained Recon Marines. He was also a pilot in the Civil Air Patrol, and David and I ended up in a rough-terrain search and rescue group.

"Later David and I took *bo* training, the Japanese art of staff fighting, and kendo, the equivalent of fencing or sword fighting. Aside from that, I've always been a voracious reader, had a vivid imagination, tremendous curiosity, and an excellent memory. I love mysteries, and spend hours day-dreaming about how I would handle various situations."

Don and Ben continued to question Janet as they readied themselves for the trek to the Jeep.

In one way, Janet regretted leaving the cabin and its beautiful surroundings, but she was glad to be headed toward a few more creature comforts. She gave one fleeting thought to the secret behind the waterfall and promised herself that she would be back.

The trip to the Lodge was uneventful. By late afternoon they were being warmly greeted by Hank and Maggie. Janet left the others to fill the McVeys in on the events of the day and headed home, promising to return for supper.

After a hot shower and a change of clothes, Janet arrived back at the Lodge to find Don and Maggie in the midst of preparing a feast. They refused her offer of help. Jim was asleep in a back bedroom. Hank and Ben were in Hank's office where Ben was on the telephone. Janet felt left out for the moment.

She wandered into the parlor and sat down at the piano. Her music had always been an emotional outlet for her. She began to play out her feelings about Sam and Dan'l, Jim and Ginny, and even Lacey and Ray Lawton. Finally, as she played the strangely haunting harmonies of David's favorite, "Rhapsody in Blue," she seemed to feel David standing behind her with his hands resting lightly on her shoulders as he had done countless times. She ended with a sense of peace, wholeness, and a healthy appetite.

Chapter 19

Later the same evening, Janet and Ben sat in front of the potbellied stove in the log house sipping spiced tea.

"Don't expect a Perry Mason drama, Janet. With Lacey's death, the inquest will be fairly short and to the point. By this time tomorrow evening you will be in a hotel room in San Francisco."

"You have no idea how little that appeals to me. I have an intense dislike for large cities and crowds of people. I used to go months at a time without ever setting foot in Dallas."

"I wouldn't have picked you as a people-hater."

"I'm not really. I like people in small groups or individually. I can't abide chit-chat or social games. I like people who can be themselves and feel comfortable with silence as well as conversation. I loathe people whose lives revolve around what wine to have with dinner, the latest gossip, who won the last football game, or what shade of lipstick is 'in' this year. There is so much more to life than that."

"Great big cities give me the feeling of being in the middle of an ant hill which someone has stirred with a stick. Everyone is dashing madly about with no apparent purpose other than making enough money to keep up with the payments on things they don't really want or need but have bought because they have let themselves be brainwashed to believe that they aren't real people without them."

"Cynicism, Janet?" Ben asked quietly.

"No, garbage. I'm just talking garbage, Ben. Put it down to mental, emotional and physical exhaustion and the last several months. Maybe I need to get away from here for a while.

"Down deep I know that every one has a dream and who's to say that the dream of owning a designer dress or a shiny new car is any less valid than my dream of owning a secluded ranch in New Mexico? I think I'd better go to bed before I get really disgusting. I'm sorry for blowing off like that."

The boat ride down the Rogue would have been pure delight if it had been for a different purpose. When Jim and Janet stepped onto the dock in Gold Beach, what small pleasure Janet had felt went out of the day. She was shaken by the open hostility of the fishermen who were standing around.

Sheriff Gates met them. Janet was even more appalled during the short drive to his office. The expressions on the faces of the townspeople they passed ranged from contempt to outright hate.

"I'm sorry, Janet," Sheriff Gates apologized. "They all loved Sam. Owen leaked the information about you to a few gossips, and a small town being what it is ..."

"They all think I killed Sam for his money."

"I'm afraid so. Don't judge them harshly. They only know what Owen has told them. They'll be ashamed of themselves soon enough. We've issued a warrant for the arrest of Richards, and I intend to arrest Owen when he reports for duty this morning."

"But won't that ruin all of Jim's work?"

"We hope not. Ben Fischer and I came to an agreement over the phone last night. We can't allow Richards to go free to kill again. We don't intend to bring the black market into it. I think Jim is in a strong enough position to survive."

Ted Nichols was waiting when they pulled up in front of the sheriff's office. He gave Jim and Janet a quick greeting, then turned urgently to Sheriff Gates.

"Owen didn't show up this morning. We checked his apartment and nothing appears to be missing. His neighbors claim that they heard him leave with someone just after midnight."

The sheriff was busy issuing orders right up until the time of the inquest.

Ben's prediction that the inquest would lack drama was wrong. Janet hadn't expected a jury or spectators. By the time the inquest was finished, she felt certain that a lot of rules had been broken, or at least badly bent. The hearing did far more than just establish the cause of Samuel Maxwell Donnelly's death. Janet knew that Sheriff Gates had exceeded the scope of the usual inquest procedures to make certain that there was no doubt about her innocence in the matter.

Janet was very uncomfortable during her testimony. Up to that point no one knew anything except the vicious gossip spread by Lloyd Owen. The expressions on the faces of the jury and spectators seemed to say that she had been tried and convicted, and they were eager to carry out an execution. Janet almost felt guilty.

It was with a great deal of relief that Janet saw the crowd's mood begin to change during the testimony of other witnesses. By the end of the proceedings, Sheriff Gates had made certain that everyone knew that Old Sam had been murdered by Edward Earl Lacey, who in turn had been murdered by Duncan "Duke" Richards, and that ex-deputy Lloyd Owen was wanted as an accessory.

Janet was surprised at how well the sheriff had covered all the bases when he mentioned they were concerned for the welfare of an anthropologist named Brownell who might have been on board the crashed airplane and possibly kidnapped by Richards. He added, however, that Brownell had probably left the plane when it refueled.

The McVeys were waiting outside as Jim and Janet came out with the sheriff. Ben and Don had disappeared. Hank passed along the message that they had business to take care of and would be in touch soon.

A crowd rapidly gathered around Janet and Jim. There were a few who were merely curious, many who were genuinely ashamed of their previous hostility and wanted to make amends, and one or two who eyed Janet with barely hidden suspicion.

They are the type who will righteously quote, "where there is smoke, there is fire," Janet thought, *and believe to their dying day that I was somehow involved.* All in all, though, Janet thought the townspeople were a pleasant enough cross-section of humanity.

Jim took a lot of good-natured kidding about his measles. It was obvious that he was tired and needed to be at home in bed, so Janet asked Hank to drive her to the landing strip where a chartered plane was waiting to fly her to San Francisco. She wanted to return upriver to the log house and retreat from the world for a while, but she would have to meet with Sam's attorney sometime and might as well get it behind her. Jim reminded her that with Richards and Owen on the loose, the initial reason for the trip was still valid.

She barely listened to the conversation between Jim, Maggie, and Hank during the drive to the landing strip. The only thing which registered was Maggie's instructions to give Fanny and Logan her love. Janet had no idea who Fanny was.

Janet was suffering from culture shock by the time the plane landed at the small airport at the edge of the city. She thanked the pilot and made arrangements to meet him the following week for the return flight.

Janet looked around for Logan Stuart, Sam's attorney. She shuddered at the sights and sounds of civilization as she walked toward the dapper little man who was smiling at her.

"I know. Terrible, isn't it?" he laughed. "A week with Hank and Maggie and I feel the same. I'm Logan Stuart, Mrs. Manning."

"Call me Janet, please," Janet said, feeling an instant rapport as they shook hands.

"If you'll call me Logan," he said, taking her suitcase and guiding her toward his ancient Rolls Royce. "I hope you won't be offended, Janet, but knowing how much you meant to Sam, Fanny and I couldn't bear the thought of you staying in a hotel. We want you to stay with us. After all, you are almost family."

"Why do I get the feeling that you were more than Sam's attorney?"

"Why bless you, child, don't you know? Sam Donnelly was my uncle. My mother was Sam's younger sister. Sam and my father grew up together and were as close as brothers. Uncle Max — he refused to be called Uncle Sam — was my boyhood idol."

"But I thought Sam was all alone, that he didn't have any family after his wife and daughter died."

"I can see that I have a great deal to tell you about Uncle Max," Logan said.

"I'm going to hold you to that. I've spent the last several months knowing only part of the story about everything that has happened to me. My life is so full of loose ends I could knit a sweater from them."

"Maybe Fanny and I can change some of that for you," Logan said as he turned into a driveway flanked by massive pillars.

The long driveway ended in a circle in front of a house which looked as if it belonged in the antebellum South instead of present-day California. In the twilight it was impossible to see all of the architectural details, but the overall effect was staggering.

"Oh, my." Janet gasped, glancing down at her faded blue jeans and flannel shirt, wondering how the high-class mistress of such a mansion would greet her.

Logan let out a gleeful chuckle. "I know, my dear. I've lived here nearly all my life and I still expect to see Scarlet O'Hara come flying down the steps every time I drive up. Don't let it overwhelm you. It's a delightfully absurd house. Ah ... here's Fanny."

"But ... but she looks just like Maggie!" Janet sputtered.

And so she did, a Maggie of a decade earlier. Her compact little figure was encased in jeans with shirt tails flying as she ran down the steps to welcome Janet.

"Janet, my dear, how glad we are to have you here," she bubbled. "Did you have a good flight?"

"Now, Fanny, the poor girl is in a state of shock. I'm afraid that no one bothered to tell her about us."

An hour later Janet was seated in the large, old-fashioned kitchen while Fanny dished up a feast amidst a continuous flow of words.

"So you see, Janet, Logan's parents brought him to Oregon every summer to spend a few weeks with Sam. After his parents died when he was nineteen, Logan practically lived there until we were married the following year and moved here to his family home. I was living with Maggie and Hank then. That's where we met. Maggie is my older sister. There are fifteen years between us, but everyone says that we're alike."

"I see that Fanny is filling you in on the family history," Logan said as he joined them.

"Yes. I think I'm beginning to put it all together. I'm glad Sam wasn't as alone as I thought he was."

"Janet," Logan said, "Sam was never meant to be a city dweller. He was born a hundred years too late. He should have been a frontier doctor or a mountain man. His heart was always in the wilderness, even before his wife died. But he loved his family and we all saw him as often as we could. I know, though, that he was happiest on some mountain trail with Dan'l by his side.

"As for Julia, the life he provided for her was the most loving and unselfish act he ever did. He gave her far more by leaving her in the care of knowledgeable and loving people than he could have done by caring for her himself.

"Sam may have thought that he was hiding out from life, but we know differently. He doctored the loggers and the Indians and took every youngster in the area under his wing. He lived the life he was suited for, and I don't think he ever realized just how much he did for others. Anyway, we all protected his privacy and never let it be known that us big-city rich folks were his relatives."

"But don't you resent Sam making me his heir? It seems like his money should go to you and your sons."

"We've always had an abundance of this world's goods, but even so, Sam provided generously for each of us years ago. We have no basis for complaint.

"Sam told me fifteen years ago that you were everything he would have wanted a child of his to be. He never changed his mind. Though you weren't aware of it, you brought a great deal of happiness and satisfaction into his life. I don't know that it is possible or necessary to try to explain how Sam felt about you or why he felt that way. He did and it filled an empty place in his life. He wanted you to be his heir and none of us have any quarrel with that. We are happy that you brought such joy to Sam."

Later they had coffee in a cozy room with book-lined walls and deep, comfortable chairs. Fanny and Logan asked Janet to tell them about her last visit with Sam and Dan'l. In turn they told Janet of their quick trip to Oregon for the simple service when Sam had been laid to rest beside Dan'l on the hilltop behind his cabin.

"I hope you understand why I wasn't there," Janet said.

"Of course, dear. Maggie and Hank explained part of the situation, and Mr. Fischer and Mr. Ross explained the rest. After we understood, we didn't even spend the night at the Lodge. It seemed best not to complicate matters with our presence," Fanny answered.

The following few days were filled with business as Logan explained the extent of Janet's inheritance and the technicalities involved in dealing with the laws in two states.

"It will take awhile for everything to be settled so that you have full control of the estate. However, there is money set aside for your use now," Logan told her.

"What I'd really like for you to do is to accept a limited power of attorney from me and continue to manage the estate as you did for Sam, at least until my other affairs are in order. Some cash would be welcome. I don't have much because the insurance company won't pay off on David's policy right now."

"How much do you need?"

"I have enough to live on for the next several months, but our home in Texas was vandalized right after I left and I need to have it repaired. The other thing may have to wait until the estate is settled. David and I were about to buy a ranch in New Mexico when he was killed. I still want it, but I don't know how much longer it will be on the market."

"I think we can handle both of those things without any problem if you will tell me who to contact," Logan said. "Now, tomorrow I would like to drive you out to see Sam's estate. It's really something."

"Logan, I hope you will understand when I say that I would rather not see it right now. None of this is real to me yet. I can't afford to start thinking about estates and money and all of this until I find out why David was murdered and get my life back on track."

"We do understand, dear," Fanny said. "And now that your business is finished, I intend to show you San Francisco."

Fanny and Janet spent the next two days sightseeing and shopping. They rode the cable cars and had lunch one day on Fisherman's Wharf and the next day in Chinatown. Janet controlled her desire to find the San Francisco office of Frederick Bryce's import-export business. She knew that if Richards and Yaeger had gotten out of the mountains, she couldn't run the risk of putting herself and Fanny and Logan into danger by being seen.

The only difficult time in her stay came the evening she telephoned her parents to try to explain Sam's murder and her inheritance. She finally promised to write a long letter, knowing that even then she couldn't tell the whole story. They were confused and concerned when she ended the conversation, but at least they wouldn't be taken by surprise when the news made its way to Texas.

At the end of the week, Janet knew that she had two wonderful friends in Fanny and Logan, and looked forward to seeing them again.

It was raining when the small plane landed at Gold Beach. Janet dreaded the prospect of a wet boat ride up the Rogue. She was delighted when she saw Jim and his Jeep waiting for her.

They spent an hour prowling through the stores and making a few purchases. Jim laughed himself into a coughing fit when Janet purchased four ice-cube trays and a styrofoam ice bucket.

"But Janet, you don't have a refrigerator."

"Oh yes, I do. It's called the great out-of-doors. It should be cold enough at night soon to freeze water."

"But why?"

"Because I hate coffee.'"

Jim stared at her in disbelief. "You drink gallons of it. How can you say you hate it?"

"I only drink it because it's always there and it's what everyone else likes. I don't mind a cup occasionally, but I lust after iced tea. Sometimes I like hot tea, but my real passion, heat wave or blizzard, is iced tea. And, by golly, I'm going to have it.'"

Jim laughed until other people in the store turned to stare.

"What do you do when you're backpacking?"

"Suffer. Someday, some brilliant, wonderful person will invent a miniature portable ice machine that I can tuck into the side pocket of my pack. I'll erect a statue in his or her honor."

"Woman, you're crazy."

"Probably, but I intend to enjoy iced tea all winter if the weather will cooperate. Here's to a long cold winter."

After a late lunch, Jim and Janet visited the sheriff's office to pick up her rifle and get the latest news.

Sheriff Gates was out, but Ted Nichols told them there was still no word of Richards or Owen.

"They brought the bodies of Lacey and Lawton out by helicopter. Ben Fischer notified us that Amos Yaeger is back in his San Francisco office conducting business as usual," Ted continued.

"Where does that leave me?" Janet asked. "Continually looking over my shoulder?"

"No. We're certain that neither Richards nor Owen is in this area. We're keeping watch on the river and the road, so it is unlikely either one could slip back in. I don't think you have anything to worry about. Caution is always wise, though."

"It looks as if you have nothing more exciting in store than the drive home," Jim said.

"That suits me. I would welcome a couple of peaceful months to spend filling a ream of paper with words. I have decided to get serious about finishing the Marcos de Niza book."

"I'm all for that."

As they waved goodbye to Ted and turned onto the river road, Janet realized there was something different about Jim.

"Your spots are gone."

Jim glanced at Janet and snarled in mock ferocity. "Don't ever mention spots to me again, J. W. Manning, or I'll hurl your bruised and battered body from the top of Gobbler's Knob."

"Oh please, please, kind sir, anything but that."

"I might be persuaded to forget that you mentioned the unmentionable if you promise to ply me with huckleberry pie."

"I've always heard that every man has his price. I certainly know what yours is."

---

258 Florence Wagner McClain

The drive, even in the rain, was pleasant as the road climbed high above the river and crossed the crest of Gobbler's Knob. Jim and Janet bantered back and forth for a few miles and then Janet told him about her week with Fanny and Logan Stuart and the stories they had told her about Sam.

"It's hard to believe that I knew Sam all of my life and never had any idea about his family or his wealth. I'm even more certain now about the source of the money which paid for my education and the trust fund which provides a comfortable income for me now. My parents were always rather vague about it and I never could understand exactly where it came from."

The two of them lapsed into silence. Each one had a lot to think about. Somewhere along the way Janet dozed off and didn't awaken until Jim stopped the Jeep in front of the log house. Janet was surprised to see lights on and smoke coming from the chimney. She gathered her purchases and made a dash through the rain. Jim was directly behind her, carrying her suitcase. The house was warm and cheery, filled with good smells. Janet's vision blurred as she placed her parcels on the kitchen counter.

"Hey, no tears, Janet. The only tears to be shed tonight are mine if you don't invite me to dinner. Maggie made a pot of her famous venison stew and left biscuits in the warming oven. I think there is even a huckleberry pie for dessert."

Janet looked at the pie, which had one missing piece, and groaned. "Oh, no. This is where I came in," she laughed.

Jim shooed her out of the kitchen to unpack while he set the table and finished the preparations for supper.

During the meal, Janet studied Jim. He was unusually quiet. When he had finished his second piece of pie, she questioned him.

"Okay, what is it that you aren't telling me?"

"What makes you ask a question like that?" he said evasively.

"Don't play games with me. I'm as deep in this as you are. The worst thing you can do to me is to keep things from me. Now what is it?"

Jim reluctantly produced a crumpled piece of paper from his pocket. "This was left in the Jeep in Gold Beach today."

Janet smoothed the creased paper and read the crudely printed message: BUSINESS AS USUAL. COOS BAY. 19.

"What does this mean?"

"I'm supposed to pick up a shipment of artifacts in Coos Bay on the nineteenth, tomorrow."

"Surely you're not going. It could be a trap."

"I have to go. If there is any hope of salvaging any part of this operation and getting Yaeger, I can't ignore it."

"I don't like this, Jim. This note means there is someone else in the area who is involved."

"It's unlikely. Remember, Janet, that entirely different people bring the artifacts to me, people who've never met Lacey or Richards. They are probably just being cautious because of all the publicity. It won't be the first time I've made the pick-up in Coos Bay."

"At least get in touch with Ben and let him know, or call Sheriff Gates. Tell them I am going with you."

"You aren't going anywhere near Coos Bay. I won't even discuss it. I doubt that I can get in touch with Ben tonight, but I'll stop at the sheriff's office on my way through Gold Beach tomorrow. I just don't think there is any reason to be concerned."

"Then why won't you let me go with you?"

"Because you are safe here. Until Richards and Owen are caught, this is where you are going to stay."

Janet was unhappy about the situation, but Jim was adamant in his refusal to allow her to go with him. She wasn't convinced that the trip would be as safe for Jim as he seemed to believe.

There are just too many unknowns, Janet thought. *Where are Richards and Owen? Does Yaeger still trust Jim, or is this his way of setting him up to be killed? Exactly where do I fit in now? Will Richards make another try for me?*

Lordy, this sounds like a soap opera. Tune in tomorrow, same time, same station, for the answers to these and other questions: will a poor little rich girl from a logging camp in Oregon find happiness as a writer and a junior G-man? Well, I'm going to give it a damn good try, Janet concluded.

After Jim left, she cleaned her two rifles and her revolver, loaded them, and put extra ammunition close at hand. Just before she went to bed, she wedged chairs under the knobs of both outside doors.

Chapter 20

Jim's trip to Coos Bay turned out to be routine. The artifacts had been left in the usual place and there was no one around. Jim hadn't been able to reach Ben Fischer. The weeks passed, but neither Janet nor Jim heard from Ben and Don.

As Thanksgiving approached, Janet began to spend more time pacing the floor talking to herself. She made good progress on her book and continued to keep up with the life and times of Mark Jamison through the crystal ball. She had responded to two frantic letters from her mother and one newsy note from Fanny Stuart. The daily rain precluded hiking, and Jim and the McVeys were busy with their own pursuits. Janet was bored.

"Okay, I'm crazy," she said aloud. "I ought to be happy that things are dull. I should be enjoying the peace and quiet." But she had tasted the thrill of high adventure and she missed the excitement, the rushes of adrenalin, the pitting of her wits against man and nature.

Part of her frustration was due to not being any nearer to knowing who had killed David and his connection with the black market. Even the knowledge that Ben Fischer and Don Ross were pursuing the connection and would contact her as soon as they had any information didn't help. She wanted to do something herself.

Two days before Thanksgiving, the rain stopped. The sunny, beautiful day prompted Janet to do something she had been avoiding. She drove to the Lodge to tell Maggie where she would be. Maggie was cooking.

"Looks as if you're expecting a crowd. It smells wonderful in here."

"Hello, dear. Yes, there will be a crowd. So few families live here the year around that we have a community Thanksgiving dinner. We have a lot of fun. I hope you are planning to join us."

"I'd love to. I'm ready for some social life. What can I bring?"

"Just yourself. If years past are any indication, we'll have food for twenty extra."

"Maggie, I'm going up to Sam's cabin. I thought someone ought to know. If it starts raining again, I may stay overnight. 1 don't want anyone to panic if I'm not home."

"Will you be all right, dear? Would you like for Hank or me to go with you?"

"I'll be fine. I just dislike the thought of going through Sam's personal belongings. We all have things we never intend for anyone else to see or read, and Sam was such a private person. I know it has to be done, though. There are things which Fanny and Logan ought to have — pictures, mementoes, family things which might be meaningless to me but treasures to them."

Maggie sat down at the table across from Janet. "Are you sure you want to do this right now? Hank and I went down while you and Jim were at our cabin and took care of the food and other things which needed immediate attention. The rest of it will wait awhile longer."

"There isn't any point in letting it wait. Besides, I need a change of scene and some exercise."

Sam's cabin was in a beautiful setting halfway up the slope of a small mountain, yet protected from the winter storms. There was a visual feast of mountains and stately fir and pine trees in every direction. Janet caught the sparkle of sunlight reflecting off the river down the slope from the cabin.

Before she went inside, she followed the path which led to the crest of the mountain. This had been Sam's favorite place to sit and look and smoke his pipe and talk to Dan'l. He had made a bench from a split log and it was polished smooth from forty years of use. Janet sat on Sam's bench and looked at the too-neat mounds. The longer she sat, the happier and more at peace she felt.

"I won't mourn for you, Samuel Donnelly. I understand so much about you now. You would have hated to live so long that you couldn't roam the mountains with Dan'l at your side.

"You left this life with one last adventure. Died with your boots on in the best tradition of the old frontiersman you were. You and Dan'l are both free now to roam your mountains and pan your gold and, if there is any justice in the universe, to eat all the store-bought candy you want. And I'm free, too. And for that, Samuel Donnelly, I thank you."

Janet sat a few minutes longer in silence, then went down the slope to the cabin. Sam's cabin was every bit as neat, colorful, and surprising as Sam had been. The living room was dominated by a natural stone fireplace flanked by bookcases. The highly polished hardwood floor was ornamented with a priceless Persian rug. The room was furnished, from massive rocker to the ornately carved sideboard, with fine antiques.

Sam, you old fraud, Janet thought. *I expected a plain mountain cabin and here is a gracious home filled with some of the most beautiful things I have ever seen.*

The other rooms were equally beautiful. The two bedroom were furnished with heavily carved four-poster beds with matching armoires and dressers which belonged in a museum. The study had book-lined walls and a beautiful rolltop desk. The dining area was occupied by a round-oak pedestal table with claw feet. There were six matching chairs. The kitchen was equipped with a gorgeously ornate wood cookstove. The cabinets were filled with fine antique china and crystal.

"If this is the cabin you have left to me, Sam, my imagination can't begin to conceive of what wonders exist on your estate," Janet whispered. "I'm just beginning to have a little glimmer of what it means to be wealthy."

Janet made a second circuit of the house, trying to imagine how Sam had managed to bring all of these things to his cabin, and done it without being seen. It was beyond her imagination.

There was nothing in the cabin which she wanted to change. Even Sam's rack of pipes was a thing of beauty and she knew she would leave it on the little table within easy reach of his rocking chair. Dan'l's cushion in front of the fireplace was as much a part of the decor as the fine furniture. Sam's idea of beauty and comfort was so in harmony with hers that she decided to leave the cabin essentially unchanged.

Janet wasn't in the mood to sort through Sam's personal papers. Instead she kindled a small fire in the fireplace, lit one of the kerosene lamps, and scanned the titles of the books in Sam's library. There were medical books and a wide assortment of the classics, books on history and archeology, geology and botany. There were mysteries and volumes of poetry, westerns, and how-to books on every subject from wilderness survival to cheese-making.

In the study, the shelves held volumes of a different sort. The subjects were predominantly philosophy, religion, strange and unusual experiences, the mind, reincarnation, and psychic phenomena. There were a few volumes which seemed more worn than others. Thumbing through, Janet saw that there were notations in the margins in Sam's handwriting and various passages had been underlined. Janet carried these into the living room and curled up in Sam's rocker to examine them more closely.

Three of the books seemed to contain the particular type of information Janet wanted. She returned the other books to their shelf. She felt a deep sense of excitement as she placed the three volumes in her day-pack and doused the fire. She took one more look around, carefully locked the door, and hurried down the river trail.

Janet had not found anything to explain to her satisfaction the crystal ball and the strange communications with Mark Jamison. She had asked herself countless times why Mark's face had appeared and how and why the communications took place. She could no longer deny that Mark had become very important to her. She had been careful not to repeat the obsessive actions which had taken place while she was hiding out with Jim, but there was a bond between herself and Mark which she had never experienced with another human being. Aside from that, she admired him as a person.

There was a strength of character in Mark that was quite attractive, but the attribute which fascinated Janet the most was the all-encompassing joy which he seemed to have in his work. He was a man who was doing exactly was he was best suited to do, with a confidence in himself which offered no apologies for being creative and imaginative in a field where those qualities were not always considered assets.

Janet was certain of one thing. Mark Jamison was a person she wanted to know face-to-face, and she believed that he was meant to be an important part of her life in some way. Mark held no romantic attraction for her. The attractions were the closeness of the mental bond and the excitement of finding a person who shared her interests and active imagination.

Janet spent the remainder of the afternoon and all of the following day devouring Sam's books. A whole new world of understanding began to unfold as she read of alpha and theta brain waves and their connections with creativity, learning, dreams, memory, mental control of physiological functions, and psychic abilities. It all began to seem logical and reasonable, and Sam's marginal notations cleared up many questions which might otherwise have gone unanswered.

The crystal ball, she learned, was not a mystical object. It was simply a focal point, a screen upon which the alpha visions of her mind were projected. Had the experience not happened with the crystal ball, it might just as easily have occurred with a window pane, a bowl of water, or totally within the visual imagery of her own mind.

Sam's book labeled as "psychic" so many of the characteristics which made her an excellent researcher that she could not refute the label, particularly when she understood "psychic" to mean only that she was expressing some of the mental potentials which were a legacy to mankind as a whole and not placing herself in the category of fortune teller or tea-leaf reader.

Janet was excited. The gateway to a whole new level of knowing and expressing herself had been thrown wide open. Over and over the writers and Sam's notes emphasized the same points: a human being is limited only by the limitations he or she accepts; human beings are unlimited spirits whose whole reason for existence is to understand and live an unlimited life. Being psychic wasn't strange and weird. Being psychic, coupled with good judgment and a large dash of common sense, was an enhancement of every facet of day-to-day living.

On Thanksgiving morning, Janet reluctantly tore herself away from Sam's books. She was filled with a sense of anticipation, as if this was going to be a very important day. *I know something of great personal significance is going to happen today*, Janet thought. *What a strange feeling. Almost, if I dare to use the term, psychic.*

Janet was tired of wearing jeans but knew that anything too dressy would be inappropriate. Most of the guests would be arriving by boat, horseback, or on foot. She compromised and chose a softly gathered wool skirt and a matching sweater in a shade of deep rose which was particularly attractive with her coloring.

For the first time in many months, Janet liked what she saw in the mirror. The tension lines were almost gone from her face and she had a glow of excitement. The rose sweater and matching lipstick brought out the natural pink of her cheeks and made her eyes look more brown than hazel. Her shining hair curled softly around her face.

"Well, Janet," she said to her image, "you're almost pretty. You're even a little thinner." She eyed her sweater-clad figure critically.

There were about seventy people at the Lodge. Janet enjoyed renewing old acquaintances and making new ones. There was a great deal of laughter, but once in a while she noted a furtive tear or two when Sam Donnelly was mentioned. She refused to allow herself to dwell on the fact that this was her first Thanksgiving without David.

Some of the people were a little reserved in manner, but that changed when they saw the warm affection shown her by Jim and the McVeys. It wasn't long before Maggie shooed her out of the kitchen toward the piano in the parlor. Janet gathered a group to join in a singsong. Each one tried to out-do the other in thinking of ancient folksy songs. Soon the walls vibrated to the sounds of "The Old Oaken Bucket," "The Ship That Never Returned," and a score of equally obscure old tunes.

After a gigantic feast, nearly everyone gathered in the huge parlor. There was much joking, laughing, and groaning. Eventually the conversations took a more serious tone as people began discussing the news of the day. Janet was shocked to realize how totally out of touch with the rest of the world she had become.

"There could have been another Pearl Harbor and I wouldn't have known it," she whispered to Maggie. "I guess I need to subscribe to a newspaper."

An hour later, Jim found Janet getting a breath of fresh air on the front veranda. "Janet, could we slip away and go down to your place for the evening?"

"Sure, but give me a minute."

Janet knew that Jim wouldn't ask her to leave the celebration without good reason. She went inside to explain to Maggie and found that she had already prepared a basket of food for them. Janet was rapidly getting the idea that whatever event she had sensed that morning was about to occur.

Janet had walked to the Lodge, so she rode back to the log house with Jim. He was very quiet. A few sprinkles of rain fell and Janet resigned herself to another wet spell. The sober skies seemed to match Jim's mood.

"Janet, why don't you change out of your glad-rags while I stir up the fire and put some water on to heat," Jim said as they entered the house.

"Oh dear, is this going to be one of those ten-cups-of-coffee, two-packs-of-cigarettes nights?" Janet asked, not quite willing to relinquish the high spirits of the day.

"Yes, Janet. I'm afraid it is."

Jim's tone sent her hurrying into the bedroom to change. "Well, I might as well be comfortable in my misery," she grumbled as she rejected jeans in favor of her velvet robe and fleece-lined squaw boots.

"Iced tea or hot?" Jim called.

"Iced," Janet answered.

"Barbarian."

At least he hasn't totally lost his sense of humor, Janet told herself, *but it isn't very nice of him to tantalize me.* The temperatures hadn't been low enough at night for her great ice-making venture to be much of a success.

Jim grinned and proffered a large glass of iced tea when Janet entered the living room.

"I liberated a bucket of ice and a half gallon of tea from the Lodge refrigerator," he explained.

"Um. Nice man. Born thief, but nice." Janet settled into the Jolly Brown Giant. "Okay, Jim. Time to talk. What's going on?"

Jim didn't answer as he walked across to the chair where his jacket hung and removed something from the pocket. "There isn't an easy way to do this, Janet. Do you recognize this?"

Janet's hands were trembling as she reached for the small leather notebook marked with three gold initials.

"D.L.M. David Lee Manning. It's David's notebook. Where did you get it?"

"Ben Fischer and Don Ross. They'll be here short-ly. They drove in late last night and stayed at the Lodge."

"I didn't see them."

"No, dear. They wanted you to enjoy the day," Jim said, awkwardly patting Janet on the shoulder.

"They think they've found out something terrible about David, don't they? Well, whatever it is, they are wrong." Janet said emphatically.

There was the sound of footsteps on the porch. Jim opened the door for Ben and Don.

"No need to ask," Ben said, crossing to Janet. She realized then that she was clutching David's note-book against her chest with both hands.

"It was David's. I gave it to him. How did you get it?"

"That's a question I'll answer in a minute, Janet. First there are some questions that I have to ask you."

"Go ahead, Ben. I'm not afraid of the truth about David."

"You told us a few weeks ago that David's last job was for an import-export company in Houston. Was it Tri-Coastal International?"

"Yes. That's Frederick Bryce's company, isn't it?"

"Yes, Janet, it is. Now, what did David keep in this notebook?"

"Confidential information. Access codes and notes about whatever job he was on. I think most of it would have been meaningless to anyone but him. Now would you please tell me how you got his notebook and what is going on?"

Ben ignored Janet's question. "The notebook had only blank pages in it, except for one notation on the last page. However, there were some impressions on the first page following the ones which had been removed. We were able to bring them out enough to see that they were notations about some large, illegal financial transactions at Tri-Coastal which were well-hidden in their computer system."

"So you've assumed that David was involved."

"We don't really know what David was doing with the information, but it doesn't look good. You may have the key to the truth."

"I don't see how."

"Look at the last page in the notebook."

Janet opened the notebook. There, in his neat script, were the last words David had ever written.

"Janet — look in the mousehole."

Chapter 21

"Oh, my god. The mousehole! I never thought to look in the mousehole!"

Janet ignored the barrage of questions and the driving rain as she ran out of the door to her Toyota. She reached under the fender over the left rear tire and tugged at something.

"Janet, what in the hell are you doing?" Jim asked as he joined her, followed by Ben and Don.

"Don't you see?" Janet said through her tears and laughter, "I had the answers with me all the time. David made rubber plugs to close the hollow end of the crossmember here. There's a wire cylinder inside to hold our valuables when we're backpacking. One spring before David made the plugs, a mouse got in and built a nest. We called it our mousehole."

Janet extracted the plug and pulled out a wire cylinder containing a roll of papers. She shoved the papers inside her robe to protect them from the rain and replaced the cylinder and plug.

Back inside the house, Janet quickly scanned the papers, then triumphantly handed them to Ben. "There, there's your criminal. I told you that I knew my David."

The papers were a detailed journal which related David's day-by-day discoveries of Tri-Coastal's involvement in the laundering of money from the black market sales of artifacts. The journal began with David's trip to Houston and ended two days before his death.

"This is exactly what they were afraid David might have done. This is why they tore apart my house and office and followed me."

"Your faith in David was certainly justified," Jim said. "You have every right to be proud of him."

"That's very true, Janet," Don said, speaking for the first time since he had arrived. "With this information about the dummy corporations, someone with David's kind of expertise should be able to recreate most of his work."

"It may take several months to unravel the whole thing, but we couldn't do it at all without this information," Ben said.

"That's all fine and good, Ben, but you still owe me one answer. Where did you get David's notebook?"

"We found it in Earl Lacey's apartment in San Francisco when we searched it the day after the inquest."

"Lacey? How did he get it?"

"It was in his trophy collection along with these and the gun that killed your husband," Ben said, reaching into his pocket and withdrawing several items which he placed in Janet's hand.

Janet looked at the items in her hand. Numbly she slipped the billfold and wristwatch into the pocket of her robe. She gripped the wedding ring tightly as Ben's words finally registered.

"Earl Lacey killed David?"

"Yes."

"I wish that I had killed that bastard," Janet stated in a very calm, matter-of-fact manner. "I felt sorry for him up there on the mountain. Now I wish that I had been the one who shot him. At least he died like the animal he was.

"Was it Bryce or Yaeger who gave the order, Ben? No, it doesn't really matter. They both deserve to die.

"Well, fellows, every man has his price. What's yours?

"One million? Two million? I want them dead. If you won't do it, I will."

Jim grabbed Janet by the shoulders and shook her. "Stop talking like that! Stop it! You're not going to kill anyone!"

"Why shouldn't I?" she shouted, suddenly feeling the most awful anger she had ever known. "They kill whenever they want and what happens to them? Nothing. Look at this ring. Do you know what it says inside? 'Janet and David — forever.' Well, they killed my forever before it had barely begun. They made me a widow." She was beating her fists on Jim's chest. "Then they killed Sam and made me a rich widow. What good is money if it can't buy revenge?"

Janet felt as if she was about to explode from the rage which was seething inside her. She wanted to hurt and destroy.

Don grabbed Jim's hand as he drew back as if to slap her. "Janet damn you, you're not going to shame Sam and what he did for you by using his — "

"Of course she isn't," Don interrupted. "Now calm down, both of you."

Don put his arm around Janet and she wept into his shoulder. "Good lord, Jim. Even I know Janet better than that. Don't you understand that she is in a state of shock? Look at what she has been through in the past several months. After all this time she can finally put a name and a face to the man who killed her husband. Of course she is angry. Of course she is going to say things she doesn't mean. The two of you come in here and put her through the third degree and casually produce her husband's personal effects without warning. What did you expect her to do? Act like she was at a ladies' tea party? Damn it, man. Get your head out of your ass!"

The angry outburst from this usually quiet man left both Jim and Ben silent and shame-faced. Janet's anger subsided. She dropped to the couch, her head in her hands. There was an uneasy silence in the room.

After a few minutes, Janet spoke hesitantly. "Don is right, you know. I didn't know I had all of that rage bottled up inside. It's out now and I'm rational again. Just consider it a moment of temporary insanity."

Jim and Ben were full of apologies, but Janet hushed them and went into the bathroom to wash her face. She slipped into her bedroom and put David's things into the drawer of the bedside table and changed from her wet, muddy robe into jeans and a shirt.

"At least I know that David was killed because he was doing something important," Janet said, returning to the living room. "I don't know why that makes a difference, but it does. I never stopped believing in his honesty in spite of all of you."

Tension was thick in the room. None of the three men knew what to say or do.

"Ben, is there anything else you need to ask me?"

"Uh ... no ... I can't think of anything."

"There are some questions I would like to ask," Don said. "Was there anyone at Southwest Data Comm your husband might have confided in?"

"No. If I didn't know, you can be certain that he hadn't told anyone else. That's the way things were with us. I know what you're getting at, though. I don't know much about computer systems, but David once told me that sometimes there are very subtle warning devices programmed into systems to allow certain key people to know if their security has been breached. I suspect that he believed he had triggered such a warning or he wouldn't have made the records he did and left the message for me."

"How could they trace the breach to him?" Jim asked.

"I would guess that they checked out several people, considering how long it took them to decide on David. He would have been a suspect because of the work he had done for the company. It wouldn't have been difficult for them to find out about his interest in archaeology and the way he felt about pot-hunters," Janet said.

"I was hoping that we might find someone who had betrayed David to Bryce or Yaeger, perhaps someone at SDC, but it looks like your idea about the warning system is probably the way it happened," Don said. "We are grateful to you for the help you've given us."

"Yes, Janet. We are grateful to you and to David. Too many lives have been taken by these people, but I think this information will help us apprehend them before more lives are lost. I'm sorry this has been so rough on you and that I handled it so poorly," Ben said.

"It has been rough on me. I've been involved in three murders in less than a year. Nothing will ever make up for the loss of David and Sam, but I have learned some valuable lessons about myself."

"What, if you don't mind me asking?" Don said.

"I've learned to trust myself and my feelings about people. Also, all my life I have been involved in how-to lessons in safe surroundings. I learned a great deal about myself in some challenging situations while backpacking and mountain climbing, but this is something different. I've had to try out some of those how-to lessons and test some of my fantasies by handling some real, life-threatening situations. There is a part of me which has found it exciting and satisfying to explore my capabilities under fire."

"I think what Janet is trying to say," Jim said, grinning, "is that she has found out that she can be just as dangerous, devious, and foolhardy as the rest of us. Somehow that doesn't surprise me, Janet. I don't think you were ever meant to live a dull, routine life. Say, is anyone else hungry?"

"Famished," Janet admitted.

Janet was content for the moment to put aside her thoughts of David and Lacey and the others involved until she was alone. Jim, Ben, and Don needed assurance that she was going to be all right and she did her best to act as normally as possible. She had already promised herself a personal revenge, and she didn't want the three of them interfering.

The four of them sat down to the leftovers from Maggie's feast. The conversation ranged from humorous to serious. The more Janet learned about Ben and Don, the more she liked and respected them. She was pleased when they trusted her enough to be very open about their work. She had only the slightest twinge of conscience when she contemplated how useful that trust might be to her in the future.

They had just started on pie and coffee when Don started laughing and almost choked.

"What's wrong with you?" Ben asked, looking at his partner quizzically.

"It probably isn't as funny as it seems. The thought crossed my mind that we've just added another chapter to Janet's book — you know, her moments of high drama separated by food orgies. I looked at the way Jim is attacking his dessert and he looked like the perfect illustration for a chapter on 'Homicide and Huckleberry Pie.'"

Janet found herself laughing with the others, giving vent to the stresses of the day in laughter instead of tears. Two or three other titles were suggested, each more absurd than the last. They all felt better from a few moments of silliness. A short while later, Ben and Don prepared to leave. "Janet, if you will allow me, I'd like to take David's journal. It will be returned to you when all of this is over. Either Don or I will keep you informed of any new developments. It will probably take several months to have anything to report."

"Take it and put it to good use," Janet said. "One question. What about Richards and Owen?"

"There hasn't been any sign of either one. I don't think you'll have any trouble from them, but we would prefer that you stay in Agness through the winter."

"I plan to stay for several months."

"By the way," Ben added. "Roscoe Carrac is playing errand boy for Yaeger at the moment. He's Jim's contact for now."

Jim stayed behind when Ben and Don left. As soon as he and Janet were alone, he put his arms around her and held her close.

"Jan, I'm so sorry for getting angry at you tonight. Part of it was a reaction from my own guilt, because I have harbored the same feelings since Ginny's death. The rest was anger at you because you turned out to be human."

Janet drew back and looked questioningly at Jim.

"It started up there on the mountain," Jim explained, "when you saluted the courage and skill of Ray Lawton and showed compassion for Lacey. All you saw in Lacey was a human being in trouble. It didn't seem to matter that he was there because he was hunting you.

"In the weeks since then, I've thought a great deal about that and I've worked hard at trying to rid myself of the bitterness and hatred which has been eating at me. Then tonight — "

Janet placed a finger on Jim's lips. "Tonight you learned that putting people on pedestals is a very chancey thing — especially this person. I have feet of clay all the way up to my knees, and don't forget it."

She kissed him lightly on the lips. "Now, get out of here and let me get some work done. But don't stay away too long."

Janet spent a long time that night sitting in the Jolly Brown Giant, holding David's billfold, wristwatch, and wedding ring, and looking at the last words he had written to her.

Now she knew why David had died and who had killed him. The questions which had plagued her had answers. The story couldn't be publicized yet, but at least that self-righteous police detective in Dallas would know the truth. Perhaps it would make him a little more human.

I have kept the promise I made to myself, Janet thought. *I know why David was killed and who pulled the trigger. Whatever Jim and the others may think, though, I'm not finished with Yaeger and Bryce. Someday. somehow, I will have my revenge.* When Janet put David's things away, she slipped the matching gold band from her finger and placed it beside David's.

J anet spent the next few days catching up on all the things she had let slide, and did a great deal of thinking about her future. She composed a letter to David's parents, as Ben had given her permission to do, outlining as briefly as possible the events which had brought a solution to David's murder. Now that she had been away from them for a while, she could understand that their hostility toward her had been an expression of their grief. She hoped that, when they understood that David's work would help bring men to justice who had caused many other deaths, the knowledge would provide some small comfort.

Writing to her own parents was more difficult. When they put this information together with what she had already been forced to tell them, there was no way to minimize her involvement. She hoped they would have enough faith in her not to panic.

When Janet had these chores finished, she decided the time had come to tell the McVeys about the treasure behind their waterfall. She chose a day when she knew Jim would be busy elsewhere. Maggie and Hank greeted her warmly, but were mystified when Janet suggested that they go into Hank's office where they wouldn't be disturbed or overheard.

"I hope there's not a problem," Hank said.

"No, Hank. What I have to tell you is the stuff of dreams."

Janet described to them in detail the way in which she had made the discovery. "There were stacks of wooden boxes wrapped in many layers of heavy oiled paper. A few of the boxes had broken open. I could see some fine pieces of porcelain, many pieces of carved jade, and a few pieces of bronze. There appeared to be some jewelry. It was difficult to tell from a distance. One object stood out from all the others. It was a Buddha covered in gold.

"I wish I could put into words the feelings I had when I saw the treasure, especially the Buddha. He seemed so incredibly old and patient, willing to wait however long it was necessary to see the light of day."

"Where did it come from?" Maggie asked. "How did it get there?"

"I think it has been there a very long time. I'm sure it came from China. My imagination is running wild with speculations. There have been cylindrical stones, much like the anchors on fifth-century Chinese ships, found off the coast of California. American and Chinese scholars are finding evidence that suggests the Chinese may have discovered North America nine hundred years before Columbus, or even earlier."

There was silence for several minutes as both Maggie and Hank were lost in daydreams of ancient days and peoples. Hank finally broke the silence.

"I know how difficult it must have been for you to keep quiet about this. I'm not sure I could have walked away from it without poking and prying just a little." He grinned and shook his head. "Why, woman, this beats any dreams I ever had of finding the Mother Lode."

"I want to see it, Hank," Maggie said softly. "It's just like something out of a storybook. I want to see it just like Janet did, before anything is disturbed."

"You shall, Maggie, my dear. You can look at it just as long as you want to. It's your own personal treasure cave."

Hank and Maggie looked at each other with smiling faces and shining eyes. Janet was glad she had kept the treasure trove a secret until now.

"Janet, I agree with you that this should be kept a secret until Jim has finished with the black market. But I don't think we have a right to keep it to ourselves forever. When the time comes, I think Maggie and I would like for you and Jim to deal with it."

"That would be wonderful. I'd like to be a part of it, but you will need someone in charge who is knowledgeable about ancient China."

They talked for another hour before Janet excused herself.

The following few weeks were busy, and Janet wanted them that way. She found herself making excuses to be with people. Maggie understood, without words, that Janet's first Christmas without David was a lonely time for her. She kept Janet busy with projects for a community Christmas party, and volunteered Jim's and Janet's services for shopping trips to Gold Beach and one to Portland to pick up items for those who couldn't get out.

Maggie asked Janet to baby-sit for the forest ranger, Roger Carter, and his wife, Marie. They left their three preschoolers with Janet for two days and nights while they did their Christmas shopping for the boys. Forty-eight hours of motherhood was enough to reduce Janet to near hysteria. When the Carters returned, Marie took one look at Janet and broke into laughter.

"Poor dear. I've never seen such a look of relief on anyone's face. I did warn you that you would have your hands full."

"They were," Janet admitted. "You forgot to tell me where to find their 'off' buttons." Janet could see humor in the situation now that Roger and Marie were back. "Now I know how you keep your figure. I think I've lost about ten pounds in the last two days. Maybe you should bring them back for a week right after Christmas."

Roger and Marie laughed as they herded the boys out the door. "Don't tempt us, Janet," Roger said, "but you wouldn't survive a week."

Janet thought Roger was probably right. The boys were full of energy and curiosity, asking hundreds of questions from daylight until late at night and poking into everything in the house. Janet spent the day clearing up the chaos they had left behind. *At least*, she thought, *for two days I didn't have time to be lonely*.

Bedtime came early that night. Janet slept twelve hours and probably would have made it fourteen, but she was awakened by the sound of the McVey's pickup. She scrambled into her robe, ran a comb through her hair, and met Hank at the door with a big yawn.

"Sorry," she mumbled and proceeded to yawn again.

"Still recovering from the unholy trinity," Hank chuckled.

"Yes. It was like having Dennis the Menace in triplicate. I don't know how Marie does it. Come on in."

"Thanks. I can't stay but a minute. Maggie sent me down to ask a favor of you.

"Whoa, wait just a minute. If it involves kids, the answer is NO! Not even for Maggie."

"No kids," Hank answered with a grin. "She wondered if you would meet the mailboat in the morning. We're expecting three guests and she wondered if you would bring them to the Lodge."

"Sure, I'd be glad to," Janet yawned. "Wait a minute. Are you opening the Lodge again? It's a pretty strange time of year for guests."

"Oh hades, Janet. Maggie'll skin me alive if she finds out I told you, but I just don't think much of surprises in some situations. Your folks are coming for Christmas. Your mother swore Maggie to secrecy, but I didn't promise a thing."

"Oh, boy. That is a surprise I didn't need. Thanks for telling me. The hysteria practically jumped off the page in Mom's last letter. She wanted me to pack up and come home immediately so she could take care of me."

Janet motioned for Hank to sit down while she stirred the fire. "Maybe it's a good thing they are coming. It's past time for me to get some things straightened out with Mom. Besides, I think she expects bullets flying and bodies behind every tree. Dad is just confused and concerned. If everything will stay nice and quiet while they are here, perhaps they will go home convinced that everything is all right now."

"We'll just have to hope for the best," Hank agreed.

The following morning as Janet sat in her pickup at the boat landing, she realized that she had forgotten to ask Hank about the third guest. When she heard the boat, she got out and prepared to be surprised. She didn't have to pretend.

"Mark! Mark Jamison!" she blurted as the tall, handsome man stepped out of the boat. She was shocked by the fear and confusion which flashed across his face when he heard her voice. "Mark, I'm — "

He interrupted with an anger which bordered on rage. "I don't want to know who or what you are. I don't know what you are trying to do to me. Just get the hell out of my life!"

With that, he turned and stalked up the footpath which led to the Lodge. Before Janet could follow, she was engulfed in hugs from her parents.

Chapter 22

After a brief visit with the McVeys, Janet took her parents to the log house. There had been no sign of Mark Jamison at the Lodge. Janet put him from her mind for the present. There were more pressing things to deal with.

Janet sat her parents down and told them the whole story of the antiquity racket and the series of events which had happened since her arrival at Agness.

"I am fully committed to seeing this situation through to the end. I don't know what I will do then, but it will be of my own choice. I can't be the person you want me to be and I can't live the life you would like for me to live. I love you both, but I'm not your baby girl. I'm an adult and I have to find my own way to live."

The Warners surprised Janet by accepting her statement with little protest.

Their visit proved to be quite pleasant. They enjoyed renewing old friendships, and the peace and quiet of the valley seemed to still their fears. They were enchanted by Sam's cabin and deeply touched by the scrapbook Janet found in his desk. It was filled with photographs, clippings, and excerpts cut from Mrs. Warner's letters to Maggie, recording the important events of Janet's life. There was even a complete collection of Janet's published articles.

Janet's relationship with her parents entered a new phase and Janet realized that it was due as much to a change in her as it was in them. She had entered a new level of maturity and confidence in her own ability to deal with whatever life had to offer. The Warners left the day after Christmas feeling confident that Janet would be all right.

After her parents' departure, Janet had time to think about Mark Jamison. She had thought there would be an opportunity to meet Mark and talk. She discovered from Maggie that Mark had been met at the Lodge by Jim, and they had immediately driven to Grants Pass to spend Christmas with Jim's family.

Janet impatiently awaited their return. Jim, however, returned alone. Mark had cut short his visit and flown back to Albuquerque. Jim was puzzled by his friend's behavior.

"I don't know what to think, Janet. Mark was moody and on edge the whole time. That's unusual for him. The only thing that made any real impression on him was meeting you at the boat."

"What do you mean?"

"It was the strangest damn thing. All he did the whole week was ask questions about you. He wanted to know every detail I could think of to tell him. I couldn't understand how he could be so interested in you and then refuse to come back and spend some time with you. And he sent you a letter."

Jim handed Janet a sealed envelope and watched with unconcealed curiosity as she opened it. The message was short and to the point.

Mrs. Manning:
Until I stepped off the boat and heard your voice, I had thought you were no more than a product of my imagination. That has given me enough problems. Please stop whatever you are doing which allows your intrusion into my life.
Mark Jamison

"Well?"

"What?"

"Aren't you going to tell me what is in the letter?"

"No."

"Oh."

"I'm sorry, Jim. It's very personal and complicated. I'm not certain that I could explain or that you would believe me if I did. Now let's change the subject."

"No. Let's not change the subject. You two are my best friends and there is something damned strange going on when you both start keeping secrets and acting the way you are. Now damn it, I want to know ..."

He didn't finish the sentence. He stared at the books on Janet's desk. "That's funny. Mark asked me if you were involved in the occult or anything like that. I told him no, but apparently I was wrong."

"Those are some books out of Sam's library. They looked interesting, so I decided to read them. Don't try to make anything out of it that it isn't."

Jim continued probing until Janet became exasperated. Their conversation ended in a shouting match. Jim stomped out in a huff and Janet was glad to see him go.

Relations remained strained between them the remainder of the winter. Whenever they were together, Jim couldn't refrain from questioning Janet about her relationship with Mark Jamison. It finally reached the point that Janet avoided Jim unless they happened to meet accidentally at the Lodge. Janet was sorry that Jim was upset, but she welcomed the long days and nights of solitude. She had several projects which kept her busy.

Because of Mark Jamison's note, for the first time Janet considered the ethics of what she had been doing with the crystal ball. She admitted to herself that it was little different from being a peeping Tom. *But there is a difference*, she protested to herself. *I didn't seek out the experience. It was dropped in my lap and no one asked my permission to do it*.

True, she had made the choice to pursue the experience and allow it to become an important part of her life. But she couldn't believe that it was without purpose.

The more she thought about it, the more she was convinced that everything which had happened to her was somehow connected with Mark Jamison and the crystal ball. She felt a twinge of embarrassment at the melodramatic conclusion she drew. She believed that unseen events were building toward some climactic event which the fates would not allow her to avoid.

Janet made the decision to continue to watch Mark. She was careful, however, not to intrude her presence into his awareness. Her perceptions sharpened and she made several exciting discoveries while watching him work. The marks on the bottom of the metate he was studying were "IOVI • OPT • MAX." Jove — biggest and best!

Janet laughed at her mental picture of an Indian woman, a thousand years earlier, finding the stone and deciding it would make a good grinding surface. It fired her imagination, also. Where had the woman found the stone? Were there others? Was it just one stone out of a longer inscription? What if the woman had used the side with the inscription and polished it into oblivion?

Janet shuddered. She vowed that she would never again pass a metate without looking at its bottom.

Janet discovered that Mark had found two more artifacts which had Romanesque features. He had also found some very old letters describing some strange artifacts with Latin inscriptions which had been found by one of the early settlers. His artifacts and the settler's artifacts had all come from the same region of New Mexico. Mark had pinpointed that particular area as the probable site of a pre-Columbian Roman settlement, but Janet couldn't determine where.

Janet promised herself that somehow, whatever it took, she was going to have a part in Mark's final discovery. Finding such a settlement had been her pet project ever since she had uncovered the first hint that such a thing might exist. She smiled at the memory of the small, crude clay tablet, inscribed with a few Latin words, which she had found in a canyon in New Mexico. At first she thought it was a joke, until she did some research and found out that requests to Roman gods and goddesses were sometimes written on just that type of clay tablet and left at the appropriate shrine. The tablet Janet found made a request equivalent to "Gaius, drop dead."

She had amassed an impressive file of information, all seeming to point toward Roman intrusion into North America many centuries before Columbus. She had hundreds of photographs of petroglyphs and artifacts that seemed to all but prove it. There had been only one problem. Her research had convinced her that the Roman settlement had existed, but the final clue to the location had eluded her. Now it seemed that Mark had the answer, but she was allowed to see only enough to be tantalized.

"It isn't fair," Janet protested aloud on numerous occasions. "I feel as if I'm being manipulated by some master puppeteer with a perverted sense of humor. I'm catapulted into one dramatic situation after another and each one is left not quite resolved just as long as possible."

Janet's feelings of frustration persisted through the winter into spring. The first anniversary of David's death passed with a renewal of her determination to make Frederick Bryce and Amos Yeager pay for David's murder. She was as much at peace with his death as she could be until time and revenge blunted the pain.

Her novel was the only project which showed consistent progress. She finished it during the last week of February and mailed it to an agent who had agreed to represent her. Then, like everything else in her life, it was a matter of waiting.

The first week in April was a turning point. Events began to unfold with great speed. Hank came barreling down to the log house early one morning and jumped out of the pickup almost before it was stopped.

"Janet! Janet! You've got to come to the Lodge quick. It's that agent fellow in New York. He's going to call back in twenty minutes to talk to you."

"What? Who?"

"That agent fellow you sent your book to. He just called with some news. I promised to have you back to the Lodge in twenty minutes. Come on."

Hank nearly dragged Janet to the pickup and pushed her in. They were bouncing up the road before Hank's message really registered. She was shaking with excitement as she ran into the Lodge. The telephone was ringing. Maggie motioned for Janet to answer it.

Thirty minutes later, Janet was laughing and crying, and so was Maggie. Hank was grinning from ear to ear.

"He actually sold my book. It's going to be published. Not only that, the publisher is interested in a whole series of similar historical books. I'm an author!"

It took Janet awhile to settle down. She called her parents and they were elated. Then she called Fanny and Logan Stuart.

"That's marvelous news, Janet. Sam would be so proud. You can't afford to make too much money, though. You'll never get the IRS paid off," Logan joked.

Janet and the McVeys celebrated for a while and then Hank drove Janet home. She couldn't concentrate on anything, so she decided to share the news with Jim. *Without his enthusiasm, I probably wouldn't have gotten serious about writing the book. It's time for our relationship to get back to normal and this is a good way to break the ice*, she thought.

As she parked beside Jim's Jeep, the other car parked in the trees at the edge of the road only partially registered. It was a beautiful day and she was going to be a published author, and for now all was right with the world. It seemed to Janet that the whole world was celebrating with her. The birds were singing and the squirrels were chattering and scolding. She sang all the way up the trail to Jim's cabin.

She pounded on Jim's door and shouted, "Hey, hey. Open up in there. This is an author knocking at your door!"

Jim opened the door. There was an odd expression on his face. "Janet, what on earth — "

Janet pushed by Jim and entered the cabin. "You are now conversing with a real, honest-to-goodness, bona fide author. Show a little respect, my good man. They bought my book and want more."

"Hey, that's great, Janet," a voice said from behind her.

She whirled to see Ben Fischer standing in the kitchen door with Don Ross peering over his shoulder.

"Ben. Don. Terrific. I didn't have any idea you were here."

The two men offered sincere congratulations as Janet turned back to Jim who, so far, had said nothing.

"Well, aren't you going to say something?"

Jim grabbed her and swung her around in a circle as he let out a whoop of delight. "You're damned right I'm going to say something. You didn't let me read the rest of it, much less tell me you had finished it." He put her down and looked her in the eye. "But then, I haven't been exactly easy to talk to, have I?"

"Forget it, Jim. We're friends and that's all that counts. Now, what brings you two up here?" she said, turning to Ben and Don.

The three men looked at each other. It was evident to Janet that they didn't want to tell her the purpose of their visit.

"Well, don't everyone talk at once. While you decide on your story, I'll just help myself to a cup of the coffee I smell."

Janet squeezed past Don into the kitchen. The table was covered with maps and papers which the three made a mad scramble to gather up and put out of sight.

"Okay. What's up? Are you going to start keeping secrets from me at this stage of the game?"

Jim looked at Ben. Ben shrugged. "Jim, we wanted to tell her from the beginning. She knows that country and may be able to help."

"All right," Jim said reluctantly. "I'm not happy about getting her involved, but it doesn't look as if I have a choice. Why don't you tell her the other news first?"

The four sat down at the kitchen table. "We were coming down to see you later," Ben said. "There are a couple of bits of news I wanted to pass along. Lloyd Owen's body was found a couple of weeks ago, in a shallow grave just south of Gold Beach. It looks as if Richards may have shot him the day of the inquest."

"Too bad it wasn't the other way around." Janet said. "I didn't like Owen, but I don't think he was the vicious killer Richards is. Any sign of Richards?"

"None." Ben answered. "Yaeger has either gotten rid of him, too, or he'll surface again and we'll get him. The other news is that David's journal has helped us put together a large part of the marketing setup for the stolen artifacts, as well as several other interesting sidelines."

"Does that mean you're about ready to make some arrests?"

Ben shook his head. "No. Unfortunately Yaeger has managed to cover himself very well and we don't have evidence which will stand up in court yet. We haven't been able to duplicate the last week of David's work. We could wreck the pipeline and put most of the small fry in jail, but Yaeger and Bryce would go free and be back in business in a matter of months. We want those two."

"And that is what this summit meeting is all about, isn't it?" Janet asked.

"Yes," Jim said. "Amos Yaeger is getting greedier. He has contacted me directly, twice. Since he was never mentioned in connection with the plane crash, and there hasn't been any publicity about the black market, he is convinced he can trust me, and you."

"Me?"

"He believes you are willing to go along with the coverup because of your feelings for me. He has no idea that you have connected any of this to David's murder. Right now we have him much more interested in something else."

"I'm almost afraid to ask what it is. The expressions on your faces tell me that I'm not going to like the answer."

Jim looked pleadingly at Ben, which prompted Ben to take up the story. "Bryce and Yaeger both like to boast occasionally about their prowess as amateur archeologists, though neither one has ever been on a dig. We decided that to get them, we had to come up with an archeological find which was unique so that they would want to see it themselves and bypass the middlemen. It has to be a new find which hasn't been publicized."

"Ben, if you can come up with something like that on demand, I know quite a few archeologists who'd love to employ you." Janet looked from face to face. All at once she had a sick feeling. "Oh, no. Mark. You're not going to do that to Mark? Yes you are. Damn!"

"Janet, it just fell into our laps. I don't know how you know about it, but Mark wrote me that he is certain he has located the site of an early Roman settlement. Yaeger would give a lot to take a team into a virgin site like that and strip it and be able to brag about it later to his cronies. Of course, we wouldn't allow him to work it for more than a week or so before we moved in and arrested him."

"Stop right now! Jim, I can't believe you would be a party to something like this. You know that even a small amount of looting would destroy valuable information. That site will be one of the most important finds of the century. It will rewrite history. That's it. You still stubbornly won't believe that it could possibly be Roman."

"Janet, listen," Jim pleaded.

"No, you listen. I want Yaeger as much or more than anyone, but this is not the way. I want him for murder, not for stealing a pot or two. That would get him a short stay in prison and a stiff fine at best. I can't believe Mark would go along with this. What does he say about it?"

The three men were very uncomfortable and silent. Jim finally spoke. "Well, we haven't exactly told him about it."

"You're unbelievable," Janet shouted.

"Now listen. This may not be the best plan, but it's the only one we have. If we get Yaeger this way it could open the door to intensive investigation of his business connections. If we tell Mark, he might start acting out of character and ruin everything. Mark is planning his initial investigation for the first of June. Some of Yaeger's men will follow him until he locates the site. I will see that Mark is safely removed from the scene, then Yaeger and possibly Bryce will come in by helicopter. I'll be with them part of the time. Ben's men will be watching and when the time is right, they'll move in and — "

"Don't tell me any more," Janet interrupted. "I don't want any part of this. Your plan is so full of weak spots it's ridiculous. What happens if Yaeger decides to have Mark killed as soon as he makes the discovery? Will you just say, 'Gee, that's too bad,' and add his name to the list of victims along with David and Sam and Ginny? My god, Jim, he's your best friend."

Jim was speechless in the face of Janet's verbal assault.

"Look," Janet continued, "give me some time to come up with an alternate site. I have one in mind, but there are some other people I have to consult." Janet had immediately thought of the treasure behind the waterfall.

"Time is something we don't have," Ben said. "We are getting a lot of pressure from upstairs to produce results soon or drop the investigation. Besides, Jim has already shown Mark's letter to Yaeger, and some of your research to back it up. We can't switch stories at this point. Weak or not, we have to go through with it. Since you know the country, you could be a big help."

"Sorry, Ben. I'm serious about not wanting any part of this. I think it's very wrong. Good afternoon, gentlemen."

All the way down the trail Janet tried to think of some acceptable alternative. There didn't seem to be one. She did decide that Mark was damn well going to have some choice in the matter. If he chose to cooperate that was one thing, but he was going to have the opportunity to make the choice.

Janet stopped at the Lodge and asked Hank for the use of the telephone in his office. A short time later she placed a person-to-person call to Mark Jamison at the number she had gotten from information.

"Please, Mark, don't hang up. This is about your Roman site. You have to listen or you're going to lose it."

"Who is this?"

"Janet Manning."

"What is this, some more of your occult mumbo-jumbo?"

"No. It's about Jim and the black market and how he intends to use you without your knowledge."

Mark was more than willing to listen to what Janet had to say. Since he had been a part of the pipeline at one time, she didn't have to waste time with explanations about that part of the situation. As Janet told him what Jim and the others were planning, she could sense his building anger.

"I agree with you, Janet. There are other ways to handle Yaeger. They have a very weak plan, aside from the fact that this find is too important to run the risk of its destruction just to get him for pot hunting. The problem is that Jim doesn't believe this will be anything more than another Anazasi site. Otherwise, I don't think he would consider using it this way."

"He does have a stubborn streak where that subject is concerned," Janet said. "I've tried to get him to just consider the possibility, but we always end up in an argument."

"Jim told me about some of your conversations on the subject. I've read a few of your articles. I must say I would like to discuss some of your theories with you sometime."

"Does that mean you won't yell at me and run away the next time we meet?"

"I'm sorry about that. I must admit that I'm still bothered by the fact that you are a real person. The idea that we have been in some type of telepathic communication is only slightly less disturbing."

"Mark, it wasn't anything I did on purpose. It just happened and the first few times made me think I was going crazy. I've read some books since then which have helped me to understand a little more about it. At least what happened, not why."

"I'm afraid that I have been guilty of having a closed mind where such things are concerned," admitted Mark. "I have done some reading on the subject lately, but it hasn't been all that enlightening. Perhaps you can tell me how this started."

"The circumstances of how you popped into my life are rather complicated and bizarre, not something I want to explain over the phone."

"In that case, we'll just have to arrange to get together sometime soon. I'm grateful to you for giving me the information about Jim's plans. I know it wasn't an easy decision for you to make. I'll let you know when I decide how I'm going to handle the situation."

They talked a few minutes longer. When Mark said goodbye, he again mentioned the possibility of getting together with Janet. She had the sudden strong feeling that it might happen sooner than they anticipated.

Chapter 23

Toward the end of April, Janet received a letter from Mark telling her that he had decided to backpack into the area pinpointed by his research during the first week in May. He hoped to find the site and have it publicized well before his expected trip in June. In that way, he could protect the site and foil Jim's plans without affecting Jim's credibility with Yaeger.

This seemed a reasonable solution to Janet. For now, also, it would keep Jim, Ben, and Don from knowing that she had betrayed their plans to Mark. She knew that her conscience would make her confess it to them sometime, but she was human enough to want that to be after Yaeger had been caught in some other way.

Janet saw Jim a few times, but their conversations were mostly about her book or community happenings. She assumed that Jim's plans to use Mark were unchanged and she tried not to be too curious about strangers in the area from time to time.

Janet was appalled that Jim would use a friend the way he was planning to use Mark. After her initial anger, though, she understood that Jim was motivated by his desire to avenge Ginny's death and the need to bring his association with the black market to a close and return to living a more normal life. She could understand, but not fully excuse him. She felt certain, also, that Ben and Don had exerted a great deal of influence on him, not realizing the importance of what was at stake.

As the first week in May approached, the crystal ball became Janet's constant companion. She watched Mark make the final preparations for his trip. She wished that she had been in a position to press him for details of his destination, but the threads of their new relationship were fragile at best.

Her excitement reached a high pitch the day Mark left Albuquerque and headed toward the southwestern part of the state. Her intuition had told her that the site of the pre-Columbian Roman settlement was somewhere in southwestern New Mexico, but that was somewhat akin to searching for a needle in the middle of the Sahara desert. She almost jumped up and down with glee when he entered the Gila Wilderness by a winding mountain road she had driven a dozen times. She was bitterly disappointed when the day ended and she had to watch him park his van and make preparations to camp beside the road.

Janet was too keyed-up to sleep. She dug into the roll of maps she had brought with her from Texas and located a geological survey map of the area. She traced Mark's route until she was certain that she could place the point of her pencil on the exact spot where he lay asleep. She added her observations of the day to the already thick notebook where she had recorded every episode with the crystal ball.

The day caught up with her all at once. She was half asleep before she crawled under the covers. Sleep brought dreams, dreams of David smiling as he spoke to her. "This will be my last legacy to you, Janet. Take it and don't be afraid." David's hands were empty and she understood that he no longer referred to the crystal ball. His last legacy to her was whatever would happen during the next few days.

Morning brought renewed excitement. Janet had a wonderful feeling of being loved and cherished. She sat down to breakfast with the crystal ball in front of her. She laughed and thought of all the times she had propped a book in front of her so that she could read while she ate.

It was mid-morning when her guesses about Mark's destination proved accurate. Mark turned off the road onto a fire lane which crossed and recrossed a meandering stream which was as familiar to Janet as her own face. He pulled his van into a grove of trees where she and David had camped dozens of times as a starting place for their backpacking trips.

She watched Mark as he checked his maps and readied his pack. He appeared to be a knowledgeable and experienced back-packer. She grinned when she noted that his walking stick appeared every bit as well-used and cherished as her own. He, too, knew the value of a good staff in difficult terrain.

Mark started down the creek, and her curiosity was boundless as she tried to guess where he was headed. This was an area Janet knew so well that she recognized individual trees and rocks. She wondered if it was possible that she and David had walked unaware across the site of a Roman settlement. She couldn't believe that they had.

Mark hiked about a mile down the creek, crossed it, and paused at the entrance to a canyon which was one of Janet's favorite places in all the world. She was mesmerized as she mentally took each step with him. She could feel the weight of the pack, the roughness of the rocks underfoot, and the bite of the cold, dry mountain air in her lungs.

As Janet followed Mark through the constantly changing terrain, her mind raced ahead to the high country, trying to think of a place which would fit the requirements of a community such as the Romans would have built. Then, halfway up the canyon, Mark began to stop and study every side canyon and gully. He would check his map and then refer to a small flat stone. Janet recognized it as a stone she had seen him examining during some of her sessions with the crystal ball. He appeared to be looking for markings of some type. He would study the boulders and larger rocks around the entrances to a side canyon, shake his head, and move on. Janet finally got a glimpse of the small stone. There appeared to be a map etched into the surface, accompanied by an inscription in Latin.

Janet was so engrossed that she failed to hear Jim drive up. She wasn't aware of his presence until he knocked on the door. She quickly rolled up the map and put it and the crystal ball out of sight. Jim was so excited when she opened the door that he failed to notice her agitation.

"Hi. I brought your mail by since you didn't show up at the post office. Janet, I've got the greatest news. A letter came from Dr. Carlos Santiago in Lima, Peru. He wants me to assist in the excavation of that Inca city they've discovered not far from Macha Picchu."

"Oh, Jim. That's wonderful. I know how much you have dreamed of something like that and the opportunity to work with someone of Dr. Santiago's reputation. I'm really happy for you. But how can you go now, with the situation with Yaeger and the black market still unresolved?"

Even as Janet congratulated Jim, she was desperate to return to her vigil at the crystal ball.

"It takes a while to put an expedition of that magnitude together. It will be at least a year, and the situation here should be resolved long before that. There could be a place for you if you would like to go, especially since you have the funds to pay your own expenses."

"Wow. I'll have to give that some thought. It isn't the sort of thing to make a snap decision about."

"Say, Janet, are you okay? I just noticed that you are in your robe."

Janet jumped at the chance to get rid of Jim without having to answer a bunch of questions.

"I feel a spring cold coming on. I thought I'd spend the day in bed with a good book and try to head it off."

"I'll go then and let you get back to bed. Sorry you aren't feeling well. I'll drop by tomorrow to see if you need anything. Maybe by then you'll feel well enough to discuss the Peru trip."

"Thanks, Jim. And thank you for bringing my mail. See you tomorrow."

As Jim drove away, Janet sat down at her desk and shook her head. "Nice going, Janet. You're becoming an incorrigible liar, as well as a betrayer of friends. What next? Oh, shut up and worry about it tomorrow."

Janet placed the crystal ball next to the enlarged contour map she had of the canyon. When Mark's image appeared, she was puzzled by his surroundings. He had left the main canyon and the terrain was no longer familiar to her. She and David had explored all of the side canyons, but Mark was in an area she was certain that she had never seen.

Janet knew the place in the canyon where she had last seen Mark. She found that place on the contour map and marked it. She checked the length of time which had passed during Jim's visit. She calculated the distance Mark could have traveled during that time and marked it on the map. Then she began to study the terrain between the two points.

The main canyon ran predominately north and south. Mark was traveling almost due west. There was only one place on the map where there was anything even faintly resembling an intersecting canyon. Janet tried to remember the area. All she could recall was a gently sloping, grass-covered creek bank, traversed by a gully no more than a few inches deep. The gully had appeared to end at the base of a cliff covered with vines and bushes. Only perhaps it hadn't been a cliff. Maybe it had been a man-made barrier. That had to be it.

She knew that Mark walked faster than she could, but by no stretch of the imagination could he have made it to the next intersecting canyon. He had to be somewhere in the vicinity of that gully. She studied the map carefully. The contour lines did appear unusual. A short distance beyond the apparent cliff there appeared to be a deep, narrow ravine which ascended sharply, then widened at one point into a rather large depression with steep high walls, then narrowed and continued until it played out high on the side of the mountain. Janet marked the place on her map and returned to her observation of Mark.

Mark was hurrying more than was reasonable for the terrain. Janet couldn't blame him. The shadows in the narrow passage were deepening and darkness would come there much earlier than in the higher elevations. As the afternoon passed, Janet mentally urged Mark on toward the wider part of the canyon. She was afraid that night would catch him where there was no place to spread a sleeping bag or even sit comfortably. She knew that it would be all but impossible to travel after dark.

Janet was vaguely aware that a violent thunderstorm was in progress outside the log house. It took second place to the possibility that a Roman, Theodorus the Renowned, had led a storm-weary group of shipmates into the Southwest to make a home in a frightening new world sometime around A.D. 775.

Daylight time was running out for Mark. Janet felt a keen sense of disappointment when he stopped and shrugged out of his pack. He ate a snack and drank from his canteen. She wondered if he intended to lean against the canyon wall until morning. She was relieved and elated when he took a flashlight from his pack, settled the pack back onto his shoulders, and began to pick his way over the rocks with the aid of the bright beam from the flashlight.

Within half an hour, the only visible light was that of the flashlight. Janet felt the tension in the muscles of Mark's neck and back as he exercised extreme care in picking a path through the dangerous rubble. One misstep could mean a broken leg or, at the very least, a broken flashlight.

The end of Mark's journey came so suddenly that it took both of them by surprise. One moment he was in the narrow defile, the next moment in the strangest place Janet had ever seen. As Mark began his exploration, Janet was no longer aware of being an observer. It was as if she walked beside him as a participant, and the darkness caused no limitation of her vision.

They appeared to be standing at the bottom of a gigantic, flat-bottomed, stone bowl. The area was perhaps two hundred yards in diameter. The walls were at least a hundred feet tall. The bottom was covered with fine white sand and a spring-fed pool was sheltered by half a dozen ancient oak trees. These were not the scrub oaks common to the area. The trunks were twelve to fifteen feet in diameter and the branches reached almost to the top of the walls. Janet had never before seen such oak trees. She could barely force her gaze away from them to continue scanning this strange place.

Mark and Janet saw it at the same moment. On the north wall there was a huge overhang half concealed by wild grapevines, and on the ledge beneath, a structure.

No Indian cliff dwelling, Janet thought, *unless a very unusual Indian indeed had developed a penchant for Greco-Roman architecture*. However crudely executed it might be, there in native stone were broad steps, a columned portico, and a huge statue of the ancient Roman god of sky and thunder — the king of the gods — Jupiter!

Janet's mind went scrambling for dates. This was from a much earlier time than Theodorus the

Renowned. My god, *how far back would it have to date to be from the time when Romans still built temples to Jupiter and their pantheon of gods? Oh hell, it didn't matter.* There he was, Jupiter seated on his throne, thunderbolts in one hand, eagle perched on the fist of the other. And the sacred oaks — it was all there. An ancient shrine to Jupiter.

As Mark played the beam of his flashlight over the scene, his shouts of delight shattered the night silence and resounded from the walls. Janet knew exactly how he felt. What colossal impudence! What cheek! What gall! What effrontery! What nerve the ancient Romans had to upset accepted history by building a temple to Jupiter in the New Mexico wilderness!

Janet wanted to laugh and cry, but most of all she wanted to be there. She finally settled down to watch Mark again. He was exhausted even in the midst of his jubilation. He dropped his pack to the sand and began to search for firewood, all the while unable to stop grinning and laughing.

Mark soon had a small blaze kindled and a pot of water heating. He began to smooth a place in the sand for his sleeping bag. Suddenly he paused, then began to dig quickly around a large object. Janet held her breath as he carefully brushed the sand away from a metallic, plate-shaped article and triumphantly examined it in the firelight. A small shield of beaten gold. In the center was the majestic figure of the Roman eagle.

Mark traced the figure of the eagle with one finger and then carefully laid the shield aside. His hands were trembling as he prepared a cup of hot chocolate and emptied a package of freeze-dried food into the remaining hot water. He put the pot at the edge of the fire and watched it as he sipped from his cup.

"Well, Janet," he said aloud, "we were right. You and I were the only ones who believed, and we were right. You should have had a part in this discovery. I wish you were here with me."

"I am," Janet answered. "I'm sorry, Mark, but I couldn't miss out on this. I've been with you since Albuquerque."

"I'm not surprised," Mark said. "I think I sensed it. This once, I'm glad. I'm also exhausted."

There didn't seem to be anything else to say. When Janet saw Mark preparing to bed down, she turned away with her own thoughts of heading toward bed. She felt as if she had hiked twenty miles with a heavy pack and then had been pulled through a knothole sideways.

Her stomach was growling and she remembered that she hadn't eaten since breakfast. She prowled through the cabinets looking for something she could eat without building up the fire. She heated water for tea in the hot pot and had eaten about three bites of smoked salmon when she heard a voice in her head urgently calling her name. She raced to the desk and cradled the crystal ball in her hands.

"Mark, I'm here. What is it?"

"Janet ... I ... "

It took a moment to orient herself to the scene. Mark lay sprawled on the steps leading to the Jovian temple. The flames of the campfire barely provided enough illumination for her to see what had happened. Mark had been unable to resist the temptation to take a closer look at the temple before going to sleep. At least two of the large slabs of stone which formed the steps had shifted under his weight and fallen to the sand. Mark's right leg was twisted at an odd angle. His nose was bleeding profusely. There appeared to be an ugly gash on his forehead. He was unconscious.

"Mark! Mark! You must wake up. Wake up, Mark."

Janet knew that as the night progressed, the temperature would fall well below freezing. Mark could not survive in his injured and exhausted state. She was determined to save him by the sheer force of her will if necessary.

Janet called his name and probed insistently with her mind. Too many people had died. Mark Jamison would not die. She wouldn't let him. She cajoled and cursed and prayed. After a ten-minute eternity, Mark stirred, groaned, and opened his eyes.

"Mark, you have to stay awake. You must. You can if you try hard enough. Try, Mark. Get your bandanna, your bandanna, Mark. The one around your neck. No, your right hand is hurt. Use your left. That's right, pull it loose. Now, press it against your forehead until the bleeding stops. Okay, that's good. Keep up the pressure. Can you tie it around your head? I know you can't use your right hand. Just hang onto the bandanna with it and work with the left. Okay. Good.

"Now your nose. We need to get the bleeding stopped. Feel your nose gently. Make sure it isn't broken. No? Good. Pinch your nostrils together until it stops bleeding."

Janet worked with Mark for an hour, pushing and prodding him to action. His nose wasn't broken and the gash on his head wasn't as serious as it had first appeared. His right hand was badly scraped and swollen from the hard blow it had taken when he tried to break his fall.

Mark's right knee was the major problem. He was certain the leg wasn't broken, but was pretty sure that he had torn some ligaments in the knee. The slightest movement was excruciating. He couldn't bite back his groans of agony as he followed Janet's instructions to slip out of his jacket and wrap it tightly around his knee. It was awkward and painful, but necessary to provide padding and support to enable him to half crawl, half drag himself down the steps.

Mark was in much better shape after warming himself at the fire and using water from his canteen to rinse the blood from his face and hands. A little first-aid cream and a Band-Aid or two took care of the minor problems.

Mark's knee had swollen rapidly and he couldn't get his jeans off without help. The only solution seemed to be to split his pant leg with his knife. Even that was complicated by the fact that he had to do it with one hand. It seemed to take forever. His knee was hideous to look at when it was finally exposed. It was blue and so swollen the skin looked ready to split. There wasn't anything either of them could do about it.

Janet urged Mark to get into his sleeping bag. Fortunately it was a rectangular bag which zipped all the way to the bottom. He rolled in and worked the zipper up from the inside.

"I'll get help to you, Mark. The Forest Service — "

"No!" Mark's voice was hoarse with pain and exhaustion. "You, Janet. Promise me. Just you. I was watched in Albuquerque. Yaeger knows from my letter to Jim that I'm somewhere in the Gila Wilderness. Just you."

Mark's voice faded and Janet knew that fatigue had over-ruled his pain. Mark was asleep.

Janet considered Mark's request. She could probably be there by the time she could convince anyone in New Mexico that she knew he was hurt and in need of help. How could she explain the crystal ball? And, if the Forest Service did mount a search for him, there was the strong possibility that Yaeger's men might move in and find him and kill him before he could be rescued. Jim? She could imagine his reaction if she told him about the crystal ball, and she wasn't sure she could trust him not to go ahead and allow Yaeger to move in on the site after Mark was rescued. No, she had to go. That was the only choice.

She didn't know of a commercial airport nearer to Agness than Portland, a six-hour drive away. It was doubtful that she could find a non-stop flight to El Paso, Texas, the only major airport near the Gila Wilderness. Even at El Paso, she would still have to rent a car and make a three or four-hour drive. Never mind the hassle of getting her guns checked through with her baggage and trying to deal with all the gear she needed to take. Too many unknowns. Too many possible delays.

It was a little over 1600 miles. With any luck at all she could make it in about thirty-six hours of driving time plus another three or four hours for gas and food and a couple of hours of sleep.

Janet spent the next two hours in a blur of activity. She packed her gear in the Toyota, made a list of what she needed to buy along the way, marked the best route on her maps, and packed food to eat on the way. She set her mental alarm for four o'clock and laid down for several hours of sleep.

Janet awakened exactly at four o'clock and checked on Mark. He was sleeping restlessly. With the care he would be able to give himself, Janet didn't think his life was in any danger from his injuries. But he would never be able to make the hike out without help.

Janet left a note for Jim, saying that she'd had a letter in her mail from a friend who was in trouble and needed her help. She promised to be in touch within a week. She had one bad moment as she drove past the Lodge. Jim's Jeep was parked beside the back door. The Lodge was dark and no one appeared to notice her departure as she crept by without headlights.

The next two days were a succession of highways and cities: Gold Beach, Crescent City, Arcata, Redding, Sacramento, Bakersfield, Barstow, Needles, Flagstaff, St. John. She stopped only for gas and food, and once for a couple of hours of sleep in a roadside park. She stayed awake on strong coffee and No-Doz tablets and almost acquired one speeding ticket between Barstow and Needles.

It was mid-afternoon when she crossed the state line into New Mexico and turned down the highway which would take her to the mountain road into the Wilderness. It was well after nightfall when she found Mark's van, parked the Toyota beside it, and rolled into her sleeping bag spread on the ground between the two vehicles.

Chapter 24

After a night of troubled dreams, Janet awoke with a sense of panic. In the predawn glow, she assembled her equipment, wolfed down a stale sandwich, and headed down the creek toward the canyon entrance.

Mark's blurred footprints were the only sign of human passage, but Janet had a momentary sensation of being some small defenseless animal about to be cornered by a pack of mad dogs.

Defenseless I am not, she told herself. She felt the reassuring weight of her .38 Special and extra shells in her jacket pocket and reached back to touch the 30-06 in the case strapped to her pack.

She talked herself out of the feeling. She couldn't see any basis for it. She knew Mark was in reasonably good shape. She had found a mental link with him without the crystal ball.

When she entered the main canyon, she tried to lose herself in the sights and sounds of the new day. Beneath the canopy of pines, the ground was covered with spring flowers. The sound of running water blended with bird songs and the hum of bees. It was a day to savor, but she felt an urgency to push herself beyond her normal pace.

Fatigue, tension, high altitude, and a pack too heavily loaded made the going unusually difficult for Janet. The trail climbed steadily, gaining a thousand feet in elevation in the first two miles. The rational part of her mind knew that she was taking foolhardy chances by hurrying, but her body seemed to move with a will of its own.

Exhaustion and a pounding head forced Janet to stop for rest and food during the late morning. A handful of vitamin E and antacid tablets helped to combat the effects of altitude sickness. After eating, she stretched out at the base of a pine tree for a few minutes of total relaxation, and began to feel better almost immediately.

There were a few wispy clouds in a sky so blue it didn't seem real. She idly watched a couple of small planes and a helicopter lazily crisscrossing the area. They were common sights during periods of heavy usage of the wilderness, or after storms when the Forest Service checked for fires. Since this was neither, Janet assumed that they were just flying for the hell of it, because it was a beautiful spring day. Something nagged at the edges of her mind, but she was too drowsy to think clearly.

After half an hour, Janet struggled into her pack. Every cell in her body protested the outrage. She forced herself to think about the excitement of seeing Jupiter's temple and its indication that a settlement had been nearby. She thought about the complexities of getting Mark safely out of this place. She had almost forgotten her aching body by the time she saw Mark's footprints in the shallow gully leading away from the main canyon.

What had appeared to be a cliff, she saw, was a cleverly constructed wall built by human hands. On a huge boulder to one side, Janet saw what Mark had been searching every side canyon for — covered by centuries of desert patina and lichens, a thunderbolt etched deep into the surface.

Twenty feet past the rock barrier, a steep, wild little passageway clogged with tumbles of rocks and dead-falls greeted Janet. The first mile was some of the roughest terrain she had ever tackled. Then the character of the ravine changed. Knee-high grass hid rocks and water seeps. The canyon narrowed until her shoulders touched both sides and she could see only a thin ribbon of blue overhead. She shuddered, pushing away the beginnings of claustrophobia.

Janet lost track of time and distance. Her mind was caught up in the ordeal of forcing one foot to follow the other. Without the slightest warning, a bend in the narrow passage gave entrance to the bowl-like area.

Nothing had prepared her for the physical reality of what she had seen in the crystal ball. The massive oak trees, the dazzling white sand, the majestic stone figure — she could only stand and stare.

"Hey, remember me? Mark. Mark Jamison — the guy you came to rescue." Mark's voice jolted her from the trance. "Rather overwhelming, isn't it?" Mark was standing, braced against a slab of rock beneath the temple, a crude cane in one hand.

"It's so damned unbelievable." Janet undid the hip belt of her pack and let it slide to the sand beside Mark's gear. She studied him as she walked toward him. "You look as if you've been playing gladiator and you lost. How do you feel?"

"Much better now," he answered, holding out his arms to Janet. "Come here. I want to make sure you are real."

It seemed natural to Janet to embrace someone she knew as intimately as she did Mark. He held her fiercely to him.

"It has been lonely, frustrating, and sometimes frightening sitting here and looking at all of this and wondering if you were really on your way or if the whole thing was an illusion. This is such an eerie place. Sometimes it seems that I can almost hear voices and see shadowy figures. That's pretty strong stuff for someone who has always prided himself on being a realist."

Janet gently disengaged herself from his arms. "I understand, Mark. I've had more than enough cause during the past year to doubt my own sanity. I've finally come to the conclusion that perhaps some of what we call illusion has more reality than the so-called 'real world.' But enough of that. We have a couple of very real problems to deal with — getting that knee patched up and getting you out of here."

"I can think of one more."

"What?"

"I finished the last of my food this morning and I'm starving."

Janet bit her cheeks to keep from smiling. She was glad Don Ross wasn't there.

Within an hour, Janet had fed Mark and tended his injuries. His cuts and scrapes were tender but appeared to be healing nicely. The swelling around his knee had subsided a little. She reduced it even more with a common folk remedy — a brown paper sack soaked in apple cider vinegar and applied as a pack. The injury still looked terrible and was quite painful.

Janet had brought an aluminum splint which she padded and used to immobilize the joint. It would protect Mark from the likelihood of further injury and perhaps cut down a little on the pain, though it was going to be awkward to handle on the walk out.

Mark tried walking with the splint, aided by his cane and walking stick. He pronounced himself satisfied. He and Janet sat down beside the campfire with cups of coffee to make plans for the following day. Janet had just lit cigarettes for herself and Mark when her attention was distracted by a strange, pulsating sound.

"Get out of sight," Janet yelled as she scooped sand over the fire, grabbed both packs and Mark's sleeping bag, and ran for the cover of the slabs of stone next to the temple steps. "Damn, How stupid. I should have known that wasn't the Forest Service."

She didn't know if they had been seen, but she didn't look back as the sound of the helicopter grew louder. Janet was almost to the rocks, Mark just ahead of her, when she felt as if someone had kicked her in the left thigh and she went down. Mark grabbed her by the shoulders and pulled her behind the rocks, then leaned out and grabbed the packs as bullets ricocheted all around.

Janet reached for her rifle case, saying some words she had never uttered aloud. "It's that damned Yaeger and his bunch," she continued. "It has to be."

"Janet, you're bleeding badly."

"I know. That son-of-a-bitch shot me." Janet levered a shell into the chamber of the rifle, but Mark pulled it out of her hands.

"That will wait. You need attention now."

Janet started to argue. Her leg wasn't hurting, only felt strange and numb, until she looked at it. She almost passed out from the pain and the sight of the ugly wound. She was losing blood rapidly. She took several deep breaths and let her anger take the edge off the pain.

"Do it quickly, Mark. Pack something over it front and back and tie it in place. Make it tight."

Janet fought the waves of pain as Mark worked as rapidly as he could with one partially disabled hand. The helicopter hovered just above the cliff on the far side while two of its passengers blasted away at them. Janet knew that it was only a matter of time until a ricochet put an end to her and Mark.

"Damn it, Mark. I won't be killed by those two. You can't shoot with that hand. You'll just have to finish with my leg while I shoot."

Mark didn't argue. He helped Janet change position and handed her the rifle. She tried to concentrate only on the helicopter through a cloud of pain which was almost beyond endurance. She angrily brushed away the tears which blurred her vision.

"Where the hell do you shoot a helicopter?"

"Tail rotor," Mark snapped as another barrage of bullets came at them. "Aim for the hub."

Janet took careful aim, trying to anticipate the movements of the chopper. Her awareness was fading in and out. She knew that she was about to lose consciousness, but she willed herself not to, just long enough.

It took five shots before she scored a hit on the tail-rotor hub. The last thing she saw before the waves of blackness took her was the helicopter spinning out of control, shearing the tops of pine trees, ricocheting off the edge of the cliff and falling to the white sand in a shattering explosion of flame.

Chapter 25

Sunshine poured through the slats of a venetian blind as Janet opened her eyes to find Jim sitting beside her, clinging to her hand.

"Hello, sport. Finally decide to join the living?"

"Jim, what are you doing here? Where is here?" Janet asked drowsily. "Mark? Is Mark all right?"

"Mark is going to be fine. He's being obstinate about allowing the doctors to put his knee back together until he sees you awake. You're in a small, private hospital in Albuquerque, and you've been asleep for the better part of two days."

"My leg?"

"You were lucky, Janet. Your leg will be fine in a few months. The bullet missed the bone, but it did leave a nasty hole and tore some muscles. Doc said you were suffering more from exhaustion than from the wound."

Janet drifted into a light sleep, quite in agreement with the doctor. She dozed off and on through the afternoon and Jim was there to answer a few more questions whenever she awakened.

"When I found your note, I wasn't satisfied with the explanation for your absence. I wanted to be certain that you had left alone and of your own free will, so I searched the house and found the journal of your experiences with Mark and the crystal ball. That's the damnedest thing I ever read. I wouldn't believe a word of it if I didn't have you and Mark here in front of me as proof. I also found your maps."

"How did Yaeger find us?"

"His men in Albuquerque had been watching Mark. When they discovered that he had eluded them, they broke into his house and searched his papers until they had a pretty good idea of which part of the Gila Wilderness he was headed toward. Yaeger put ground and air search teams into the area. One guy spotted you entering the Wilderness, but you lost him somewhere along the way. The smoke from the campfire was what pinpointed you and Mark from the air."

"Where were you?"

"After I read your journal, I stopped only long enough to call Ben Fischer and arrange for him and Don to meet me down at the creek where you left your vehicles. I've been about four or five hours behind you all the way, hoping that you would stop long enough for me to catch up with you.

"Ben and Don brought four men with them. We were attacked in the main canyon by some of Yaeger's men. Two of the agents were wounded and one of Yaeger's men was killed. Ben and Don are fine."

"Jim, what about the helicopter? Who was in it?"

"Yaeger, Richards, Carrac, and one of Yaeger's pilots."

"Are they ... ?"

"Yes, Janet. All four of them are dead." Jim cupped her face in his hands and made her look him in the eye. "Janet, you didn't have a choice. They were there to kill you and Mark, and anyone else who got in their way."

Janet turned her face away from Jim and was silent for a long moment before she answered. "I know you're right, Jim. Part of me is glad I killed them, but another part of me is going to have to take a little time to get used to the idea that I took four lives."

"Better do it right now, Jan. The newspapers have had a field day. There was a reporter at the ranger station when we called for help. You and Mark have been splashed all over the headlines. You're quite the heroine. You even made network news on television."

"Oh, no." Janet groaned as Jim handed her one of a dozen newspapers. There were screaming headlines and pictures of Mark and her being carried to a waiting helicopter. There were pictures of the Jupiter statue and the oak trees. Some enterprising soul had done his homework and Janet's whole story was there — David's and Sam's murders, the inheritance from Sam, the soon-to-be-published book. Janet wanted to crawl into a hole.

"What happens now?"

"The authorities have been satisfied for now. They'll want a statement from you later."

"You didn't tell anyone about the crystal ball, did you?"

"No. We let everyone think that you and Mark had made arrangements to meet there. The canyon is under guard until a team of archeologists arrive. This particular black market is finished, along with the weapons and drug dealing. Unfortunately, Frederick Bryce covered his tracks well. There is nothing to prove that he knew of Yaeger's activities or the involvement of his import-export company with the black market. Now, the waiting room is full of reporters and one set of newly-arrived, very anxious parents. Mark is about to tear down the hospital to see you. In what order would you like to deal with all of this?"

"I'd prefer not to deal with any of it, but I suppose I'd better. Mark first, then my parents. The reporters are going to have to wait a long time. First though, I could do with a hairbrush and some lipstick."

"You certainly could," Jim laughed. "Your mother brought a whole assortment of fripperies — face goo, warpaint, perfume, and fancy nighties. Shall I call a nurse to help you?"

"No, please. Just once over lightly with a damp washcloth, a little lipstick, and a few swipes of the hairbrush. I'll use the rest of it when I get this damned needle out of my arm."

Jim gently washed her face and brushed her hair. When she was ready, he stood beside the bed and looked down at her.

"Janet, there is something I have to say just this once, then I'll never mention it again unless you do. I never did stop loving you. I'll always love you. I can't fight this strange bond between you and Mark. It's something strong and special and I don't know what it means for your future. I just want you to know that I love you and I'll always be around if you need me."

Jim kissed her on the forehead and left the room before Janet could say anything. Her eyes were shiny-bright with tears when Jim returned a few minutes later, pushing Mark's wheelchair. He carefully positioned the chair beside Janet's bed and left.

There was a long silence as Mark and Janet looked at each other.

"I hear you have been a real stinker," Janet finally said.

Mark grinned. "I had to be certain that they weren't lying to me. I had to see you awake and know that you are all right."

The smile left Mark's face as he continued. "If you had seen yourself, you would understand. My god, I felt so helpless and so responsible. You were still and pale, and covered with blood and sand. The only way I knew that you were alive when Jim found us was because you were still bleeding."

Janet held her hand out to him. "I'm going to be fine. I hate the publicity, but to tell the truth, life had gotten a little dull. I could have done without the bullet, and I'm not thrilled about killing those four even though I thought I wanted revenge. But I wouldn't have missed the rest of it for anything. What are you doing?"

Mark had struggled out of the wheelchair and was leaning over the bed. "I'm going to kiss you." And he did, thoroughly.

He straightened up and looked down at Janet's flushed face. "You are the strangest, weirdest, most unpredictable, most thoroughly bewildering female person I have ever known. If I hadn't seen you in action, I'd think Ben Fischer and Jim and the newspapers were the world's greatest liars. The stories Ben has told me ... I don't know whether you are a witch, a battle-hardened soldier, or the personification of virtue and femininity. I don't know whether to run like hell, or handcuff myself to you so you can't get away." He sat down in the wheelchair and looked at her with a perplexed expression.

"That has to be the most unusual speech anyone has ever made to me." Janet couldn't suppress her laughter. "I have to admit that our relationship so far has been a little bizarre, but I'm not certain whether you mean to flatter me or insult me."

"To be honest, Janet, I'm confused myself. I know that I don't want you to disappear from my life until I have a chance to get to know you. I've been doing some thinking. We both have surgery and several months of convalescence ahead of us. Jim has agreed to play nursemaid for me. I'm hoping that you will stay in Albuquerque and let us have that time to get to know each other."

"I think I'd like that very much," Janet answered, not adding that Jim's promised presence was the deciding factor for her.

Mark smiled and seemed relieved. "Looks like some of the others are going to have all the fun with Jupiter's temple and searching for the Roman settlement. But who knows, when we get our heads together, we may discover another strange and wonderful site waiting out there somewhere for us."

Janet laughed. "Mark, do you know anything about ancient China?"

Note from the Author

Agness, Oregon is a real place. With the exception of the McVey's secret hideaway and Samuel Donnelly's cabin, it is described as I remember it from the two wonderful summers when I lived in Janet's log house on the banks of the Rogue River.

All of the characters are products of my imagination and are not based on any of the fine people who live in and around Agness and the other locales.

The black market in stolen Indian artifacts is a serious and continuing problem, wreaking a high toll in knowledge and money.

The psychic incidents are based on personal experience and the experiences of people close to me.

Florence Wagner McClain

About the Author

Florence Wagner McClain is a parapsychologist, amateur archeologist, photographer, historian, and expert woodsperson who has traveled and lived all over the United States. Now living near Denton, Texas, she spends her time in historical and archeological research, writing, and exploration of the Southwest. Experienced in search and rescue treaining and wilderness survival, a local newspaper has described her real life adventures as "topping those of the fictional Indiana Jones." She is the author of A Practical Guide to Past Life Regression, also published by Llewellyn.